THE TRAITOR AND THE THIEF

THE TRAITOR AND THE THIEF

GARETH WARD

WALKER BOOKS
AND SUBSIDIARIES

LONDON • BOSTON • SYDNEY • AUCKLAND

The Traitor and the Thief is the winner of the Storylines Tessa Duder Award
for Young Adult Fiction sponsored by Walker Books Australia.

First published in 2017
by Walker Books Australia Pty Ltd
Locked Bag 22, Newtown
NSW 2042 Australia
www.walkerbooks.com.au

The moral rights of the author have been asserted.

National Library of Australia Cataloguing-in-Publication entry:
Ward, Gareth, 1968– author.
The traitor and the thief / Gareth Ward.
ISBN: 978 1 925381 50 4 (paperback)
For children.
Subjects: Orphans – Juvenile fiction.
Spy stories.
NZ823.3

. COVER IMAGES: mechanisms © Agor2012/Shutterstock.com
boy silhouettes © basel101658/Shutterstock.com
adult silhouettes © alex74/Shutterstock.com

Typeset in Garamond
Printed and bound in Australia at McPherson's Printing Group

MIX
Paper from
responsible sources
FSC® C001695

The paper in this book is FSC® certified.
FSC® promotes environmentally responsible,
socially beneficial and economically viable
management of the world's forests.

In memory of Lesley Ann Ward,
who taught me the value of imagination.

CHAPTER 1
THE STOLEN NECKLACE

Sin shadowed the steamtram, hiding in the clouds of vapour spurting from the machine's giant pistons. He couldn't afford to get caught. Not now. Not today. The Fixer would never forgive him. He crouched lower. Built short and stocky like a pit bull, with a temperament to match, he wanted to front up to the Red Blades, not run and hide. But the Fixer said you had to pick the fights you could win, and he was alone on the other gang's turf.

Sweat trickled down his angular cheeks, leaving pale tracks. He'd run three blocks with the tram and his lungs burned from the steam and smoke. He brushed a tangle of sooty black hair from his eyes, and tried to pick out the Gothic stone archway that offered sanctuary. The tram slowed, then shuddered to a halt. With a near-deafening hiss, steam billowed from beneath the carriage. Sin darted through the clouds and into the covered market.

Russet iron columns spiralled skywards, supporting the Corn Market's unique and much acclaimed flurohydrous roof. Created by the eccentric inventor Nimrod Barm, a turquoise solution swirled between ironglass sheets providing an ever-changing vista.

Sin skulked through the market, checking over his shoulder, but this was the Fixer's patch and the Red Blades wouldn't dare follow him here. His nerves calmed; he took a deep breath and instantly regretted it. The smells of science wafted from the booths: the sulphurous results of chemical reactions hanging in the air like a pungent perfume. He coughed and the secret harness containing his brassanium keeper pulled tight against his chest. The Red Blades had tried to take it, but it was worth more than his life. It *was* his life: his only clue to his abandonment as a baby fourteen years ago. It held a mystery that he was determined to solve. With a final glance behind him, he pushed into the crowd gathered around Phileas Pines' Technological Timepieces, the press of warm bodies a fleeting moment of companionship. Soft velvet and wool brushed his bare arms, the expensive fabric's touch exquisite compared to his own rags.

From the booth, the top-hatted Phileas Pines held forth. "Ladies and Gentlemen, witness the chronological magnificence of our new 'Radiant Active' watches. Crafted with the finest uranium, these luminous masterpieces are to die for."

A saggy-faced punter in a tweed suit jostled past and Sin felt a promising bump from the jacket pocket.

The world quietened, drowned out by the thump of his quickened pulse. *Time slowed.* Something Phileas Pines would have declared impossible. Sin couldn't control it, but often, when he most needed it to, the world around him seemed to pass at a snail's pace. Sin's hand glided beneath the punter's jacket. His fingers touched metal, sensing the shape of the fob watch, before exploring for a securing chain or pin. None found, he grasped his prize and eased his hand clear.

The bustle of the market returned, the sounds, colours and smells jarring his heightened senses. He thrust the watch into his pocket and hurried away.

Weaving through the market-goers, Sin inspected his prize. The glass fitted poorly, the hinges squeaked and the patterning was stamped, not engraved. It wasn't one of Phileas's artisan masterpieces as he'd hoped, but a cheap imitation, mass-produced in a steam press in one of the new tenement factories. The Fixer wouldn't accept it as payment. He'd laugh, then beat Sin seven shades of purple, then laugh some more.

Sin prowled past more stalls. Normally, the sounds of

Coxford's famous craftsmen working leather and metal into technological wonders filled him with a sense of awe. But today every hammer fall was like the tick of a clock, slicing away the little time he had left before his debt was called in. He'd gambled and he'd lost. He needed to find another crowd.

Doctor Donodroid's Mekanikal Marvels was always a popular attraction. Coxford's finest would stand enthralled watching the humanoid automata clunkily navigate the booth, making pots of tea they would never drink and cutting geometrically perfect cucumber sandwiches they would never eat. Sin's attention was drawn to an imposing lady in a corsetted brocade dress. A large ruby set in a platinum pendant nestled in the lady's cleavage. Sin's fingers twitched; it would easily pay off the Fixer. Lifting the necklace would be tricky but given ample distraction, feasible. He scanned the market for Sheriffs and prepared to make his move.

A dandy in a scarlet leather coat and bowler hat cut across Sin's path and insinuated himself alongside the woman. A vertical scar bisected the man's right eye, lending him a roguish air. Scarface tapped the woman on the shoulder and smiled disarmingly. "Forgive me, my lady, but as the sun sets you may wish to direct your eyes heavenwards."

A steamwhistle shrilled. In the market's cellars hidden

pumps whirred to life and violet fluid flooded between the roof's ironglass plates, forming hypnotic eddies and whirls.

The lady craned her neck, peering upwards at the unfolding spectacle. The gentleman moved his hand to the back of the lady's head and with a tender touch guided the direction of her gaze. "See the glow at the apex. The chemicals luminesce as they mix." His hand moved lower and unfastened the necklace.

With a *pop* and a flash, the entire roof burst into light. The woman gasped, holding a lace handkerchief to her lips and, in that moment, the man snaked the jewellery from her neck and into his pocket.

Sin twiddled the brassanium hoop in his ear as he stalked Scarface through the bustling market. Thieving from a thief was never a good idea, but he needed that necklace.

He ducked down a side aisle and approached one of the market's newspaper hawkers.

"*Evening Press*. Teutonians preparing for war," shouted the boy.

"Lend us a paper, Jordie," said Sin.

"What for? Ye can'ae read."

"Don't matter. I just need one."

Jordie reached below his barrow and retrieved a folded paper. "Ye can 'av yesterday's, an' ye owe me."

"You're a gent, Jordie," said Sin, taking the paper and hurrying back in pursuit.

The lithographic image on the front of the news-sheet showed a platoon of pointy-helmeted Teutonians digging trenches. The headline said something about war but the other words meant nothing to Sin and he wasn't bothered anyway. It wasn't his problem. He flicked to the back of the paper, where the lithograph showed a picture of a horse, and he folded it in half.

The crowds thinned and Sin picked up his pace, getting ahead of his quarry. At the next intersection, he slowed to a dawdle and studied the paper. Timing it perfectly, he stepped into the junction and collided with Scarface. *Time slowed.* His fingers slid inside the thief's jacket, brushing across a shield-shaped coin before alighting on the necklace. He clasped the jewel and chain, then withdrew his hand and normality returned.

"Careful, youngling," said Scarface, "my old bones aren't so strong these days."

Sin doubted this was true. The impact had been surprisingly firm, like hitting a wall.

"Sorry, guv'nor. Lost in the racing results. Bloody nags will be the death of me." Sin doffed his cap and thrust the necklace into his breeches.

"Oh, I doubt it will be the horses," said Scarface.

Sin darted away, the hardened edge to the man's parting words sitting uneasy with him.

* * *

Industrial smog choked the streets. Sin pulled a tattered neckerchief from his pocket and secured it over his face. The thin fabric was a poor substitute for a proper filter mask that according to the advertisement billboards chemically scrubbed every breath clean, but it was all a street urchin like him could afford. At least the greasy smoke would hide him should Scarface or the Sheriffs come looking.

He drifted down Magpie Lane, his footfalls muffled by the fog, his eyes scanning the shifting shadows. Something clattered on the cobbles behind him and his heart jumped as a figure emerged from the gloom.

"I didn't get a chance to introduce myself when we bumped into each other earlier," said Scarface. "I'm Eldritch Moons and I believe you have something of mine."

Sin didn't question how the man had found him. He just ran. Nobody knew the alleys and backstreets, the sneakways and cut-throughs, better than him. Eldritch had found him once but Sin was damn sure he wouldn't find him again. Not in this pea souper.

Sin pelted down Crooked Row, his feet hammering the cobbles. A sharp left into Tanner Street then hard right into Crosses Court and he slowed to a trot. Sucking in air through the neckerchief, his chest falling and rising like a blacksmith's bellows, he approached the ancient monument at the square's centre. Chemlights hanging on rusted chains coloured the smog into wraith-like apparitions.

A shadow flitted behind the stone cross and Sin froze. It couldn't possibly be him. He glimpsed a flash of scarlet between the stonework then his pursuer stepped into view. A leather and brass respirator obscured the lower half of Eldritch's face, but Sin could tell he was smiling.

This was wrong. The man wasn't even out of breath. Eldritch should be shouting and swearing, sweating and panting, not acting as if it were all a game. He was like a cat toying with a mouse, letting it run away, thinking it would escape when there was only one possible ending. Well, Sin wasn't a mouse. A rat maybe, and rats were cunning. Sin shuddered and a trickle of sweat ran down his ribs as he surveyed the court. To his left and right stone arches lead to two of Coxford's historic gates.

Sin sprinted across the square and bolted through the left-hand arch.

Eldritch's voice, muffled by the respirator, followed him. "That way's a *dead end.*"

The towering facades of Archimedes College boxed Sin in on both sides and ahead, at the street's end, Patriot's Gate blocked the way. Standing over twenty feet tall and fashioned with cruel thorn-like barbs, it seemed impenetrable. However, you didn't survive for years on the streets without picking up a few tricks. Sin gripped two of the gate's vertical bars and twisted. They spun easily, as if oiled, and, thanks to the metal's geometric curve, a narrow gap opened up. Like a circus contortionist he squeezed through, before returning the bars to their original positions.

Eldritch emerged from the fog, whistling a tune behind his mask. "With you in just one moment, young fellow," he said. From the folds of his coat he pulled a brassanium hemisphere and secured it over the gate's lock. The device's internal clockwork clicked and clanked and the gate began to shudder.

Sin stared at Eldritch and backed away. He wasn't scared. Definitely not scared. The streets belonged to him, not this swaggering dandy.

The device gave a final loud crash and the gate swung open. Eldritch stepped through and stopped. His expression hardened. "This is the part where you run."

Carved stonework, brick walls and concrete slabs flew past as Sin navigated a meandering path through the grey-fogged city. He leaped wooden fences, negotiated sharp iron railings and pushed through hedges, determined this time he would be impossible to follow. Legs and lungs burning, he dropped onto the towpath of the Cherwell Canal that divided the city's industrial district. Exhausted, he slunk into the black recess of the Ashmole Tunnel and rested his back against the sooty curved brickwork. He pulled the neckerchief away from his mouth and sucked in the damp tainted air. He'd not run like that since the big dust-up with the Barrel Lane crew. He'd been stabbed in the arm that day and had leaked claret all the way back to the Fixer's lair.

Eldritch stepped onto the canal bank, silhouetted in the tunnel's entrance. He rotated a dial on his bowler hat and the rim illuminated, bathing him in a column of light. "Most excellent work, my young thiefling. You lead me a right merry dance, but for you the game is lost."

Sin looked for an escape route. Eldritch blocked the entrance and stumbling further into the pitch-black tunnel would be futile. That left only one option. It wasn't a good option, and possibly a fatal one, but it was an option all the same. He took a deep breath, pinched his nose and plunged into the canal. The dark oily waters closed above his head. His feet sank into the sludgy bottom, the mud cloying at his boots, threatening to trap him. Panic seized him like a fever. His legs thrashed wildly and he surged upwards, chasing the bubbles escaping from his mouth. With flailing arms, he breached the surface and splashed his way to the far bank.

"That was either very brave or very foolish, and really quite unnecessary," shouted Eldritch across the canal.

Sin hauled himself onto the towpath. The acrid taste of the canal water burned the back of his throat. He rolled his tongue over his teeth and spat. "Nearest bridge is a mile. Don't reckon on you taking a dip in your swanky pants suit."

"Indeed not." Eldritch unbuttoned his coat and reached inside. The garment issued a loud hiss then hidden seams within the leather ballooned and hardened, turning the coat into a set of bat-like wings. Eldritch stretched out his arms, grasped the wings and kicked his boots together. Smoke billowed from the soles and he glided over the water, brilliant blue flames spurting from his heels.

Sin knew he should get up and run, but the icy water had sapped the last of his strength. Besides, there was no way he could escape from this strange techno-thief. He retrieved the pendant from his pocket and held it out to Eldritch. "Take it. It's yours."

"No. Actually, the jewel, it is mine," said a voice from the dark of the canal tunnel. The woman from the market stepped into view. Her pale skin shimmered in the light from Eldritch's hat. She hooked the chain with an elegant finger and secured the necklace around her neck.

Eldritch tipped his hat. "May I introduce my colleague, Baroness Lilith Von Darque."

Lilith fixed her hypnotic blue eyes on Sin. "Well done. You are the most elusive urchin we have ever hunted."

Sin shuddered. Lilith's stare was colder than the sodden clothes clinging to his body. He'd heard stories of the Hunt, all the gangs had, but he hadn't really believed them. It was crazy to think someone was hunting and killing street kids for sport.

"You've got the necklace. I ain't got nothing else. What say you just let me go?"

In an instant, Lilith was alongside him, her fingers encircling his throat, forcing his head backwards. "It wasn't the necklace we were after."

A sharp pain needled Sin's neck and he slumped to the bank, unable to move. A pleasant warmth spread throughout his body and his world darkened. If this was death, then it wasn't so bad. Far away, he heard voices.

"Well, what do you think?"

"I think it's him."

CHAPTER 2
FRIEND OR FOE

Sin's vision blurred in and out of focus and his head throbbed. He'd never given much thought to the afterlife, but he'd expected more clouds and angels and not so many fish. Overhead, a neon-striped specimen drifted past, its flared tail undulating. Sin's stomach churned and a wave of nausea hit him. He blinked, beads of sweat pricking his brow.

"Here, drink this," said Eldritch. He eased the rim of a teacup to Sin's lips. The warm liquid was sweet and flowery but not unpleasant. It was certainly preferable to the taste of canal water that lingered in his mouth.

"It's Earl Grey," said Eldritch. "I find most things seem better with a good strong cup of tea."

"Am I dead?" croaked Sin.

"The simple answer to that is yes, no and maybe."

His head clearer now, Sin eased himself upright. He sat on a luxuriant bed in a room where the walls and ceiling were decorated with gigantic round aquariums. Teak and polished brass surrounded the tanks giving the impression of portholes in some elaborate undersea craft. His sodden street clothes had been replaced with a set of soft pyjamas. His hand went to his chest; his keeper was missing. They'd stolen from him! Taken the only thing he had, the only thing he cared about. A snarl formed on his lips and he lunged forwards.

With fingers strong as tungsten rods, Eldritch pushed Sin back onto the pillow. "Calm down." He motioned to the bedside cabinet where the ribbed brassanium tube and leather harness rested.

Sin relaxed. His keeper was safe and there was no way they could have opened it.

Eldritch released his grip and handed Sin a teacup, while expertly balancing his own cup and saucer on his knee. "You need to hydrate after the drugs we gave you."

Sin touched his neck. The skin where the needle had penetrated was sore and swollen.

"Experience has taught us that sedation saves a great deal of unnecessary aggravation. Please accept my apologies for any harm caused," said Eldritch.

"You're the Hunt," said Sin, his eyes widening.

"The Hunt is a myth we allow to perpetuate because it suits our purposes. It's a touch melodramatic, but we wanted to see you perform under pressure. We had to be certain you were up to the task. Please be assured that you are now safe. A doctor has examined you and the nurses have given you a good scrub down. I'm afraid due to 'visitors' your haircut is somewhat severe, however it will grow back."

Sin ran his hand over the shaved stubble. It felt odd, but at least it didn't itch any more.

"You are a guest of the Aquarinomic Hotel, another of Nimrod Barm's monumental achievements."

Guest? When a gang member was thrown into jail the Fixer would say they were guests of the King. Sin glanced at the brassanium-plated door with its heavy nautical hinges and spoked ship's wheel handle. It was elegant and unnecessarily sturdy, unless …

"Am I a prisoner?"

"Good gracious, no. You can choose to leave now, but you will be required to drink milk of amnesia to wipe these events from your mind. That is the 'no' option of your 'Am I dead?' question."

Sin took a slurp of tea, the cup rattling in the saucer as he replaced it. "And the yes?"

"A proposition will be set out in full tomorrow. If you accept the terms of the deal, you will have an entirely new life. The Sin of old will be dead." Eldritch tilted his head.

"Although, what we offer is not without risk and it *may be* that you die for real."

Part of Sin wanted to leave now. He couldn't reconcile this smiling dandy with the man who had harried him across the city. It was like Eldritch was two different people and that made Sin suspicious. Then again, Sin could be charming and kind when it suited his needs, hiding the street thug from view. Perhaps he and Eldritch weren't too different. And he had to respect the man's skills. He was a hard case for sure, possibly even tough enough to give the Fixer a run for his money. Yeah, he was scary bad and, unlike the Fixer, he hadn't hurt Sin. Well, apart from the injection, and that had been the lady. So maybe he should stay. The room had a warm bed and now his head was clearer, the tropical fish fascinated him.

"So I just wait here until tomorrow?"

"The hotel is ours. You're welcome to make full use of its facilities and meet the other potential candidates."

"You've got other street kids like me?"

"Some. We recruit from a variety of sources and you may find it helpful to meet the more scholarly candidates." A smile twisted Eldritch's lips. "You could do a lot worse than befriend the young lady in the opposite room."

Sin nodded, but his thoughts were elsewhere. "Are there any more of the Fixer's crew here?"

"No. We select from across the gangs and no more than one from each."

With no turf and no bosses, Sin wondered how that would work. Badly, he suspected, but not for him – he could hold his own against any of them.

"There is only one Cast-Iron Rule." Eldritch drained his teacup. "You are to be in your hotel room between the hours of ten in the evening and seven in the morning. We will not tolerate the breaking of this rule."

Sin stretched against the soft down pillow. "Keeping me in bed isn't going to be the problem."

Eldritch patted him lightly on the shoulder then walked to the door. "I'm glad I found you. There are clothes in the wardrobe and the dining room really is top-hole." He let himself out, whistling a cheery ditty as he went.

The moment the door closed Sin reached for his keeper. Six numbered rings encircled the top of the brassanium tube. He rotated each ring to align the numbers into a combination seared into his brain: six, two, three, one, one, five. With the faintest of clicks the keeper's lid sprang open. Sin reached inside and retrieved a torn photo. It was ripped from the bottom of a larger image and showed a young woman in a white coat, her belly gently rounded. This was the lady he believed to be his mother. Despite her smile, her eyes were tinged with sadness. As if she knew her unborn child would grow up strong and capable but alone. He turned the photo over and looked at the single word written in faded ink: *Eve*. With the tip of his finger he traced the writing then slid the photo back into the keeper and secured it closed.

The newness of his pyjamas made the buttons difficult to undo, so after loosening a few, he pulled the top over his head and tossed it onto the floor. He checked the straps on his harness then buckled it around his torso, feeling the reassuring tightness of the leather against his skin. The Fixer had given him the keeper when he'd first joined the gang so he could run secret messages across the city. As he'd moved up the hierarchy, his duties changed, and so now he used it to keep his most precious treasure safe. He slid the tube into the holder and placed his hand over the leather, pressing it into the gap between his pectoral muscles. Feeling whole again, his only clue to his past secure, he opened the wardrobe.

Sin gawked in wide-eyed wonder. The wardrobe was crammed with garments from Walters on Turl, Coxford's finest tailor. He'd scurried past the shop on many occasions, avoiding the burly yet finely dressed security guards who ensured the likes of him never harassed their well-to-do customers. Choosing what to wear was going to be a dilemma; he'd never owned more than one outfit.

He pulled a garish Italian silk shirt from a hanger and slipped it over his broad shoulders. The fabric tickled, feather-like on his skin.

He strutted the room in expensively woven suits, tweed jackets, boating blazers and all manner of exotic patterned breeches and blouses. However, at heart he was more pit bull than peacock, so he settled for a grandad shirt, moleskin trousers and a pair of rugged trench boots.

Sin's leather soles squeaked on the polished wood floor as he left his room. More aquariums lined the corridor, brassanium-plated doors interspersed between them.

A short, plump girl in an emerald-green cocktail dress emerged from the room opposite. She smiled at him, dimples forming in her cheeks. "You must be the runner they brought in last night. Everyone's gasbagging about it. Is it true you nearly gave old Eldritch the slip?"

Sin shrugged. "Dunno, maybe."

"That's so danderific. They're going to pick you for certain." The girl twirled one of her blonde pigtails. "I'm Zonda. We can be friends, if you like."

Sin didn't have friends. Life as a cutpurse was hard and you formed an uneasy arrangement of alliances. Measures of who owed you and who you owed. But this wasn't the streets and Zonda had talked about Eldritch with a familiarity that didn't come from being chased across the city. Maybe that was why Eldritch had suggested Sin befriend her. She certainly knew more than he did, and that made her useful. He wasn't sure he trusted Eldritch, though the blighter had gone hard out to recruit Sin and he couldn't see any reason why Eldritch would lead him astray now. And besides, there was something about Zonda he liked.

"I don't normally do friends," said Sin, "but for you I'm going to make an exception."

Zonda lifted a satin sleeve. "Splendiferous. You may take my arm."

Sin hesitated. In his world, the only time you took somebody's arm was to break it, which he suspected was not the social etiquette here. Tentatively, he hooked his arm through hers.

"Do you know where the dining room is? Me stomach thinks me throat's been cut," he said.

"Oh, that's simple; you just follow the fish."

Peering at the aquariums, Sin scratched his head.

"No sillies, look." Zonda pointed to a brass plaque, adorned with rows of labelled buttons in the shape of coloured fish. "You just choose where you want to go."

Sin's hand hovered over one of the buttons, a green perch.

"That's the Conserva-Observatory," said Zonda, "which has smellerificly fragrant flowers. I think we should go for the dining room." She pressed a blue fish and a mekanikal trout lowered into the adjacent aquarium and began to swim away from them.

"I expect it's on an ironglass rod which is rendered invisible by diffraction of the water," said Zonda as they followed the fish.

Sin had never heard of diffraction but he nodded agreement.

"See the way the mouth's open?" said Zonda indicating the fish's head. "I think water flows through it driving an impeller that creates the swimming motion. At least that's how I'd build it."

"You could make something like that?"

"Easy-peasy, stinky cheesy. Now, making one you could travel in under water, that would be difficult. I bet Nimrod's done it though."

"No danger. He'd be showing it off in Coxford. The gentry would be queuing up for rides."

"Maybe." Zonda tilted her head and smiled. "I'm hoping to meet him. Rumour is he's here at the hotel."

The fish reached the end of the aquarium. In the next tank an identical one appeared and continued on its journey. A guppy briefly chased the trout then lost interest. Sin tapped the ironglass and the guppy shot into some swaying reeds. "So we can go wherever we want by following the fish?"

"Sure. But if you get a red herring ignore it. Nimrod's little joke. You could end up anywhere."

The peaceful gurgle of the aquariums was broken by a scream and a muffled thump. Around the next corner, a muscled bruiser of a boy pummelled a foppish white-haired weakling. Sin recognised the bruiser as a Red Blade and his fists clenched. The bruiser landed several more punches and the weakling crumpled to the floor.

Zonda raised a hand to her mouth. "How heinous. We should endeavour to offer abettance."

Sin stared at her blankly. "In English please."

"I said we should help."

Sin's eyes flicked back to the boy who curled in a ball on the floor while the Red Blade kicked him. "Why?"

Zonda's grip tightened on his arm. "He's getting hurt."

"Do you know him?"

"That's not the point." Zonda let go of Sin and clapped her hands together. "Desist immediately, you rapscallion."

The bruiser snorted. His gaze slid over Zonda and alighted on Sin. He straightened, all interest lost in the groaning boy at his feet. "You're the Fixer's lieutenant."

Sin drew level with Zonda. "If this goes sideways, gap it."

Zonda stared at him blankly. "In English ple—"

The Red Blade charged.

Time slowed. Sin ducked under a wild haymaker punch, slammed his fist into the bruiser's stomach and shouldered him to the floor.

Time snapped back. The lights from the aquariums fluoresced, leaking tendrils of colour into the corridor. Sin squinted and swallowed, the sound of the bruiser's pain sharp in his ears.

"Come on, let's eat," he said, stepping over the writhing Red Blade.

CHAPTER 3
MUM'S THE WORD

The dining room was a cavernous hemisphere of riveted steel and ironglass designed to give the impression of eating under the ocean. Above one half swam turtles, octopuses and all manner of peculiar tropical fish. The other half was muddy and murky with dark, ominously undulating reeds. A pike surged from the gloom and snatched a gudgeon in its jaws before darting back into the shadows.

"That's the actual River Thames," said Zonda. She guided Sin to a huge circular white-clothed table surrounded by myriad chairs. At its centre shone an elaborate brassanium chemcandelabra.

Sin considered the two worlds overhead: one bright and beautiful, the other sinister and dangerous.

Zonda gave a little cough as she waited beside a gold

chair. "In polite society it's customary for the gentleman to seat the lady."

His stomach rumbling, Sin recalled his last meal. Dirty urchins fighting over stale bread and rotting cabbage, the only seat mouldering sacking. "Oh right, I kinda forgot," he said and pulled out the velvet-cushioned chair.

He took his own seat next to Zonda, heart beating faster as he considered the array of silver knives, forks and spoons arranged before him; they'd be worth a fortune on the street. He jumped, a foreign-accented voice interrupting his thoughts of theft.

"Your menu, sir," said the waiter, handing him a leather-bound folder with an air of ill-concealed disdain.

Sin knew his letters and a good many words, yet the writing was all fancy curls that squirmed on the page like fish market eels. He watched Zonda's eyes darting back and forth. His grip tightened on the menu. He should scarper, find the pantry and nick some scoff. Zonda placed her hand on his arm. Her touch was feather-like but it secured him in place. "I've eaten here before. Perhaps you'd like me to make some recommendations?"

"If you want. Get some meat. Can't normally afford meat."

Zonda beckoned the waiter over, the names of culinary delights rolling off her tongue. The waiter scribbled in his notepad then, with a shallow bow, left for the kitchen.

"So tell me about your run-in with Eldritch," said Zonda, fixing him with her big green eyes. "From the way everyone's tittle-tattling it sounds posituitively incredabubble."

Sin took in the details of her face: the slightly upturned nose, the rosy hint to her cheeks, the natural smile of her lips. He wasn't used to having feelings, or if he was they were anger, hatred and fear. The way Zonda treated him made him feel something different. She made him feel like he had worth.

Toying with a loose thread on the tablecloth, he said, "I ain't proud of it. They dangled that big old jewel as bait and hooked me like fresh fish. The Fixer would box me ears if he knew."

"Who's the Fixer?"

"He sort of takes care of street kids. Puts a roof over your head and gives protection. It ain't for free mind, you've got to pay your taxes or he'll come down hard. That's why I needed the jewel. I got gypped in a poker game and me debts were rung in."

Zonda clasped her hands together. "How fantabulously exciting. Just like a Bertie Brasspipe novella."

Sin had never heard of Bertie Brasspipe, but he somehow doubted the stories involved vicious beatings. Fortunately, he was saved from airing his suspicions by the return of the waiter carrying a tray covered with a silver dome.

With a flourish, the waiter removed the dome and placed the tray between them. "*Escargots a la Bourguignonne. Bon Appétit,*" he said in a thick Fromagian accent.

Sin's mouth watered at the garlicy smell. He lunged for the bowl, but his hand came to a sudden halt as his eyes caught up with his nose. "What the ... snails?"

Zonda gripped a shell with a set of silver tongs, and levered the meat free with a two-pronged fork. "You asked for meat," she said and popped the snail into her mouth. Sin watched her chew, his own mouth hanging open.

"These are exquisitissimo. You should try one," said Zonda.

Sin leaned backwards. "No danger. We had it tough on the streets but never so bad we had to eat slugs."

"Your loss. So how did Eldritch catch you?" Zonda asked.

Sin recounted the chase while Zonda worked through the snails. The waiter brought crusty bread rolls, which Sin ripped apart and devoured, not bothering with the accompanying butter florets.

His hunger partly sated, he sat back while the plates were cleared. "So that's how I got here. How about you?"

"Nothing nearly so dramatic. I'd been completing the 'Complicated Conundrums' section in the *Coxford Times* and sending them to the competition address at the back of the newspaper. Someone obviously liked my answers because a letter arrived inviting me to attend selection."

"Selection for what?"

Her reply was curtailed by the arrival of a cluster of waiters bringing trays of meat, potatoes and dishes of vegetables. Zonda piled her plate high then checked over her shoulder. "I'm not supposed to say, but we're being selected for COG."

"What's COG?" asked Sin, through a mouthful of beef.

Zonda winced and held a finger to her lips. "Not so loud. Do you want to get us thrown out before we've started?"

"I don't know. No one's telling me what the hell I'm doing here."

Leaning closer, Zonda whispered, "Covert Operations Group."

Before Sin could question her further, a girl bedecked in a velvet dress and double-buttoned corset prowled over to the table. She was flanked by an entourage of four well-heeled boys who jostled each other to be closest to her. In the chemcandelabra's soft light her skin appeared near flawless. The only blemish was a tear-shaped mole positioned so perfectly below her left eye, it seemed impossible nature created it. One of the boys pulled out the chair next to Sin and the girl sat, brushing hair the colour of Indian ink from her face. "Do you mind if we join you?" she said, her silver-spooned accent gilded with a continental hint.

Zonda's expression hardened and the corners of her mouth turned down. "It appears you already have."

"I was talking to Eldritch's pet," said the girl. "I presume it speaks."

Sin was used to fronting up to thugs and bullies, but something about the girl unnerved him. She was like a snake: poised, waiting to strike. He slammed his fork into a slice of beef, skewering it. "Yeah, I talk."

The girl clapped her hands together in mock delight. "Oh, actual words. I was expecting maybe a series of grunts."

On the streets Sin would have slapped someone down for talking to him like that, but here, he didn't know how to respond. He shoved the chunk of meat into his mouth and chewed.

While her entourage sat, the girl beckoned over a waiter. "Two bottles of Erasmus Bonds Tonic Water," she commanded.

The girl twiddled a sapphire-encrusted ring on her finger. "The boys and I are going to the Phantasmagoria Magic Lantern Show in the hotel's theatre at midnight. Do you want to come?"

Sin swallowed the meat. "Eldritch said we had to be in our rooms by ten."

The girl flicked her hair, sending a waft of lavender perfume across the table. "So I was right. You are his pet?"

"No. It's just–"

"It's just that you're Eldritch's little hound. I'm surprised he didn't give you a collar in that big old wardrobe of clothes. Or is that what you're wearing under your borrowed shirt?"

Sin's hand went to his keeper and the girl smirked.

"The boys aren't scared to go. Do you have the cogs to join us?"

It was ridiculous to think he was frightened. He'd known real fear in the gang, fear for his life. Of course he wasn't scared of a shadow puppet show, but for some reason he felt compelled to prove himself to this girl. It was like she knew how to push his buttons, knew how he hated to back down.

Zonda grabbed his arm. "Don't do it. She's not worth it. Believe me, I know."

The girl's nostrils flared. "No one asked you, Chubbs."

Sin's fists clenched. He'd had enough of this girl. His chair shot backwards as he stood. "Stay sat down or I'll put you down," he said, pointing at the boys. He squared up to the girl. "Apologise."

Zonda tugged his arm. "Forget it."

The girl looked up and her oddly familiar blue eyes drilled into him. "I'm sorry, I don't understand. I'm not fluent in urchin."

Sin brushed Zonda's hand away. "You called her

35

chubbs and that's bang out of order. It's just a bit of puppy fat, that's all."

The girl smiled wickedly. "That's her name. Zonda Chubb. Did you not know?" She took a sip of tonic water. "Perhaps I should introduce myself, to avoid further confusion. I'm Velvet Von Darque. I believe you've met my mother."

Blood rushed to Sin's face. What an idiot he'd been. Zonda had shown him only kindness and he'd embarrassed her. It was obvious there was history between the two girls and he'd been suckered into saying something stupid. He turned to apologise, but Zonda was gone.

CHAPTER 4
EAVESDROPPING

Sin rushed along the corridor, cursing under his breath. Eldritch had told him to make friends with Zonda and he'd blown it. He reached her door and rapped his calloused knuckles against the wood. From inside he heard her sobbing. "It's me, Sin. Look, I'm sorry."

The sobbing quietened. He knocked again. "Come to the door and we can get this proper sorted."

The door thudded as something was thrown at it. "Go away."

Sin hesitated. "I thought we were going to be friends."

"Go to the Magic Lantern Show with the popular girl. You can all be friends together, until she gets bored of you."

The door thudded again and there was a "Hrumpff," with an air of finality from inside.

Sin turned to his own room and saw the plaque with the coloured navigation fish. Maybe he could sort this. His hand hovered over the buttons, then he pressed the green perch. He'd never seen the appeal himself but he knew the market's flower girls did a roaring trade to the toffs buying bouquets for their ladies. Sin had no money so he couldn't buy flowers, however he was a thief and he knew where he might nick some.

* * *

The Conserva-Observatory was a giant hexagonal conservatory that formed the hotel's roof. Metal lattice struts interlaced with curved ironglass panels rose to a lens-like dome that magnified the stars above. Steam from the hotel's pressure boiler drifted through cast-iron floor vents creating a warm, humid environment for the exotic flora within.

Sin sneaked along a damp flagstone path that curved towards the central viewing area. The air was hot and earthy and the towering ferns and fronds reached for him, their shadowy fingers scratching at his clothes. A fragrant smell hung in the air and Sin let his nose guide him. Set deep in a low-walled flowerbed a glossy-leafed bush presented starburst pink flowers to the world. He jumped over the wall and brushed past a clump of giant spotted toadstools.

With an audible *puff* they sent a dewy mist into his face. Sin wiped his sleeve across his eyes, the world blurring as he reached the bush. Humming filled his ears and bright lights peppered his vision. Fingers trembling, he plucked a flower from the plant. The sound of the Conserva-Observatory doors opening cut through the buzz in his head. He froze. Footsteps and whispered conversation drew closer. Foliage obscured the speakers but he recognised one of the voices. Lilith Von Darque.

"They can't possibly know. How could they?" said Lilith.

The second speaker's voice was low and rasping. "You underestimate Eldritch."

A wooziness gripped Sin, his senses intensifying. Aromatic tendrils snaked from the flower, tickling his nose, and a sneeze began to form. He cupped his hands over his face but the tingling grew worse.

"I can handle Eldritch," said Lilith.

"Yet you helped him hunt down the boy?" croaked the voice.

"It wasn't my fault."

"We agreed he shouldn't be recruited."

"Eldritch was tracking him. I think Nimrod did something to the necklace. He wanted to be certain the boy wouldn't escape."

"We should tell the boy now."

"No! We promised to wait. We promised Eve."

"There's no honour in skulking and spying," spat the voice.

"And yet you are so good at it," said Lilith.

The owner of the voice laughed with all the humour of a mass grave.

Sin held his breath, the tension in his chest growing. His lungs begged for oxygen but he refused to breathe. He counted the passing seconds in his head, each one seeming further and further apart as the chittering in his ears surged louder.

"And the exchange?" asked the voice.

"The Chinasians and Ruskovians are interested but they want more than rough sketches. I'm still waiting for other bidders."

Kaleidoscopic swirls filled Sin's vision. He clamped his arms arounds his head, rustling the leaves on the bush beside him. The voices stopped. Dead quiet filled the Conserva-Observatory. Sin crouched lower, his chest tight, his lungs screaming at him.

"We should get back before the Committee misses us," said Lilith.

The footsteps receded and Sin heard the Conserva-Observatory doors open then close. He gasped, the air's heady scents threatening to overwhelm him. Dropping to the earth, he curled into a ball among the vegetation and shuddered. Perspiration covered his brow and he began to shiver, overwhelmed by the toadstool's toxins. The rasping voice replayed in his head, echoing, distorted. There was something about it that terrified him. It was like he'd heard it before, linked to some terrible memory, just out of reach. His body convulsed and darkness overtook him. Outside, Coxford's bells pealed ten of the clock.

CHAPTER 5
CAST-IRON RULES

Sin awoke in his room with no recollection of how he'd got there. Sweat-soaked bedsheets twisted around him like a straitjacket. His lips felt gummy and his cheek stuck to the pillow where he'd dribbled in his sleep. Peeling his face away from the damp cotton, he disentangled himself and staggered to the bathroom. He spun a tap shaped like a starfish and looked in the mirror, waiting for the water to run hot. Minuscule red veins meandered across the whites of his eyes, an after-effect of the toadstool he presumed. The last thing he remembered was the voices in the Conserva-Observatory. Had they been talking about him? Unless they used the necklace to lure all the street kids they must have been, but why? And why was Nimrod so keen to recruit him? He was nothing special.

A bell rang and a confusion of feet hurried along the corridor. He selected a new set of clothes, quickly dressed and laced his boots. There was a hesitant knock at the door. He eased it open to find Zonda smiling sheepishly at him. The flower from the Conserva-Observatory now graced her hair, complementing the frilled tea gown she wore. A vague recollection scratched at his mind: staggering past the fish tanks and dropping the flower outside Zonda's room.

Zonda held out a lace-gloved arm. "Friends?"

Were they friends? He'd only just met her so how could they be? He'd known some of the Fixer's gang for nearly five years and they weren't friends. Sure, the crew had loyalty, but that came down to safety in numbers, a pack mentality and a fear of the Fixer. Here, he had nothing to fear; he was tougher and meaner than any of the other kids he'd seen in the dining room. The scent of the flower in Zonda's hair tickled his nose, triggering another memory. The owner of the malevolent voice — that was someone to fear. Maybe he did need a friend. Maybe he needed a new crew, one with different skills and different values. Maybe that was why Eldritch had encouraged him towards Zonda.

"Friends," agreed Sin, offering his arm. "So where the fish are we going?"

"To the ballroom," said Zonda, depressing a yellow carp button on the wall.

As they followed the fish, Sin contemplated ways to

discover more about Zonda and Velvet without provoking another sobbing fit. The Fixer had a knack of wheedling information from people. *Start with a compliment*, he always said.

"That's a nice dress you're wearing," hazarded Sin.

"Do you think? I wondered if it was a tad too frillericious."

"Oh no. You've definitely got the style to pull it off. Not like that other girl, what was her name?"

"Velvet?"

"That's right, Velvet," said Sin, nodding to himself. "How did you say you knew her again?"

Her eyes narrowing, Zonda said, "We shared the same governess for a while. I did all the work and got the best marks. Velvet got all the praise and the best report."

"That don't seem fair."

"As I tried to warn you last night, there's nothing *fair* about Velvet Von Darque."

* * *

A giant octopus head formed the ballroom's ceiling from which eight brassanium support girders shaped like tentacles arched to the floor. Suspended from the octopus's beak, a sparkling chemcandelabra threw an aquatic glimmer across the dance floor.

The neatly rowed chairs filled with excited candidates suggested they must have been last to arrive. Only three empty seats remained, adjacent to the aisle in the front row. On one rested a brass *reserved* sign so they occupied the other two. Before them seven throne-like chairs were arranged on a dais. A ship's bell chimed and the hall fell silent. Heels click-clacked on the parquet dance floor. Sin turned to see Velvet strutting down the aisle. With a sense of inevitability, he watched as she drew alongside, removed the reserved sign and took the seat next to him.

A megaphone voice echoed around the hall. "Please stand for the Committee." Chairs scraped back, then a hush fell over the candidates as an eclectic mix of characters walked onto the raised platform. At their centre was a Herculean man-machine, the whole of his right side remade with precision steam engineering. His mekanikal leg hissed and clanked as he turned to face the audience. On the organic side of his face he wore a look of manic intensity, his bushy moustache quivering. Flanking him were Eldritch and Lilith. To Eldritch's right a tall wiry man dressed in a black rag coat and crooked top hat scowled at the candidates. His face was painted white with a red band surrounding his small mean eyes. Next to Lilith a portly gentleman in a tweed suit tinkered with a piece of clockwork. The two end chairs remained empty.

Zonda nudged Sin. "Spin my cogs! The cove in the tweed – that's Nimrod Barm."

The goliath's head tracked mekanikally in their direction. "I am Major C. As second-in-command at COG, I will lead today's proceedings. If you are successful, I will also oversee your training for the next five years." His head moved again as he surveyed the audience. "I would like to welcome you, and indeed bid farewell to anyone who was not in their room after ten last night. Those remaining may sit. Those leaving can do so via the central doors."

A confused murmur ran through the crowd. A handful of candidates made their way out while others remained furtively in their seats.

Sin had no recollection of what time he'd returned to his room but he was adamant he wasn't leaving. He looked at Velvet, a sense of relief steeling over him. "I guess you'll be off then. Waste of time reserving your seat."

Velvet lifted her chin. "I'm going nowhere."

"You were going to the theatre. You made the others go."

"Nobody made them go."

Sin guessed this was true enough, yet Velvet had manipulated them. She'd manipulated him too. If it wasn't for Zonda, he'd be joining the others filing out of the hall. "That don't make it right. You broke the rules."

Velvet fiddled with a sapphire earring. "Rules mean nothing when you have money, power and privilege. That's doubly so when you're a Von Darque. Not even the rules of nature apply."

Lilith stood. "We know who you are. Leave now or there will be consequences."

More candidates departed, the cold smile on Lilith's face convincing them that she would very much enjoy the consequences and they would not. "Let that be lesson one." Lilith held up a finger. "Many of you are here because you seek danger and flaunt rules. However, in every organisation there must be control, so to help you with this we have Cast-Iron Rules. We will not tolerate the breaking of these rules."

Sin glanced sideways at Zonda. He couldn't picture her as a risk-taker or rule breaker.

Major C straightened and a jet of steam shot from his back. "The Empire is on the brink of global war. It will not be glorious or heroic as oft presented in the news-sheets, but fetid and ignoble." He clinked a metal finger against his brassanium half skull. "I am no coward. I have given my service and my body to our great country. Alas, war has changed. The honour of the soldier is replaced by the technology of killing and now we maim and slaughter with industrial efficiency. We few at the Covert Operations Group seek to maintain the fragile peace by putting a spanner in the war machine's works."

Gears mashed as Major C about-turned and marched

to the side of the dais. "Now I would like to introduce you to the founder and chairman of COG. A man without whom we could not exist: Professor Nimrod Barm."

Nimrod retrieved a pair of glasses from his pocket and pushed them onto his nose before walking to the front of the stage. "I founded COG because too many good men and women have died in the pursuit of military conquest." He gestured to the two empty chairs. "If you join us, you too may die, but your sacrifice will save the lives of millions. COG does not fight for the Empire; it fights for humanity. We do not work for the Britannia Government, or indeed any government. There are those in parliament, in industry and in our military who actively seek war. We must work against them, against our own country, breaking the rules and committing treason so peace may prevail. This is what I ask of you."

Eldritch stood next to Nimrod, his leather coat flapping about him. "Over the next five years you will receive the very best training in spy craft, combat, science and survival. You will undertake COG missions, here and abroad, in an attempt to stop what we fear will be the war to end all wars. If you survive and if we succeed in maintaining the peace, you can retire with a generous pension." Eldritch turned to the man in the rag coat. "Staff Noir, time please."

The man adjusted his top hat and joined Eldritch. From the folds of his coat he produced a large bone-white hourglass and placed it on the dais. "Leave or stay. You have three minutes to decide your fate," he rasped.

Sin shivered, recognising the voice. Noir was the man from the Conserva-Observatory and he appeared every bit as evil as he sounded. How could he possibly be one of the good guys? How could any of them? The only one who seemed vaguely normal was Nimrod Barm, and everyone knew he was mad as a bag of frogs.

Zonda clutched Sin's arm, an anxious expression on her face. "You're staying, aren't you?"

Every day on the streets Sin faced danger and the possibility of death. Here he'd get food, lodging and coin. Of course he was staying. The Committee were odd but they couldn't be any worse than the Fixer. Well, maybe Noir could. A fragment of conversation replayed in his mind. *We promised Eve.* That couldn't be coincidence, they knew something about the woman in the photograph. Something about his mother? And he was going to find out what.

Sin fidgeted in his chair. So what did he know? Noir didn't want him recruited but Nimrod had sent Eldritch to make sure that he was. Eldritch had directed him to Zonda. So was Zonda part of the plan to make sure he joined? She definitely knew more than she was letting on. Could he use her to fish for information?

Sin half-stood from his chair as if contemplating

leaving. "I'm not sure if I'm staying. That man with the white face, he don't seem right."

Zonda rested her hand on his forearm and drew him back to his chair. "Apparently," she whispered, "Noir was once a great stage magician until something went wrong with an illusion and he got hideously burned. That's why he covers his face with white makeup."

"Do you think he's dangerous?"

"Honestly, I think they're *all* dangiferous."

"But you're going to stay?"

"Definoso! We get to be taught by Nimrod Barm. That's just posituitively terrifertastic."

"What about the other stuff, the danger and the spying? That doesn't seem like you."

"Just because I wear dresses and have pigtails, doesn't mean I'm not tough."

Sin remembered the sobs he'd heard from her room. He'd only ever cried once, when Karl Jaeger had ripped the head and limbs from his teddy bear. It had been his only possession when he'd been abandoned at the orphanage as a newborn. The bear had been too badly damaged to repair, but hidden among the stuffing he'd found the photograph of his mother.

Sin rubbed a hand across his chin. "Guess I'll stay. Just to see how tough you are."

The final grains of sand dropped into the bottom of the

hourglass. Nobody else had left the ballroom. Sin guessed they were all like him and had nothing to lose, or were like Zonda and Velvet who already seemed to know what they were joining.

Eldritch spoke again. "From this point onwards you do not talk about COG to anyone who is not a member. This is a Cast-Iron Rule. The consequences of breaking it will be terminal." He leaped from the dais, his coat billowing. A grin spread across his face. "No need to look so terrified. Nobody dies on the first day."

CHAPTER 6
PIPE-WAY TO THE PALACE

The candidates thronged after Eldritch as he hurried through the staff-only areas of the hotel. Here, there were no aquariums or elaborate decorations, just brick walls lined with service ducts and steam pipes. Although his counting wasn't the best, Sin tallied sixteen other candidates, an even mix of boys and girls. He no longer held Zonda's arm but he stuck by her side as they descended a narrow flight of steps beneath a low-arched ceiling. They emerged into a high-vaulted circular chamber, the clatter of feet echoing around them. Half-sunk into the floor, a heavily riveted pipe, the height of three men, bisected the room. The air was damp with a pungent tang that reminded Sin of his recent swim in the canal.

The pipe rattled and gurgled as a chemlight mounted

in the ceiling swirled from red to green. Eldritch heaved on a sturdy iron lever attached to a console of fluctuating dials. Pistons hissed into life and the top section of the pipe rotated open. A brassanium and ironglass fish the size of a small steambus bobbed in the trough of water created by the half-pipe.

Zonda gave an excited squeal and shook Sin's arm. "I told you Nimrod could make one."

Sin stared at the fish, feeling a combination of awe and terror. He'd occasionally travelled by horse and cart at the Fixer's bidding but never in the enclosed confines of a steamtram. And at least on a steamtram you could jump off at any time. In the fish he'd be trapped, underground, under water.

"That's pure mental. I ain't going in that."

"Not so tougheroony, after all?" said Zonda.

Eldritch span a wheel on the console and the windowed side panels of the fish slid open allowing access to the plush cushioned seating inside. "Fill up from the front," he shouted.

Zonda dragged Sin to the fish. His stomach knotted. Every instinct screamed at him to resist. He pushed down his fear, stepped inside and shuffled to the fish's head. Dropping onto a padded curved bench opposite Zonda, he peered through an ironglass porthole representing the fish's eye. Outside, none of the other candidates had moved.

"Don't all rush at once," said Eldritch, pushing the reluctant candidates towards the doors.

Velvet strode through the crowd and stepped into the fish, trailed by a clique of followers. She stretched her shoulders back, and her tightly corseted bodice creaked. Her boots tip-tapped against the metal chequer-plate floor as she sashayed to the rear of the fish.

Sin didn't like Velvet and he didn't trust her, but there was no denying she had a certain bad girl allure, and with her mother on the Committee, she had powerful connections. He returned his gaze to Zonda who squirmed excitedly in her seat like a kid in a sweet shop. Should he jump ship? He didn't want to admit it but he probably had more in common with Velvet than Zonda. He could be self-centred and downright evil when provoked.

The last seat now filled, the fish's side panels locked back into place and the chemlights in the roof brightened. Outside, Eldritch pushed the lever and the pipe rotated back into position, sealing closed with a clunk of finality. Across from Velvet, the foppish boy with the mop of curly white hair, who Sin had saved from the Red Blade, mumbled to himself, rocking back and forth.

Valves opened and water rushed into the pipe. The fish creaked, swaying as the murky water crept above the sill on the ironglass windows. The boy rocked faster, arms clutched around himself.

Velvet dragged a ringed hand against the ironglass, the gems eliciting a sound like nails on a blackboard. "Mother says the Committee refuses to travel by fish. Something to do with one sinking once."

The boy leaped up, his eyes wild, his breathing fast and ragged. He yanked the door's handles. "I need out, I need out," he screamed.

Zonda pushed herself to her feet and glared at Velvet. "I hope you're pleased with yourself."

Velvet smiled demurely.

The doors refused to budge and the boy collapsed to the floor. His eyes rolled back in his head and his chest rose and fell rapidly as his breath came too fast and too shallow. Zonda kneeled beside him, cradling his head in her lap. "Has anyone got a paper bag?" she asked, her voice squeaking with panic.

Sin had seen the Fixer deal with panicked gang members before. "Lift his chin," he said. The prone figure was now shaking uncontrollably.

Zonda raised the boy's head in her hands and tilted it upwards. Sin bunched his fingers into a fist and punched the boy in the jaw, knocking his head out of Zonda's grasp.

"What the Hades are you doing?" she cried.

Sin flexed his hand. "Knocking some sense into him."

The boy's twisted body lay still. The convulsion ceased and his breathing returned to normal. Zonda rolled him onto his side and checked his pulse. "I think he'll be okay."

The boy stirred and Sin grabbed him under the arms. "Can you sit next to him?" he said to a rakish girl with a long, thin face.

She nodded, possibly too frightened to speak. Sin lifted the boy onto the seat and wedged him between the girl and Zonda. Massaging his knuckles, he returned to his place opposite.

Zonda glowered. "Did you have to punch him quite so hard?"

Sin shrugged. "It was just a tap. He'll be fine." He could feel his knuckles already beginning to swell but it didn't harm to create a statement. *This is how I help people. You don't want to see what I do to the ones I want to hurt.*

Dirty water now filled the pipe, swirling past the windows. The fish lurched, rocking from side to side as it started to swim. A gramophone horn lowered from the ceiling and began to broadcast a message. Despite the crackly quality of the recording, the Irish lilt of the woman's voice was calm and soothing. "Welcome to the pipe-way. You are currently some fifty feet below the bustling streets of Coxford. The pipe-way was originally constructed to provide safe passage from the city during Zeppelin bombing raids. It is now used for travelling to the COG training establishment. We sincerely hope that in these troubled times it will not be required to return to its original purpose. The journey will take a little over fifteen minutes. Please enjoy this music while you travel."

A scratchy silence followed as the shellac auto-changer swapped platters and the sound of Sir Jedwood Elgar's "Steam and Happenstance", played by the Londinium Pressure Pipe Orchestra, filled the carriage.

Zonda turned to the rakish girl. "Thanks for helping. I'm Zonda, and the Marques of Queensbury over there is called Sin."

The girl pushed a barley sugar to the side of her mouth and said, "Pleased to make your acquaintance. I'm Mercy Goose." She thrust a paper bag at Sin and, reddening a little, said, "Sweet, Sin?"

Sin reached into the bag. "Nice one, Goosey." He flashed her a smile and she reddened some more.

As the last of Sin's barley sugar melted away the music stopped and the voice returned. "You will shortly be leaving the pipe-way to continue your journey free floating. Do not be alarmed; this hardly ever goes wrong."

They shot from the pipe, black water now surrounding the fish. A weightlessness filled Sin's stomach. The floor angled upwards and the fish began to rise. The water went from murky brown to mottled blue, then light flooded the interior. The fish breached the surface nearly leaping clear of the water before settling to an even keel. They were in the middle of a lake surrounded by rolling grassy slopes. Directly ahead of them, at the top of a hill, stood an impressively columned stately home the size of a small village. The stonework appeared golden in the summer sun and the long regal windows sparkled.

"Welcome to Lenheim Palace, former residence of the Duke of Marlborough, donated to COG by our leader Nimrod Barm. This will be your home for the next five years," said the voice.

Sin stood and pressed his face against the window. "Have you ever seen anything like it?"

"It's beautiferous," said Zonda.

Velvet snorted. "It's a hovel. Mummy's castle in Ransilvainia is far more impressive."

Sin's gaze travelled along the length of the palace. It had more windows than he could count. How was it possible for one person to own all that? "I thought Nimrod Barm was a crackpot inventor. How can he buy a palace?"

Zonda tapped the window. "He invented ironglass. The patent for that alone would buy the palace with change to spare. He has over seven thousand other patents; he's probably the richest man in the Empire."

"Not richer than the King?" said Sin.

"Technology is the new King. Nimrod Barm could buy the throne."

Guided by unseen mekaniks, the fish drew alongside a

reed-bound jetty, onto which the candidates disembarked. A lady in a flounced layered dress welcomed them, her words flavoured by a thick Fromagian accent. "Bonjour. I am Madame Mékanique and I will be responsible for your welfare during your stay."

She motioned towards the palace. "Your new residence has an East Wing and a West Wing and you will be divided into two groups accordingly. The first name I call out will go here, the next name here, and so on and so forth," she continued, gesturing left and right. She pulled a list from a pocket and began reading: "Ace, Asp, Brazil, Carnaige, Chubb, Von Darque, Goose, Grundy, Hope, Irk, Jenkins, Maggot, Nobbs, Shank, Trimble, Wagtail."

The candidates took their assigned positions and Madame Mékanique folded the sheet of paper. She looked up to see Sin standing alone.

"Candidate Sin. We are not knowing if it is your first name or your last name, so Monsieur, you may choose. East Wing or West Wing?"

Zonda smiled and waved eagerly at Sin. Next to her slouched the white-haired boy, rubbing his chin. Both groups were an even mix of boys and girls, but Zonda's group, the East Wing, were a motley crew. Velvet was clearly the queen of the West Wing, by luck or some sort of scheming her cronies had been selected with her and they radiated an air of superiority. They were definitely the stronger group, the ones most likely to succeed, the group he knew he should join.

Madame Mékanique tapped her foot. "So, Monsieur Sin, what is it to be?"

CHAPTER 7
TESTING TIMES

Sin collapsed onto the bed in his newly assigned room. Despite his exhaustion, he took a moment to enjoy the blanket and the gentle bounce of the mattress. The day had been a whirlwind. Sin had arrived at the palace with only the clothes on his back, his keeper and his trusty set of lock picks. So the morning had been spent collecting clothes, books and equipment from the Quartermaster. Then in the afternoon they'd had exams.

Sin had never sat an exam before and would be happy if he never sat one again. They'd been told the papers had been individually assigned to account for the candidate's varying levels of education, but even so he'd struggled to get the words to make sense or do the sums in the exam they'd called mathematics. In the end, while the other candidates scribbled away frantically he'd covered most of his exam papers with pictures, something he had a natural flare for. He'd drawn the brassanium fish they'd arrived in, the flowers in the Conserva-Observatory and his encounter with Eldritch on the canal bank. He'd also started to draw his new room with its giant arched window, plush carpeted floor and fabulous antique furniture, but the bell had rung and papers were collected before he could finish.

Afterwards, many of the candidates had eagerly compared answers. Sin had ignored them, he wasn't bothered. So long as they didn't throw him out before he could investigate Lilith and Noir's connection to the photograph in his keeper, he was golden. He'd considered fronting up to the magician but the man petrified him. There was something about his white face and raggedy black clothes that exuded evil.

Sin started as a loud knocking rattled his door. "Are you decent?" yelled Zonda.

Was he decent? Well, that was the ultimate question, wasn't it? And it had nothing to do with whether he was wearing his breeches. He was a thief, a liar, a bully and a cheat. Those were the cards he'd been dealt. Maybe if he'd grown up in a well-to-do family like the foppish Jasper Jenkins, or been the offspring of Olympic athletes like Mercy Goose, things would have turned out different. Instead, he'd been abandoned on the church steps in a box of Sinclair's Medicinal Spirits and he couldn't change that. The Sisters of the Sacred Science Church had never missed an opportunity to remind him of his sinful heritage and maybe they were right. Sin by name, sin by nature.

"I'm as decent as I'm ever going to be," answered Sin.

Zonda pushed tentatively into the room. "Tomorrow's itinerary's been posted. You've got remedial maths and English. Six in the morning before brekker."

"I guess they didn't like my drawings."

"I'm sure they thought they were fantabulous, I really do, but generally on an exam paper they prefer the answers to the questions."

"I couldn't even read the questions, so that was never gonna work."

Zonda slumped into a leather-backed armchair adjacent to a Tedwardian desk and huffed. "It'll be my turn to be humiliated after brekker because it's an introduction to the assault course, and then later in the week we've got combat training."

"They'll probably go easy on us, first time out."

"I think not. It says we're going to be in competition with the West Wing and the losers get to do punishment duties. So not only do I get to be humiliated in a generalist manner, I get to be specifically humiliated by having my face rubbed in it by Velvet."

"You don't know, you could do all right."

"If you're serious, you're delirious. I mean look at me."

Sin shrugged. "You'll just have to play to your strengths."

"That was the point when a gentleman would have asserted I had an hourglass figure."

"You do have an hourglass figure." Sin rolled onto his front and grinned. "It's just your hourglass has a few extra minutes in it."

Zonda gripped one of the chair's cushions, an expression of disbelief on her face. "At least I can calculate how many extra minutes, unlike some." She hurled the cushion with surprising accuracy, landing it squarely on Sin's nose.

Sin sat up, rubbing his face. "There you go, Zon, a bit of fighting spirit. So long as combat training is cushions at ten paces, you'll be fine."

"Sin, you are a complete and utter dough-brained maggot." Zonda pouted, but her eyes were smiling. "Thanks for joining East Wing."

Sin shrugged again, not letting on how close he'd been to choosing the West Wing. Only Eldritch's advice directing him towards Zonda had swayed his decision. "As my test results showed, I'm not so smart," he said.

"You were plenty smart enough to survive on the streets. That sort of courage has got to be good at COG."

"It ain't courage. I didn't have no other choice. I joined COG because it's the first time anyone's given me a way out." He gently tossed the cushion back to her. "That's what I don't get about you and Mercy and pretty much all the others. You had it all nice and cushdie. What you wanna leave that for?"

Zonda clutched the cushion to her chest. "It's about doing the right thing. Stopping the war."

"We're just kids. How we gonna stop the war?"

"Using kids is the whole pointerooney. No one's going to suspect us of spying or working undercover."

"Don't make no sense to me. The Fixer's crew was mostly kids and the Sheriffs always suspected us."

Zonda frowned. "There's a considerable disparity between petty thievery and international espionage."

"Do you like using big words because it makes you sound clever?"

"No. I like using big words because I *am* clever."

"Yeah, we'll see how clever you are on the assault course tomorrow."

Sin ducked and the cushion hurled by Zonda sailed over his head. He may not be educated, but he was a quick learner.

CHAPTER 8
CHEATERS SOMETIMES PROSPER

"The Gears of Excellence trophy is awarded to the fastest candidate completing the assault course on test day," barked Sergeant Stoneheart. A healthy few inches over six feet tall with the physique of a Zulu warrior she looked out of place dressed in a pristine white blouse, tan jodhpurs and shiny leather boots.

"Fail to complete the course on test day and you're out of COG." The metal plates on the soles of her boots clicked as she prowled between the candidates, sizing them up.

The assault course that filled the hangar-sized gymnasium started simply with a brassanium plated wall, monkey bars and a rope swing, but as it progressed the obstacles became more bizarre. Canvas umbrellas hung below a series of giant intermeshing cogs, rows of cannons guarded a rubber mat that ran up a steeply inclined slope, and two mekanikal horses sat on a set of rails that swept over a series of jumps.

Stoneheart's face appeared, an inch from Sin's nose. "Are you listening, boy?"

"Yes."

The instructor's eyes narrowed. "Yes, what?"

"Yes ... I am ... listening?" said Sin.

"You will refer to me as Staff, is that clear?"

"Yes, Staff," answered Sin.

Stoneheart spun on her heels and paced through the candidate's ranks. "You will refer to me as Staff and to yourselves as COG and your last name. This is to remind you that you're all parts of a bigger machine." Stoneheart clacked to a halt and planted her feet apart in front of a fearful-looking Zonda. She flicked the end of her riding crop onto Zonda's shoulder. "If you fail, the whole machine fails, which is why you will be tested to destruction so we can discard those of you who are weak and break."

Zonda's face turned deathly white with an unhealthy hint of green. Sin half expected her to puke. He smiled encouragingly, but Zonda focused only on Stoneheart. The instructor scrutinised Zonda with ill-concealed contempt. "Name?"

"COG Chubb, Staff."

"Front and centre, Chubb. Let's see what you've got."

Zonda shuffled to the start line as Stoneheart retrieved a battered stopwatch from a chain around her neck. "There are two rules. ONE: You must complete every obstacle. TWO: No one can help you during your run."

Zonda picked at the hem of her baggy gym smock as she stared at the ground, her shoulders hunched. Stoneheart twisted the button on the top of the stopwatch, returning the hands to zero. "COG Chubb, you go on my mark. Three, two, one, MARK."

Wild-eyed panic on her face, Zonda sprinted from the line. She executed the worst attempt at a jump Sin had ever seen and thudded into the wall with an audible *whoomf.* Kicking at the metal, she heaved herself upwards then her arms gave out and she slid into a crumpled heap.

"COG Chubb, that is a fail. Get off my assault course."

As Zonda limped back to the candidate's ranks Stoneheart sneered in disgust. "There are no second chances in the real world. When you're being chased down by a squad of mounted Teutonian Dragoons you either get over that wall or you get run through with a lance."

She reset her stopwatch and turned back to the candidates. "Test day's in four weeks, but you could be sent on missions at any time, so we're going to have a little competition this morning to motivate you."

The candidates ran the course two at a time, East Wing versus West Wing. The team that won would go to morning tea, the team that lost would carry sandbags to the lake and back. Stoneheart picked the draw, skilfully matching the candidates so that as the last two prepared to run the score was level at seven each.

Sin walked to the line, where Velvet limbered up. She turned to him and tapped a finger against his temple. "I know you're short a few cogs up top so I'll do the maths for you. I win. You get zero points. We get tea and crumpets. You get to chaperone Chubbs to the lake."

Sin slapped Velvet's hand away. "If your legs ran as fast as your mouth, I'd be worried."

A clanking echoed through the gymnasium. Major C marched towards them, steam spurting from his mekaniks.

"Attention," commanded Stoneheart and the candidates brought their feet together, their arms rigid at their sides.

"Thank you, Staff," said the Major, hissing to a halt in front of them. "A COG agent needs to be multi-skilled. You may be dancing a waltz at a foreign embassy before cracking a safe and then escaping across the rooftops." The Major's eyes focused on Zonda. "If Sergeant Stoneheart is hard on you, it's because I've told her to be. You cannot afford to fail." He about-turned and clunked over to where Sin and Velvet waited. "Ms Von Darque and the boy who nearly outpaced Eldritch. I think we can give these two a proper test, don't you, Sergeant?"

"Yes, sir." Stoneheart retrieved a flat metal card

peppered with holes from the pocket of her riding blouse. She slotted the card into an octagonal column at the start of the course and the gymnasium floor rumbled. A siren sounded and the mekanikal contraptions around the course came to life. Pistons wobbled obstacles, landing platforms moved side to side and padded beams, balls and boxing gloves rotated, swung and punched, ready to foil an unwary candidate. Sin stared at the steam-powered mekaniks. The obstacles were just like the rooftops of Coxford with its swings, jumps and climbs – they were child's play – but the mekaniks, they were going to hurt like hell if they hit you.

Stoneheart reset her watch. "Candidates ready. Three, two, one, MARK."

Sin sprinted hard and sprang at the wall, planting his hands on top. He somersaulted over and, maintaining his momentum, barrelled towards the monkey bars. To his surprise, Velvet matched him.

By the course's midpoint, they were still neck and neck as they traversed balance beams over a water pool. Velvet crouched and flicked out a shapely muscled leg, kicking Sin on the ankle. He wobbled, arms flailing as a rotating spar caught his knees, toppling him into the water below.

Sin waded to the side of the pool and, ignoring the heavy pull of his sodden clothes, heaved himself out.

Spurred on by rage he powered into the course, determined to catch Velvet.

The last obstacle was the boxing net. Velvet scrambled on her belly, already halfway through as Sin dived beneath the rough rope. Piston-powered boxing gloves rained down blows, the pain fuelled Sin's anger, driving him onwards. Velvet was now only yards in front, slowed by her desire to avoid a battering. Sin's ears rang, a shock of colour flooding his vision as toughened leather slammed into his head. Dazed, he pulled himself clear of the net but Velvet was already over the line.

"Victory to the West Wing," shouted Stoneheart.

Gears grinding, Major C stomped from the course.

His body battered and bruised, Sin limped past the finish line. He thumped his fist against his chest venting his rage. He wasn't angry at Velvet for cheating – fair play to the girl. He was angry at himself for not cheating first.

With a self-satisfied smirk on her lips, Velvet held her hand in front of her face. "Zero," she mouthed, touching her finger and thumb to make a circle.

* * *

A sandbag over each shoulder, Sin hobbled down the gravel track. Next to him shuffled an unburdened Zonda. "This isn't fair," she complained.

Sin inhaled a breath of fresh, clean air. Across the lake majestic oaks stood, centuries proud on the gently rolling grass hills while the weeping willows bowed at the water's edge. A smile crept onto his face. "I've a soft bed, warm clothes and as much food as I can eat. Seems pretty fair to me."

"But Velvet cheated, we shouldn't have lost."

"We didn't lose, we won."

Zonda eyed him suspiciously. "Err, wrongarooney. Fewer points and a punishment run, that's losing."

"Do you want to fail the assault course on test day?"

"Of course not."

"This is like my remedial maths, extra practice. We're getting fitter and stronger while the West Wingers gain nothing. So we won."

"We won," Zonda repeated. "We won. This will help me get over the wall, so we won." She hefted a sandbag from Sin and clutched it awkwardly to her body.

"What are you doing?" said Sin.

Zonda smiled through the exertion. "I'm not letting you steal my winnings."

CHAPTER 9
ICE COOL CHALLENGE

Still aching from the morning's punishment run, Sin marched with the other candidates onto the shooting range. The tendons pulled taut on the backs of his hands, the polished wood stock of the steamrifle he grasped felt alien and frightening. The gun's cylindrical pressure boiler was warm against his chest, unlike the cold sweat prickling his palms and fingers. He was a stranger to guns, only ever having seen them from afar, carried by the King's Militia in the streets of Coxford. The Fixer had claimed to own a Teutonian revolver but Sin suspected that was a lie as no one had ever laid eyes on it.

Sin ran a finger along one of the copper pipes. There was something unnerving about the gun. The muzzle flared beautifully from the clean straight lines of the dark steel barrel. The steam hardware curved with geometric precision. It was like a work of art.

"Dinnae be scared of the weapon, she'll nay bite you if you treat her well," said Staff MacKigh. He was a short, barrel-chested Scotsman with luminous ginger hair and tattoos. He locked his own steamrifle into his shoulder and aimed it down range. "This is the NB78 steamrifle. It is the canniest weapon in the Empire. It makes a distinctive retort when fired, which is why we call it the Banshee." He squeezed the trigger and the steamrifle screamed. Halfway down the range a target fell with a clunk. "This little beauty saved my hide in the Ceylon Tea Mutiny of '79. Get to know her and she'll serve you well too."

Claude Maggot leaned towards Velvet. "It's just a gun," he whispered, his face scrunched into a disparaging expression.

MacKigh's body stiffened. "It's a steamrifle or a weapon, ne'er a gun. And if you'd defended a sangar from three hundred screaming Chinasians, you'd appreciate there's nae 'just' about it." The shade of MacKigh's face now matched his hair. "COG Maggot, hold your weapon above your head and run to the fifty-yard mark and back. GO!"

Maggot jogged onto the range. MacKigh squeezed the trigger and his weapon screamed. A target next to the terrified candidate dropped. "Faster, Maggot," yelled MacKigh. The Scotsman lowered his steamrifle and addressed the group. "It fires a standard nail sabot round, which is lethal at up to three hundred yards." He held up a rusted nail about two inches long that tapered to a point. "This one was removed from my shoulder after the battle of Tetley Hill." He loosed two more rounds down range and Maggot doubled his pace, sprinting back to rejoin the candidates.

MacKigh flicked on the steamrifle's safety. "As COG Maggot will now tell you, the nail makes a distinct sound when fired at you."

Between pants, Maggot said, "A very distinct … zinging … sound, Staff."

"At COG we are about preventing war but sometimes you have to fight for peace."

MacKigh pulled a large silver guinea from his pocket. "I call this the ice cool challenge. The candidate who hits this at the furthest distance wins an ice-cream supper for their wing." He flicked the coin in the air. "So who's got the stones to start the bidding?"

Sin kept his mouth shut. He probably couldn't hit the coin from ten yards. Heck, he probably couldn't even get the steamrifle to shoot. MacKigh hadn't taught them anything yet. He guessed this was to determine the candidate's abilities like the tests in the other subjects.

Well, like the maths and the reading he was starting from zero. He looked around the East Wingers hoping someone was a crack shot. Much as he'd talked up their defeat on the assault course he was smarting about losing to Velvet and being beaten by the West Wing twice in one day would be unbearable.

"COG Trimble, East Wing, one hundred yards, Staff," said Esra in a plummy accent. He held his steamrifle confidently, and it was obvious that he'd shot before. Maybe only pheasants on his father's estate but at least he knew how to handle a weapon.

Velvet glanced at Sin. She brushed some non-existent dust from the satin trimmings on her dress and lifted her steamrifle. Shouldering the weapon, she sighted down range. "COG Von Darque, West Wing, one-fifty, Staff."

Sin had no idea if Velvet's stance was correct, but the way she planted her feet leaning into the weapon, she looked confident. Mind you, Velvet tended to look confident whatever she did.

"COG Goose, East Wing. My parents shot in the Olympic team. I think two hundred yards shouldn't be out of the question, Staff."

Sin smiled as Velvet lowered her weapon and her nose wrinkled. Good old Mercy, not only generous with the barley sugars but hopefully an expert markswoman too.

With one hand, Beuford Wagtail waved his steamrifle

in the air, the weapon's weight a trifle to the large-framed Americanian. "COG Wagtail, West Wing. My pa taught me to shoot before I could walk," he said in a southern drawl. "I normally hunt with something bigger than this little peashooter. Still, it'd be a damn shame if I couldn't put a hole clean through your silver dollar at two hundred and fifty yards, Staff."

Velvet patted Wagtail on the back and made the zero sign with her hand towards the East Wingers.

Sin fought the urge to say three hundred yards just to take the smirk from her face. You had to pick your fights and this was one where he was literally outgunned.

"COG Chubb, East Wing, three hundred and fifty, Staff."

Uproar broke out among the candidates. The West Wingers jeered and catcalled while the East Wingers tried to get Zonda to recant.

"You can't do that. Let Beuford take his shot and if he misses Mercy can nail it," said Esra.

"I've definitely got this," said Mercy.

Velvet muttered something to Trixie Asp, a pretty West Winger with a blonde bob and a smile spread across her face. "You're obviously desperate for the ice-cream but think of your figure," Trixie said to Zonda.

Jasper Jenkins placed a hand on Zonda's arm. "We know you want to help, but maybe now isn't the time."

"SHUT IT," shouted Sin, and both sides recoiled in silence. "Zonda's made her bid; let her take the shot unless any of you have the pistons to bet further." His challenging glare swept across the West Wingers. "Thought not. Zonda's shot it is then."

MacKigh flipped the guinea in the air and caught it. "I appreciate the wee lassie's enthusiasm but the NB78 only has a range of three hundred yards."

Zonda stood to attention. "Incorrect, Staff. The weapon has an effective lethal range of three hundred yards. Captain Chubb of Second Battalion King's Steam Cavalry shot Zulu Chief Chianga through the eye at five hundred and fifty yards. As I don't need to kill the guinea, just hit it, three hundred and fifty yards should be fine, Staff."

Sin realised he was holding his breath, waiting to see how MacKigh would respond.

The hue of the Scotsman's face deepened to an impressive crimson. MacKigh slowly brought his feet together and his arms to his side, in a position of attention. "I stand corrected, lassie. And if you can hit that coin at three hundred and fifty yards I will nay only buy you an ice-cream supper, I will wear a pink frilly dress for the remainder of the week because I say it canae be done, you wee Sassenach."

Hoisting her rifle, Zonda said, "I think you'll look fabuloso in pink, Staff."

Maggot ran the coin to the three hundred and fifty yard post, balancing it carefully on top. Staff MacKigh fished in the breast pocket of his tunic and pulled out two rounds. "You get one practice shot to zero the weapon, then one attempt at the coin, lassie."

With well-drilled precision, Zonda clicked both nails into the magazine, then tapped it against the rifle's stock.

"You know it's a soldier's myth that it settles the rounds," said MacKigh, pointing to the rifle.

Zonda slotted the magazine into its housing and it latched fast with a solid clunk. "So at the battle of Tetley Hill, you never did it?"

MacKigh grinned. "Every time, lassie, every time."

Sin felt unsettled by the change in Zonda. Velvet may have looked competent with the steamrifle but Zonda appeared positively dangerous. It wasn't just that she knew her way around the weapon; for someone of Zonda's intellect that would have been easy to learn. It was more the way the steamrifle became a natural extension of her body.

The ruffles on her frilled dress flattened as Zonda adopted a prone position at the firing line. Mercy kneeled beside her and tossed some blades of grass in the air. "Moderate left to right crosswind," she said.

Sighting down the barrel, Zonda dialled in the sights to three hundred and fifty yards.

A hush fell over the candidates. Sin's gaze darted

between Zonda, MacKigh and the target. The instructor didn't think it was possible, but if she landed a good practice shot, she'd be in with a chance. Zonda's finger pulled tighter.

Velvet sneezed and Zonda yanked at the trigger. The weapon twisted in her hands and screamed.

"Miss," said Mercy. "Practice over."

"Oops, sorry," said Velvet, holding her hand to her face as if mortified. "I hope I didn't put you off."

Sin watched Zonda as she stared down range. To the unaided eye, the coin was nothing more than a bright sparkle. Zonda lowered her head to the eyepiece and pulled the weapon tight into her shoulder. The barrel moved rhythmically up and down with her breathing. Sin tensed as Zonda exhaled, tightening her finger on the trigger. The last of her breath left her lungs and the trigger pulled taut. The weapon screamed and the nail flew down range.

CHAPTER 10
SACRIFICIAL PAWNS

The setting sun's rays drifted sluggishly through the high arched windows of the East Wing common room. Well-stocked bookcases lined the walls, while an eclectic mixture of seating and cushions provided ample space for the candidates to relax. Sin slouched on a battered leather sofa eating ice-cream and studying a book. It was a simple story with pictures about a dog and a ball – a big red ball. His finger traced along the words. The dog was called Spot and it was running after the ball. Sin's chest burst with pride; this was the first book he'd ever read and he was doing it all by himself. Spot caught the ball and brought it back to a boy called Tom. Sin turned the page, eager to discover what happened next. He finished the story and snapped the book closed. A broad smile spread across his face. He could read.

Lottie Brazil, a serious-faced, dark-haired girl with an overindulgence of freckles, rested her far weightier tome on her chest. She spooned a generous helping of melted chocolate fudge sundae into her mouth and turned her head towards Sin. "So did Spot get the ball?"

"Spot fetched the big red ball for Tom and was given a bone for being a good boy."

"Ah, so some sort of redemption tale."

"Yeah, it was a long tail, a long waggy tail. How's your book going?"

"It's jolly scary. A mad scientist called Frankenstein has created a monster by combining dead people's body parts." Lottie turned a page. "Alas, no dogs or balls."

From the armchair opposite, Stanley Nobbs sniggered. Lottie looked down her nose at him. "Really?"

Stanley shifted position, his beanpole body folding into the chair's contours. "Raised in the gutter, weren't I?"

"But now you have an opportunity to better yourself, to do good, to stop a catastrophe."

Stanley slurped some ice-cream. "Nah, I'm just here 'cos Eldritch caught me and promised free nosh."

Sin tapped his fingers against his book. "I'm guessing Eldritch didn't chase you across the city, Lottie. So how come you're here?"

"I'm not really supposed to talk about it. My father's stationed in Bucharest as head of the diplomatic corp. He says the politicians aren't going to stop the war so it has to be done via the back channels. He's been helping COG for years."

"So you knew what you were letting yourself in for?"

"Not really. Father's connections got me on a secret COG selection course but it was mostly academic tests and team games."

Stanley lifted his face from the bowl, his nose covered in melted ice-cream. "So why'd you join?"

"It was either this or a young ladies' finishing school. Running assault courses and shooting steamrifles takes the biscuit over embroidery and filling out dance cards any day of the week."

It sounded like reason enough to join, thought Sin. Except on a mission the enemy would be shooting back. No one really understood what it was like to face down death until it happened, and when it did, Sin wondered if Lottie would wish she'd opted for the dance cards. He swung his legs from the sofa and ambled over to where Zonda was challenging Jasper Jenkins to a game of chess. "Finished me book."

"So I heard," said Zonda, her attention not straying from the board.

A faint scent of strawberries wafted from Zonda's hair as Sin perched next to her on the arm of the chair. He liked strawberries. In the summer the barrow girls would push their carts around the streets, hawking woven punnets to the toffs. If they had any left at day's end he'd blag a handful for the price of a smile or, if he'd been lucky, a stolen trinket. He eased closer, inhaled deeply and pointed at the board. "Never did get me head round chess. Half the bits were missing from the set at the orphanage and we normally ended up chucking them at each other. Who's winning?"

Jasper tugged at a curl of hair, pulling it over the livid bruise on his cheek. "It's a might more complicated than *you'd* understand. I've employed a Sicilian defence while Zonda's attempting the Sebastopol gambit."

Zonda dipped her hand into the remnants of her banana split and pulled out a chocolate swirl. She popped it into her mouth and licked her fingers clean before advancing a pawn. Jenkins moved his horse, taking the pawn.

"He got you there, ay?" said Sin, nudging Zonda's arm.

From the back of the board, Zonda pushed her queen into the knight's square and removed it. "Checkerooney." She raised her eyes to Sin and they hardened. "Sometimes you have to sacrifice a pawn to take the king."

There was something in her expression, or possibly an edge to the tone of her voice, that made Sin feel uncomfortable. It was like being savaged by a kitten. His thoughts drifted back to that afternoon when the silver guinea had spun from the post, struck by the nail. There had been no delighted squeal from Zonda or other girly emotion. She had simply pulled the magazine from her rifle and drawn the bolt back, making the weapon safe. In that moment, Sin had seen something different in Zonda. It was like on the smoggy streets of Coxford when you saw the dark outline of a gentleman, then a swirl in the mist would make everything clear, just for a second, and it wasn't a gentleman, but a Sheriff and suddenly you needed to run.

Jenkins knocked his king over. "Well played," he said and offered his hand.

Zonda grasped it daintily and smiled, her green eyes soft again. "Thank you, it was a pleasure."

"No, the pleasure was all mine," said Jenkins, holding onto Zonda's hand for a little too long as far as Sin was concerned. There was something about the boy that wound Sin's spring. Below the dandified veneer and flawless manners lurked a malicious streak, Sin was sure of it.

He plucked the queen from the board and said, "Don't make no sense her being the most powerful. Should be the king who's in charge."

"You're confusing power with importance," said Zonda. "The queen may be the most powerful but remove her from the game and it continues. The king is the most important; every army needs a rallying figurehead and without him the game is lost. Look at Nimrod. He's by no means the most dangerous member of COG, but as the founder, he's the most important. We'd be doomed without him."

Unlike the cheap wooden chess pieces from the orphanage, the ivory queen was heavy in Sin's hand. Heavy with the burden of being the strongest, maybe. The weight of responsibility, that's what the Fixer had called it when he'd given Sin the job of toughening up the weaker members of the gang. He'd been good at it too and had turned the scrawniest of runts into hardened scrappers. He considered Zonda, an idea forming. "Do you trust me?" he asked.

Zonda toyed with a black knight. "You know what? I posituitively do."

"Nice one. Meet me back here after lights out and be wearing your gym kit."

* * *

Three hours later, Sin stole back into the common room. The rays from his chemlamp sparkled from the crystal bowls left over from their ice-cream supper. Zonda was already waiting for him, dressed in her gym smock.

Turning the lamp down to barely a glimmer, Sin said, "Follow me."

They crept through the palace, Sin's footfalls

undetectable, the thump of Zonda's feet worryingly loud. Sin stopped below a portrait of a knight in black armour, his sword dripping with blood, a pile of slain enemies at his feet. "There's tons of ways to walk quietly, you need to find one that works for you," whispered Sin. "I like to place my heel down then roll the rest of my foot on to the ground." He took several steps, overemphasising the motion as Zonda copied the walk. "Yeah, that's better," he said. She wouldn't be working as a sneakthief any time soon but the improvement was enough that they might avoid discovery.

They navigated to the gymnasium, the padding of their feet the only sound in the deserted hallways and corridors. Sin turned a brass wheel on the wall and the overhead chemlights brightened. "You're going to need two things to complete the course: more strength and better technique." He guided Zonda past the wall to the second obstacle, the monkey bars. "Strength will come with time but I can teach you technique now." Sin reached up to the first bar. "You hold it like this, fingers over the bar, thumb underneath. Both hands go on the same bar then one hand to the next bar and the second hand joins it."

Zonda swung over the water pit, her face turning beetroot-coloured with the exertion. One hand slipped from the bar and she flailed backwards. Sin clutched her waist and pulled her tight against him back to safety. Her body trembled as she sobbed. "I can't get over the wall and I can only do two monkey bars. How am I ever going to pass the whole course?"

Sin shuffled her backwards, away from the edge of the chasm. "Hey, where's the steely-eyed soldier I saw this afternoon on the range?"

"She doesn't exist." Zonda sniffed. "Father taught me to shoot and I was good at it. It was the one thing about me he was proud of, so I practised and practised. It's simple physics really: distance, velocity and gravity. You just do the maths." Zonda gesticulated at the assault course. "But this isn't me. I want to pass, I posituitively do, it's just too hard."

Sin turned Zonda around to face him. "The book you're reading at the moment, it's hundreds of pages long, right?"

Zonda frowned. "I suppose."

"I've just read a five-page book with pictures, about a flipping dog called Spot. Everyone thinks I'm a dullard. The book Lottie's reading is thicker than my head. I could look at it and give up reading right now, but I don't, because tomorrow I'll read six or seven pages, the day after that ten and then maybe, one day, I'll read as well as you and Lottie." Sin wiped a tear from Zonda's cheek. "Two monkey bars is your Spot the dog, but tomorrow, it'll be three. You don't need to worry about the whole course, just one piece at a time."

"I don't think you're a dullard. In fact, you might just be the smartest person I know."

"What, cleverer than Nimrod Barm?"

"Okay. The second smartest," said Zonda, wiping the back of her hand across her eyes.

Sin clasped her shoulders. "You didn't see Velvet when that coin pinged from the post – face like a sucked lemon, it was priceless. Staff Stoneheart is wrong. You're not a weak COG, you're a different-shaped one, and a machine isn't made from all the same pieces."

As Zonda reached again for the monkey bars, Sin caught his reflection in the water below. How did he fit into the machine? The streets had made him tough and resourceful, but so were thousands of other kids. He hadn't been recruited by accident, he'd been targeted. Not for the first time, he wondered why.

CHAPTER 11
I SPY

The faint sulphurous aroma that pervaded the technology lab tasted like rotten eggs in the back of Sin's throat. He peered at a blackboard covering the wall behind a long and cluttered desk. His lips moved as he silently sounded out the words chalked on the board: *An Introduction to Technology with Nimrod Barm.*

With childlike enthusiasm, Zonda picked up a steam motor from a workbench and gave it an experimental spin. "This is fantabulous. Have I died and gone to heaven?"

Sin lowered his eye to a tapered brass telescope that pointed out of the window. "Not unless your idea of heaven includes an introduction to technology with Nimrod Barm."

"It probably does," scoffed Velvet. "Either that or a giant cake shop."

"Actually, I'm more of an ice-cream girl," said Zonda.

"You are too." Velvet clicked her fingers. "Do you remember that time when Miss Derwent took us to Geovanni's Gelato Parlour?"

"No," said Zonda.

"You must remember. You got Strawberry Surprise on the end of your nose and walked around Coxford looking like some sort of circus clown. I don't think I've ever laughed so much."

"You laughed. I got stung by a bee."

"That's right. Your face swelled right up." Velvet pinched her own nose. "And you couldn't talk properly for a week," she concluded, making her voice nasal.

Trying to keep himself from grinning, Sin panned the telescope across the lake. "This is amazing; it makes everything seem real close."

Velvet smacked him on the back of the head, banging his face against the eyepiece. "It's just a telescope." A cruel smile crept onto her lips. "Although, you'll find it useful to get a good view of my back as I win the Gears of Excellence trophy miles ahead of you."

Sin rubbed his eye. "The only reason I'd be watching your back is so I don't have to see your ugly mush."

Velvet framed her face with both hands. "Radiant

beauty. Your insults are as dumb as the rest of you." She shouldered past Zonda and flounced off to sit with the other West Wingers. Sin hated to admit it but she had a point. Maybe not radiant beauty, more cruel magnificence, but she had it in spades. Movement outside caught Sin's attention: a figure sidled along the hedge in the formal gardens. He redirected the telescope and peered through it.

Lilith Von Darque checked over her shoulder then slunk to an alcove in the hedge. She eased onto a rustic arbour seat and again looked about furtively. Grasping the folds in her dress she hitched up the hem and reached down to a circular buckle on her boots. While pretending to tighten the strap, she took an envelope from her boot and slid it beneath the bench.

Zonda pulled Sin away. "Come on, we need to sit down."

He glanced back at the window, however without the telescope, the gardens were just a blur. What was Lilith up to? Whatever it was, it was well dodgy.

The balding head of Nimrod Barm appeared from behind the desk. "Ah, good, you're here. Please do find a seat, everyone, I've just got to get the spindle-drive fitted back into this wotjamacallit." He vanished back below the desk, his voice muffled. "That's got it. Champion."

Sin pulled out two stools at the back of the class but Zonda took his hand and guided him to the front row.

"Don't be a sillies. We want to sit here."

"We do?"

"Absolutamon."

Nimrod reappeared with a socket wrench in his hand, which he waved at the blackboard. "Welcome …" He stopped and focused on the wrench, his brow furrowing with confusion. "No, hang on, that's not right." He deposited the wrench and picked up a telescopic rod. "Welcome, candidates. I'm Nimrod Barm." He indicated his name on the board. "And I'm a mass murderer."

A collective gasp escaped the room. Nimrod clenched the rod, his knuckles whitening.

Sin had met murderers and he'd no doubt that the Fixer had killed more than a few, but Nimrod, he didn't seem like the type.

The portly scientist slammed the rod down and gripped the edge of the desk. "I haven't personally killed anyone, nonetheless my inventions have ended more lives than I care to dwell on. The blood of hundreds of thousands of poor unfortunate souls is on my hands and that is one of the reasons I founded COG. We must stop the next war or millions will die."

Sin didn't know how many a million was, but he'd once been in a big gang fight with the Barrel Lane crew where there must have been at least a hundred of them scrapping and that had been pretty scary.

Zonda raised her hand. "Sir, you can't be held accountable for the actions of others."

With trembling fingers, Nimrod removed his glasses and pinched the bridge of his nose. "That's exactly what I told myself in my youth. I was just the inventor, the artist, the creator, never the user." He blinked and replaced his glasses. "I was proud and arrogant, the great Nimrod Barm. My country needed me to design better guns, bigger shells, more efficient ways to maim and kill and I complied. I thought all technology was good technology; the advancement of science was to be applauded. I know better now."

From the pocket of his tweed trousers, Nimrod removed a red and white spotted handkerchief and wiped a solitary tear from his cheek. "I can't put the genie back in the bottle, but between us we can stop those who are wishing for war." He screwed the handkerchief into a ball and dropped it into a steel crucible. A match flared at his fingertips and he tossed it on top of the material. There was a loud bang and the crucible shuddered sending a ball of flame mushrooming upwards before burning out.

A wave of heat and sooty smoke washed over Sin and Zonda. Sin nudged her under the table. "Real glad we sat at the front now."

Nimrod tapped the crucible with the telescopic rod. "I call that the flamekerchief. It works well as a distraction or an incendiary fuse and also ..." Nimrod stared into space "... for blowing your nose." He pulled a lever on the desk and, with a hiss of steam, a map of Europe descended from the ceiling. A loud crack echoed through the lab as he whacked the pointer against the map. "The Teutonians fear the Ruskovians and want to invade the Fromagians. The Fromagians fear the Teutonians and want to invade the Swisstalians. The Swisstalians fear everybody. The Ruskovians fear the Britannians and the Britannians fear nobody but want to invade everybody. In short, we have our work cut out."

His eyes fixing on the class with frightening intensity, Nimrod said, "There has never been a time in our history when the outbreak of all-encompassing war in Europe was more likely."

Sin had lived all his life in Coxford. He'd never been to another city, let alone another country. It was way too big for him to comprehend. How was he, or indeed any of them, going to make a difference?

"Unlike these empires," said Nimrod, gesturing towards the map, "we do not have armies. But COG has something far more valuable: a network of well-trained, well-motivated and well-resourced spies. Rather than the blunt instrument of military might, we will send you on missions to strike with surgical precision, sabotaging the war machines of the most powerful empires in the world. As COG agents you will achieve more than any army ever could."

The way Zonda gazed in awe at Nimrod, hanging on his every word, worried Sin. He'd seen the same look in some of the newbloods in the gang, lapping up the Fixer's banter, believing the crew was the toughest and that they couldn't lose. And it was the truth, the gang was the toughest, and the gang didn't lose, but that weren't no comfort to the same starry-eyed kids as they lay dead in the gutter.

The map disappeared back into the ceiling as Nimrod strolled to the front of the class.

"The purpose of these lessons is to give you a firm scientific grounding. Your missions may require you to work undercover and destroy experimental technology. If you understand the machine, you know where to best throw the spanner."

Zonda raised her hand again. Somewhere behind, Velvet tutted.

"Yes, COG Chubb?"

"Wouldn't it be better to steal new technology rather than destroy it?"

"Often you're alone, in a foreign country, and so it becomes impractical. However understanding the science can be invaluable. A quick sketch and some scribbled notes may allow us to reverse engineer the technology."

Glancing over his shoulder, Sin contemplated the likeness of Velvet to her mother. *The Chinasians and*

Ruskovians are interested but they want more than rough sketches. That's what Lilith had said in the Conserva-Observatory. She was from a foreign country. If COG stole technology from overseas, then surely other countries must do the same. Was Lilith stealing from the century's greatest inventor, Nimrod Barm? Whatever she'd been up to in the garden, it was well suspect. He needed to check under that seat.

Nimrod struck the bench with his pointer. "So let's start with something simple. Who can name the three basic sources of motive power?"

Zonda's hand shot up and she issued little excited gasps, stretching upwards. Sin looked around the class, most had their arms raised. The only three who didn't were the kids from the streets, the runners as they called them. Himself and Stanley Nobbs from the East Wing, and Skinner Grundy, a thickset bruiser from the West Wing.

Nimrod smiled encouragingly at the three runners. "Come on; think about it. Even if you don't know you can work out two of them."

Sin kept his arms by his side. Why pick on the street kids? It wasn't fair. He should ask one of the schooled candidates who knew this stuff. He should ask Zonda, she'd be delighted to answer. Grundy's hand tentatively lifted and Sin thought he was off the hook, then Nimrod aimed the pointer straight at him and his heart jumped.

Why was Nimrod picking on him? He must have seen his test results. He must know he had no education. Was he trying to show him up in front of the class? It was hard enough for him as it was, knowing everyone was cleverer than him. Picking on him was just giving the likes of Jasper Jenkins even more reason to rub his nose in it.

"Sin, name a source," said Nimrod.

"Tomato?" answered Sin.

The class burst into laughter. Even Zonda couldn't suppress the smile from her lips. Red pins of embarrassment prickled Sin's face. He bit down hard, anger in his eyes. Fists clenched, he kicked his stool backwards and stormed from the lab.

* * *

Sin paced his room, boiling with rage. He wanted to smash something or fight someone, or even get a beating, anything to take these feelings away. He'd nearly thrown his chair out of the window but he wanted to stay at COG so he'd fought the urge. The echoes of the laughter replayed in his brain and the anger roiled. One particular laugh cut through the cacophony of merriment, stinging his ears and piercing deep into his soul: the delighted cackle of Velvet Von Darque.

There was a knock at the door.

"Leave me alone," he shouted and kicked the bed.

The door pushed open. "I came to see if you were all right," said Nimrod.

"Oh, I'm just flipping danderific, can't you tell?"

Nimrod removed his tweed jacket and draped it over the chair. "I'm sorry I put you on the spot like that. I was hoping you would get the answer. I was wrong to do so. The mistake was mine, not yours." Nimrod's voice hardened. "Look at me, Sin."

Fury still burned within him yet he turned his head towards the scientist.

"I want you to understand that I am genuinely sorry for any hurt caused."

"What do you care about a toerag like me? I'm just a cog in your machine."

"I care because I *was* a toerag like you."

"You? You're soft as fresh horse doings."

Nimrod pulled the shirt tails from his trousers and lifted the material clear of his back. Pale white scars crisscrossed the skin. "My shoulders are worse. Hard as it may be to believe, as a child I was diabolical at chemistry and the Sisters weren't kindly if you didn't know your scripture or your periodic table."

Sin ran a hand over his own shoulder, feeling the ridged scarring. "You were raised by the Sisters of Sacred Science?"

"Until fortune smiled on me and a kindly Coxford

professor took me in. I was younger than you, but I got a chance in life. This is your chance, Sin. Take the blighter with both hands and don't let it go."

"You started off like me, unable to read and write?"

Nimrod waggled his glasses. "I started off worse than you. I could hardly see until the professor fixed my eyes."

Sin cocked his head to one side, cricking his neck. "So what are the three basic sources of motive power?"

"Steam, clockwork and chemical, with chemical being the primary source. I can explain the theory in your detention after dinner this evening."

Sin straightened his neck and squared his shoulders, glowering at Nimrod. "Detention?"

"You can't storm out of class and not expect consequences. Besides, I'm not supposed to give private tuition, but I can give as many detentions as I like."

The bad-tempered expression melted from Sin's face as the penny dropped. Nimrod patted Sin's shoulder. "You're going to do fine here, Sin. I'll make sure of that. Now you need to get to the arena for combat training." Nimrod retrieved his jacket. "And a word of advice. If Staff Von Darque asks you to hit her, try your hardest to do so."

CHAPTER 12
MURDEROUS MACHINES

The arena was a hexagonal hall set apart from the main palace. Racks of every conceivable weapon lined the walls, from samurai swords, to Teutonian crossbows, to inventions of Nimrod's that didn't officially exist. Lilith and Eldritch faced off on a circle of white sand at the centre of the arena. Dressed in their everyday finery, they looked more like they were out for a Sunday afternoon stroll than preparing for gladiatorial combat.

Sin hurried towards the throng of candidates who huddled around the brassanium and ironglass safety screens that enclosed the arena. He spotted Zonda shifting nervously from foot to foot, the ruffle on her dress fluttering like a swarm of irritated butterflies. Velvet stood statuesque beside her, cool as a cucumber sandwich. He eased between them and pressed his face to the ironglass. "This should be good. Eldritch chased me down in Coxford without breaking a sweat."

"A man trying to hurt a woman is never good," said Zonda.

Velvet turned. "Mother fought hard to get women accepted into COG, we can't afford to be seen as shrinking violets."

"I just don't think violence should be the answer."

"True enough," said Velvet, "but unfortunately it's men asking the questions."

Lilith swung her silk parasol as Eldritch removed his bowler hat. She caught the parasol's point and levelled it, rifle-like. A steel harpoon shot from its centre in an explosion of steam. In an instant, the brim of Eldritch's hat expanded to four times its size, forming a buckler shield. He dodged sideways, swatted the lethal bolt away and raised his walking stick. The cane's ebony outer sheath fired at Lilith. More of a distraction than a serious threat, Eldritch took the opportunity to attack with the internal blade now revealed. Lilith pirouetted away and the folds of her dress raised outwards in a spinning circle of razor-edged fabric. Eldritch withdrew, his rapier poised. Lilith spun to a halt, parasol raised. Discarding the bowler hat buckler, Eldritch circled Lilith, feinting with the rapier, testing her defence. He twitched the blade right and lunged. Lilith's parasol cut down, blocking the attack. Eldritch thrust his left hand towards Lilith's throat. A contraption concealed in his coat sleeve delivered a bayonet to his hand and he pressed the blade against her windpipe.

"I yield," said Lilith, her eyes burning with hatred.

Steam erupted from the base of the safety screens and they sank into the ground.

Eldritch lowered the bayonet and turned to the candidates. "A COG mission without confrontation is a good mission. We prefer stealth and guile but there are times when combat is unavoidable." Eldritch flicked his wrist and the bayonet disappeared up his sleeve. "If you have to fight, you do whatever it takes to win. There are no rules or chivalry; that will only get you dead."

Lilith planted her parasol in the sand. "Although still in training, when the need arises, you will be sent on missions. So we have to ensure you are ready." She gestured at one of the East Wingers, a chunky boy with cropped hair. "You. Come here."

Jimmy Ace seemed hesitant as he stepped into the ring. Lilith looked him up and down. "You boxed for your school?"

"Yes, ma'am, I got a blue."

Lilith pointed to her chin. "Hit me just there."

"But we're not supposed to hit ladies."

Lilith's hand shot out and the heel of her palm struck Jimmy on the jaw. His feet lifted and he crumpled backwards onto the sand. Lilith ignored him, addressing the remaining candidates. "There are no rules or chivalry. Let's try again. COG Wagtail step up."

Beuford Wagtail cracked his knuckles and walked up to Lilith with a gunslinger's swagger. "Yes, ma'am," he said.

"Same as before, hit me just here."

Beuford drew his arm back and threw a haymaker punch. Lilith squealed and cowered, her arms held defensively in front of her face. Beuford pulled the punch, his meaty fist hanging in midair. Lilith's leg flicked from beneath her dress and she kicked him in the clockworks. There was a collective intake of breath from the boys as Beuford sank to the ground, moaning in agony.

"Girls, when we fight, we are not ladies. Men will hesitate and underestimate you; be sure to use that to your full benefit." Lilith beckoned to Sin. "COG Sin. Your turn."

Wary as a cat on the hunt Sin prowled into the ring. He guessed he had an advantage over the other candidates. He'd never been in a fight with rules, or if he had, there was only one rule: survival.

Lilith indicated her chin. "Same again, hit—"

Sin didn't wait for her to finish. No rules. He sent his fist flying in an uppercut. Lilith arched backwards, the punch missing her chin by a whisper. Sin went to follow up with his left but Lilith stepped away applauding. "Well done, COG Sin. I yield. You may stand down."

Sin backed away cautiously, unsure of whether this was still a test and certain he didn't want to end up like Beuford and Jimmy.

Eldritch, having disposed of his rapier, returned to the ring. "Boys with me, girls with Staff Von Darque."

Sin and Stanley helped Jimmy and Beuford to their feet and followed Eldritch to a training area at the side of the arena. Eldritch removed his coat and rolled up his shirtsleeves.

"The foreign news section of the *Coxford Standard* reports that tensions are high along the Ruskovian border after a brigade of Chinasian Manchus were in lively skirmishes with a division of Cossacks." He pointed to a scar on his forearm. "A memento I gained from a Cossack Shashka during the Balkans campaign. The Ruskovians are a formidable foe but you underestimate the Chinasians at your peril."

Eldritch spread his feet apart and bent his legs, lowering his body. "We have very little time to get you mission-ready. Pay attention, work hard and kung-fu may just save your life." His arms snapped back and forth in a series of well-executed punches, making his fists a blur. "Right, boys, lesson one: Zhang Yu, arms of the Octopus."

* * *

Sweat dripped from Sin's brow. They'd spent the last hour kicking, blocking and punching while shouting strange words like "ki-ah". His arms were bruised and his legs ached, but he was beginning to see the benefits of a more disciplined approach to fighting. He was partnered up with Jimmy, who despite the smacking he'd got from Lilith, was an accomplished fighter. Eldritch sauntered over. "COG Ace, go practise with another group. COG Sin, I want to see what you've learned." Eldritch held up his hands palm outwards. "Hit my hand."

Sin slammed his right fist into Eldritch's palm. "Good. Raise your shoulders and twist your hips. The power comes from your whole body, not your arm. Again."

Twisting as instructed, Sin punched once more.

"Nice." Eldritch gestured to the practising candidates. "The skills you possess put you way ahead of the others, and I'm not just talking about fighting. You have talents honed by necessity. It was the same in the army. The good soldiers survived the bad and the weak died. A sort of unnatural selection to misquote Darwin."

"But I ain't educated, like the others."

With a grip like a clockwork clamp, Eldritch clasped Sin's shoulders and leaned closer. "I know the truth of who you are." He fixed Sin with a manic stare, then a smile spread onto his face. "You are a diamond in the dirt. Let COG shape you and polish you and you will shine oh so very brightly."

Sin had never thought of himself as a diamond. Most of his life people had treated him like he was horse crap. Maybe Nimrod had instructed Eldritch to give Sin a pep talk, worried that he might quit. And it had worked, sort of. Sin did feel better about himself, however that last bit, that had been strange. Nimrod had made Eldritch recruit him and he still didn't know why. If he confronted Eldritch he'd have to confess to spying on Lilith and Noir in the Conserva-Observatory, when he was supposed to be in his room. That was a whole nest of wasps he didn't want to kick. He could always ask Nimrod during detention, but that would be tipping his hand. If Nimrod had wanted him to know surely he would have told him already.

Eldritch let go of Sin and clapped his hands together. "That's excellent work, boys. Now, can anyone here ride a bike?"

Stanley's hand shot in the air. "Me, Staff."

"Apologies, got my words mixed up. I meant to say would anyone here like a fight. Well done for volunteering, COG Nobbs, please step into the ring."

Stanley shuffled onto the sand, a look of apprehension on his normally cheeky face.

A strange mekanika contraption trundled into the ring.

It was like a punching bag on wheels, with a multitude of piston-powered, boxing-gloved arms. On the round padded target that represented the contraption's head someone had painted a smiling face.

Eldritch tinkered with the dials on the rear of the device. "This is the Battler Boy. I'm putting it on the easiest setting today so you can get a feel for it." Eldritch stepped away. "You need to get ten hits in two minutes to win." A bell rang and a puff of steam escaped from the Battler Boy. It punched all six of its gloved hands together and rolled towards Stanley.

"Come on, Nobby, you can take it," shouted Sin.

Stanley had an unusual style but one which suited his lanky body. He weaved about the ring then darted in with a couple of quick punches and skipped away before the battler shot back with a gloved piston.

"One minute gone," called Eldritch.

Stanley sprang towards the Battler Boy and landed a punch to the mekanika's head. The battler responded with a slow right and Stanley ducked left. A jet of steam spurted from the battler's back and it unloaded a left jab. The glove thudded into Stanley's cheek and he reeled backwards, shaking his head. The battler advanced, throwing a series of punches at its dazed opponent. Stanley caught another slug to the chin and his legs wobbled.

"All-in, Stanley, all-in," yelled Sin. It was a street term

used by the Fixer but Sin was sure the other crews used it too.

Stanley lowered his head, screamed, and charged. In a show of berserk rage, he hit the battler with a whirlwind of fists, knees, elbows and a rather impressive headbutt. The battler's bell rang twice and, with a sad hiss, it deactivated, arms falling limply by its sides.

Outside the ring, the boys cheered, viewing their classmate with a new-found respect.

For good measure Stanley kicked the battler twice more then swaggered from the ring. Sin held out his fist, which Stanley bumped with his own. "That's how she rides," he said, the grin returning to his face.

Beuford lifted his chin. "Ya'll don't do bad for a scrawny guy."

"Had to impress the ladies, din' I." Stanley winked.

Lilith strode over to the ring trailed by the girls and a second battler. "You will often be sent on missions in pairs so it is important to learn to work as a team." She guided the battler into the ring. "COG Sin, you impressed me earlier. Let's see if you can do it again."

He'd impressed her, but fighting wasn't about showing off or scoring points, it was about survival. Sin shrugged out of his jacket and handed it to Zonda. Her fingers trembled as she grasped the collar. Sin placed his hand on hers. "Relax. No mekanika's going to get the better of me.

Besides, what's the worst that could happen?"

Eldritch fiddled with the controls on the back of the second battler's head. He signalled to Lilith. "I think we'll make this one a little more challenging, so pick someone good."

"Better than good, I'll pick the best," said Lilith. "COG Von Darque. Do not disappoint me."

Velvet strutted into the ring and joined Sin. "Hope you're better at fighting than you are at science."

Sin rolled his shoulders and cracked his neck. "This I'm schooled for."

A bell rang and Sin advanced on the nearest battler. He fended off a couple of nasty punches and began hammering the mekanika's targets. Unlike Stanley, he kept in close, absorbing blows to the body and dodging anything aimed at his head. In a matter of moments, he landed a series of well-executed combinations and the battler deactivated. Sin sauntered towards Velvet who danced around her battler.

In an explosion of steam, the ironglass safety screens shot from the floor, trapping Sin and Velvet in the ring. Startled cries rang out from the candidates, several of whom had been knocked backwards to the ground. Sin glanced at Zonda, her face a mixture of shock and panic. He smiled and shrugged. It was no drama – he'd just pummel the other battler then wait for them to drop the screens.

Behind him, the dormant battler hissed back to life.

Sin turned. The boxing gloves fell to the sand, discarded by the battler, and a series of long blades emerged from the hollow arms.

Sin retreated. This was grim. Previously, he'd blocked most of the mekanika's punches and the few licks that got through were nothing he couldn't handle. Sharpened steel changed everything. He couldn't block the blades, and muscle offered little protection from razor-edged metal. Slow time, slow time, slow time, he thought but the battler surged towards him, blades flailing wildly. Sin dived sideways and pain sliced his shoulder. He rolled across the sand leaving a trail of red.

Outside the screens, Lilith screamed at Eldritch. "What have you done? You've put one into weapons mode?"

If there was a reply, Sin didn't hear it. His focus narrowed on the battlers as they closed in on Velvet, shepherding her into a corner. He leaped onto the back of the blade-wielding mekanika and ripped away the leather and horsehair padding to reveal a confusion of pipes and gears beneath. Velvet pressed her back against the ironglass screens, the mekanika's blades slashing within inches of her face. Hot metal scorched Sin's hands but ignoring the pain he seized a handful of pipes and heaved. The muscles in his arms bulged taut then a giant cloud of steam erupted from the mekanika and Sin fell backwards onto the sand. Through the haze he saw Velvet deliver a combination of well-aimed blows. The gloved battler deactivated and the ironglass screens sunk back into the ground.

Having checked that Velvet was unhurt, Lilith zeroed in on Eldritch. "What the hell do you think you're doing?"

Eldritch held his hands out placatingly. "It wasn't me. I assure you."

Sin clamped his palm to his shoulder, the warm blood painful on his scalded hands. Although the cut wasn't deep enough to be dangerous it stung like a whiplash. He took in the lifeless battlers. Why hadn't time slowed? What was different from all the other times? He may have saved Velvet but somehow he felt he'd failed himself. If he couldn't rely on his ability, then it was like playing Ruskovian roulette, not knowing when his luck was going to run out.

Zonda rushed to Sin's side. "You're hurt."

"It's just a scratch. Like I said, what's the worst that could happen?"

CHAPTER 13
ESCAPE FROM DETENTION

Sin peered through the telescope at the formal gardens. He hadn't yet managed to check under the bench, his plans having been thwarted by an afternoon spent in the sick bay. The cut to his shoulder had been glued and bandaged, while a gooey green cooling gel applied to his hands had miraculously removed all signs of the scalds. Madame Mékanique had insisted he rest for the afternoon under observation. Finally, after ensuring he'd eaten an evening meal of her special medicinal soup, she'd released him from the infirmary and he'd gone straight to the lab for detention.

Nimrod clattered through the doors, an ornate toolbox in one hand, a slice of Battenberg cake in the other. "Of all the things I wished I'd invented, I think Battenberg cake has to be top of the list. Alas, that credit goes to another."

He deposited the toolbox on the bench and depressed a button. Clockwork whirred and the box unfolded, trays and compartments appearing almost magically. "Mr Kipling, a master baker and brilliant poet. Some people are just over achievers." Nimrod scooped tools from the bench and loaded them into the box. Retrieving a chisel, he sliced his cake in two and handed half to Sin. "This evening, detention is going to be a practical introduction to mekanika. We need to investigate what went wrong with my Battler Boy."

* * *

The arena was deserted, save for the bladed battler that lay inert on the circle of sand. Nimrod plonked his toolbox next to it and Sin helped him roll the battler onto its front. A ripping sound drifted across the arena as Nimrod removed the padding from the battler's head. "Velkrow, another invention I missed out on." Nimrod placed the padding to one side and examined the control panel revealed beneath. "I met Velkrow Evans once. A tiny Welsh man with wiry hair. He said he got the idea from cockleburs that were forever attaching themselves to his head." Nimrod fished a screwdriver from his pocket and prodded the panel. "Oh dear." He directed Sin's attention with the screwdriver's tip. "This is the control bar. You can see it's on intermediate boxing."

"So Eldritch was telling the truth. He had set it right?"

"Yes, but see here, below the bar. The control rod has sheared off, so no matter what you select, it remains on the sword-master setting." Nimrod began unscrewing the control panel. "The thing is, that control rod is made from brassanium, so it would take a monumental degree of force to snap it."

"You think someone bust it on purpose?" asked Sin, helping to remove the screws.

"No other logical explanation presents."

"Why would someone do that?"

"It would be naive to think the government aren't aware of us. Those that are baying for war may want to send a message."

Sin rubbed his shoulder. That message was inscribed on his skin. "Zonda reckons you're richer than the King. Can't you just use your money to prevent the war?"

"Money can get you many things, but it would be a very sad day for democracy indeed if moneyed men and wealthy businesses controlled our government."

"But with all your coin you could hire the best soldiers and spies. Why recruit kids?"

"Soon, when you go on undercover missions, you will appreciate pounds, shillings and pence aren't motivation enough. Money only buys loyalty until someone pays higher. You have all been selected because you bring special skills to COG."

This was the opportunity Sin had been waiting for. "Why me? I'm just an urchin; I'm nothing special."

Nimrod put his hand on Sin's shoulder. "You survived for years on the streets. That's pretty extraordinary."

"Don't make me special, plenty of others survived too."

"They're not you, Sin. You have the potential to be the best COG operative we've ever seen. Even better than Noir."

So the magician was their top agent. Why would Nimrod think he could be better?

"I don't understand, sir. You don't even know me."

Nimrod smiled and tapped the side of his nose. "Let's just call it a scientific hunch."

Sin slotted the screwdriver's blade under the control panel's edge and levered it clear.

"Well, would you look at that," said Nimrod. He snatched a magnifying glass from his toolbox and held it over the damaged control rod. "Cut marks. Someone went through this with a hacksaw."

A loud clatter issued from the far end of the arena, startling them. Sin leaped to his feet. "Stay here, I'll check it out." He sprinted in the direction of the noise. A dull ache throbbed in his shoulder but otherwise it seemed good. He slowed his pace as he neared the arena walls, which were covered in racks of weapons. He could easily picture one of the cruel blades in the hands of the saboteur, ready to complete the message they'd started earlier. On the floor rested a chunky spear, apparently having fallen or been knocked from a rack. Sin approached with caution. The Fixer often used what he called a "come on". They'd place a bizarre object in a back alley and when some poor unfortunate went to investigate, they'd jump him. Sin scanned the surrounds but there was no hiding place from which to launch an ambush. He bent to pick up the spear and noticed the faintest of scents hanging in the air. He inhaled deeply. Visions of barrows and market girls filled his head and the sweet memory of overripe strawberries tantalised his tongue.

He replaced the spear and returned to Nimrod, who now had the battler in pieces. "Just a weapon slipped from a rack," said Sin.

"Right-ho. Let me explain how the battler works."

Sin could tell Nimrod was keeping his explanations simple, but even so he glazed over at times when the words or concepts held little meaning to him. As they replaced the damaged parts, Sin tried to identify the different metals by their unique feel. The copper steam pipe was warmer and softer on his palm than the cold, hard brassanium control rods, while the steel of the clockwork mainsprings was smooth and oily.

Nimrod snapped the control plate back into place and with Sin's aid they screwed it back down.

"Good as new," said Nimrod.

"Apart from that flipping great hole I ripped in the padding," said Sin, pointing to the ragged-edged leather that still bled horsehair.

"The saddle maker can fix that. We need to look at the boiler room."

* * *

Nimrod led Sin down a concealed flight of concrete steps on the outside of the building and unlocked the sturdy oak double doors. "The heart of any building, or indeed ship, airship or other vehicle, is its boiler. If you really need to throw a spanner in the works, that's the place to do it." He pulled the door open and they headed inside.

The air was hot and humid. Colour-coded pipes ran along the walls, interspersed with wheeled valves and pressure gauges. They traced the route of a thick conduit to a massive steel sphere that perched like a giant egg on a nest of pipes. Behind the sphere, the arena's ironglass safety screens rested on massive pistons that would raise and lower them through the floor above.

"This is an experimental design of mine. A violent chemical reaction heats the water so there's none of that laborious mucking about with coal." Nimrod slapped the sphere and a hollow thunk echoed around the basement.

"If the Sky Navy knew about this little beauty, they'd shoot me dead and steal it in an instant. Imagine how far they could fly their blimps and their bombs if they didn't have to carry tons of coal." The scientist tilted his head, momentarily lost in thought. "But it's the steam console we're interested in. Someone must have tinkered with it to raise the screens and trap you with the battlers."

Nimrod disappeared behind a cluster of pipes. "Here we are. Oh. Oh dear."

The console contained rows of brass-rimmed dials and gauges. Although Sin hadn't the faintest idea what they represented, the fact that their needles were all in the red was not a good sign.

"Is the boiler going to explode?" asked Sin.

Nimrod wiped beads of sweat from his forehead with a handkerchief. "Boilers rarely explode these days, dear boy, too many safety features. No, it will dump steam if the pressure gets too high."

"So we're safe?"

"From being ripped to pieces by exploding boiler shrapnel, yes." Nimrod hesitated, then tapped one of the gauges with his knuckles. "From having our skin peeled from our bodies by a deluge of venting steam, probably not. I think perhaps we should vacate the area."

They hurried to the exit and Sin slammed into the oak doors, pain piercing his shoulder. The doors hadn't budged.

"I didn't lock them," said Nimrod, his brow furrowing. He jiggled the key in the lock. The doors held fast.

Maybe he was imagining it, but Sin was sure it was getting hotter. Needle pricks itched his palms and he tried not to think of the scalding pain in his hands from earlier, or how that would feel magnified across his entire body. Steam hissed from a pipe at his ankles and he flinched away. "How long have we got?"

"A couple of minutes. Maybe less."

"You designed the boiler, you must be able to switch it off."

Nimrod scuttled back down the passage. "I didn't design it with saboteurs in mind." He lowered himself to the floor and sat cross-legged, contemplating the mess of pipes. "I need to think for a minute."

Steam jetted from pipe joints across the basement. Sin wiped a hand across his forehead. "Are you barmy? We don't have a minute!"

"Go check the dials and let me ponder in peace," snapped Nimrod.

The needles on the console climbed further into the danger bands. Sin felt helpless. Someone had tried to kill him this afternoon and now it looked like they were intent on finishing the job. He was used to his life being dangerous but this was different. On the streets you knew who your enemies were, and if someone had a score to settle they were up-front about it. Here the enemy was invisible, hiding behind mekanika and science. It wasn't right. It wasn't decent.

With a loud crack the ironglass on one of the controls splintered and steam gushed forth.

Nimrod stirred. "Sin, this is going to require some technical finesse." He rummaged inside the toolbox and pulled out a large wrench. "I need you to smash all the pressure gauges. Try denting the metal around the outside so the ironglass pops out. It won't be easy but it should buy me some time to shut down the boiler."

Gripping the heavy wrench with both hands, Sin slammed it into the side of the nearest dial. The blow reverberated along the pipe and sent a wave of pain through his injured shoulder. He gritted his teeth, pushing down the pain, and struck again. Steam spurted from the dial and the ironglass sprang free in a pandemonium of steam.

"Good lad," said Nimrod. He lifted the toolbox and threaded his way into the nest of pipes below the boiler.

Sin's forearms burned and sweat dripped from his body. Every dial he destroyed added to the oppressive heat. If the Sisters had been telling the truth about the crucible of Hell, then surely it must feel like this. His ears ached from the discordant screech of venting steam and his lungs felt raw. Nimrod emerged from the swirling mist, his face a ruddy pink, his glasses opaque with condensed steam. "It's no good, the reaction's gone critical. There's nothing more that I can do." He took a grimy handkerchief from his waistcoat pocket and rubbed his glasses clear.

Sin lowered the wrench. "Your handkerchief."

Nimrod pushed his glasses back onto his nose. "What about it?"

"Is it a flamekerchief?"

"I really don't know, dear boy. It might be."

Sin held out his hand. "Give it here and start praying that it is."

Nimrod passed him the handkerchief. "I'm a scientist. I don't believe in God."

"Don't mean he don't believe in you," shouted Sin, sprinting to the oak doors. He twisted the material into a wick-like tube and fed it into the lock so only a small tail protruded from the keyhole. An errant thread hung from the material. He teased it free and trailed it down to the floor.

"You got a match, Professor?" said Sin.

"Even better than that. I have a Zinc Acid Pyrotechnic Originator," said Nimrod, pulling an ironglass and metal contraption full of liquid from his pocket.

Sin took the device from Nimrod with an air of reverence. He'd seen them for sale at the Corn Market, but costing in excess of twenty guineas, they'd been as unobtainable as Phileas Pines' watches. "You've got a ZAPO lighter, that's well rich. How long you had it?"

Nimrod brushed some dirt from his sleeve. "Pretty much ever since I invented it."

Sin depressed the gas paddle and the zinc and acid reacted producing a hydrogen flame. He held it to the bottom of the thread and a bright orange sparkle fizzled towards the handkerchief.

From the direction of the boiler a shrill whistle sounded.

"I'm guessing that ain't good," said Sin.

"It's the steam-dump warning."

The flamekerchief exploded in a ball of fire and the oak doors flew open, a charred black hole where the lock had been. Behind him Sin heard a cacophonous hiss. He glanced over his shoulder to see a billowing white cloud roiling towards him.

"Gap it," he shouted and grabbed Nimrod's arm.

Dragging the scientist, he stumbled outside and up the steps as a torrent of steam erupted through the doors. Sin pushed Nimrod safely aside, out of the steam's path. The scientist staggered to a halt and rested his hands on his knees as the white cloud dissipated harmlessly into the air. "That was close," said Nimrod between wheezing breaths.

"I hope all your detentions ain't like that, Professor," said Sin, rubbing his ears, which still rang from the explosion. He stared into the darkness surrounding the arena. His sense of relief at escaping was now replaced by a feeling of foreboding. Was the saboteur out there, watching them? Waiting to strike again?

CHAPTER 14
NIGHT TERRORS

Collapsing into a padded leather armchair, Sin leaned back and gazed at the elaborate plaster decoration on his room's ceiling. Raw from the steam, his skin prickled and his shoulder ached. He contemplated falling asleep where he slumped, but images of Lilith skulking along the hedge flashed through his mind and he knew there'd be no rest until he checked under the bench. His original plan of scoping out the garden during the day had been thwarted, so now he was left with plan B: sneak out under the cover of nightfall. It was a simple plan and in essence straightforward, but there was one major complication: the grounds were off limits after lights out. That was a Cast-Iron Rule.

Sin locked his bedroom door and pocketed the key. The flamekerchief explosion and steam dump had attracted a good deal of attention, but fortunately it was on the other side of the palace and so should work in his favour. He slid the room's sash window open and clambered onto the wide stone ledge. Despite being only one storey up, it was still a lethal drop. The height didn't bother him. He'd spent many nights running the rooftops of Coxford where, much like the palace, the fancy stonework made for easy climbing. He moved his foot to a recess in the masonry and gripped onto a decorative carving. The stone was rough on his fingers but solid, unlike the flaky sandstone of some of Coxford's older colleges. He stretched for a lower handhold and his fingertips sunk into slimy bird poo. In a flap of feathers, a wild-eyed pigeon burst from its roost. Startled, Sin's fingers slipped from the stone and he lost his footing. Dangling from one arm, Sin winced as pain lanced through his injured shoulder. His hand spasmed and he tumbled backwards.

The sound of the pigeon became distant, the ringing in his ears died and *time slowed*. The stonework drifted past as he fell, the pockmarks and weathered carvings suddenly appearing far more detailed, his eyes viewing the world with a magnified clarity. He targeted the passing handholds and clutched at the sides of a column. The rough stone chafed his fingers but he slowed enough to kick his toes into adjacent footholds. The pigeon's wing beats returned and pain coursed through his shoulder.

Blood thumped in his head and he inhaled deeply, fighting the urge to scream. His legs began trembling. In the gang they'd called it jelly legs and he knew he didn't have long before the adrenaline rush faded and he'd lose all strength. He hurried downwards, conscious that now speed was more important than safety.

Dropping the last few feet onto the gravel path, his legs gave way and he crumpled in an undignified heap. A figure rounded the corner at the end of the East Wing and patrolled towards him. He didn't have the strength to stand and there was nowhere to hide. He shuffled back into the lee of a protruding column and pressed himself flat into the shadows. The figure marched closer. There was something peculiar in the way it moved, the motion unnatural and precise, the timing of each stride as regular as clockwork.

The mekanika's matt black head scanned left and right, its eyes pulsing red. In one hand it hefted a jagged-edged blade. Sin's heart pounded and a sudden cold gripped his body. Could it sense his presence? Would he be geometrically sliced like one of Doctor Donodroid's cucumber sandwiches?

The mekanika drew level and Sin heard the busy whirr of cogs emanating from below its dulled metal skin. Its head turned, red rays reaching into the shadows. Sin held his breath.

A dizziness overwhelmed him as the mekanika looked away and it continued along the path. He bent double, his stomach churning and his mouth dry. What was he doing here? He should climb back to his room and be done with it. That was the smart thing to do. He reached up for a handhold, tempted by the sanctuary of the open window. The Fixer's voice played in his head, taunting him: *A few days of regular meals and a warm bed and you've gone soft as butter.* Sin clenched his fists, took a deep breath then darted across the path into the cover of the gardens.

He slunk through the grounds, tormented by an uneasy feeling that itched the back of his neck. Under the Fixer's direction, nefarious nocturnal activity had become almost routine and this should be a walk in the park, yet something had him on edge. Sure, the close call with the mekanika had spooked him, but in the past he'd had dust-ups with the Sheriffs and it had never left him feeling like this. He ducked into shrubbery and settled between two bushes. There was no rush. He had all night and he needed to trust his instincts. Calming his breathing, he opened his mouth, swallowed, and listened to the noises of the night.

Leaves rustled and the sound of feet padding on grass drew near. Sin tensed, catching a flash of movement between the bushes. Costumed in a floral pink puffer dress, Zonda moved through the grounds in a caricature of creeping. Was she following him? He could have sworn he'd detected her aroma of strawberries in the arena by the fallen weapon. Whatever she was up to she was going to get them both caught, or even killed.

"Zon, over here," he hissed.

She froze, surprised, then tiptoed towards him. It was like watching the world's least stealthy meringue. He dragged her into the bushes. "What the blazes are you doing?" he whispered.

Zonda placed her hand on his arm. "I'm stopping you leaving."

Sin tilted his head. "I'm not leaving."

"Oh. What the blazingeroo are you doing?"

"I can't explain now."

Zonda stared at him like an expectant puppy. "I can come with you and help."

This was turning into a joke, only there was nothing funny about being diced by a mekanika or thrown out of COG. "No. I need you to stay here and ... keep watch. It's very important. Can you do that?"

"Absolutamon. I shall be like the watchiest of watch-dogs," said Zonda, turning her head from side to side.

Sin crept into the formal garden and flowed along the hedge, silent as a shadow. Drifting into the alcove, he sunk to his knees and rolled onto his back. The underside of the arbour seat was dark, but pinned to the slats the pristine white envelope with its wax seal was clear enough. He removed it and eased back one edge of the flap, careful not to break the embossed shield of the wax seal. Through the gap he spied several sheets of paper, of which the topmost one contained some sort of complex diagram. He'd been right: Lilith was up to something, but what? Back in his room he should be able to remove the seal intact with a hot knife and examine the contents before resealing it. Delicate work, but he'd done it many times before, intercepting sensitive mail for the Fixer. He slid the letter into his jacket pocket and eased away from the bench.

Something jarred his senses and his head jerked up. The splashing of the fountain, which acted as the garden's centrepiece, had quietened. It was a small detail and could have been due to a gust of wind, or drop in water pressure, but experience offered a more likely explanation. Someone, or something, had walked in front of it, blocking the sound's path.

Sin slithered on his belly across the grass to a low box hedge and peered cautiously over the privet leaves. Adrenaline spiked his veins and cold fear gripped him for the second time that evening. Noir stood at the fountain, his raggedy cloak wrapped around him. From inside his top hat he removed a sheet of paper. Sin stifled a gasp. It was from one of his exams, the one with the drawing of the Conserva-Observatory.

The magician clicked his fingers and a crackling ball of fire appeared in his hand. He held the paper above it, transfixed as it burned to ash within the flickering flame.

Using the low hedge as cover, Sin snaked away from the fountain. The man terrified him; he exuded an aura of evil. A little way off an alarm sounded, the single deep note repeating over and over. Zonda screamed and Sin leaped to his feet and sprinted. Fists clenched, he pounded through the gardens as all around more alarms blared.

A mekanika guard stomped through the bushes slashing plants with its sword. Zonda crawled from the undergrowth, her dress ripped, a livid cut on her forearm. The mekanika's eyes pulsed, throbbing in time with the alarm note resonating from its torso. It stepped over Zonda, blade raised, ready to strike.

Arms outstretched, Sin barrelled into the metal beast, and boy and machine crashed to the grass. The mekanika thrashed wildly, like an upturned bug, unable to right itself. Sin rolled away, dodging the jagged blade and pushed himself to his feet. He gripped Zonda under the arms and hauled her upright. "You hurt?"

"My dress is ruined. This is not as fun as I thought."

"We need to gap it. Follow me."

Zonda resisted his pull. "No, you follow me." She guided him from the grass and onto a narrow flagstone path that lead away from the palace.

The alarms, nearer now, reverberated with a deep bass tone that seemed to resonate through his body. Sin glanced back at the palace. "You sure about this?"

"Definoso."

The path dipped sharply below ground level, the earth retained by brick walls. Curving back on itself, the culvert ended at a sturdy wood door. Zonda heaved the door open and they stepped inside. The air was bitterly cold. Large slabs of ice rested on thick stone shelves around the walls. Zonda turned a brassanium dial and chemlamps in the low-arched ceiling came to life.

"What is this place?" asked Sin, his breath forming vapour clouds.

"It's the palace's icehouse." Zonda pulled the door closed and locked it. "We can get to the kitchens from here."

"How did you know about it?"

Maybe it was the chill temperature but the colour seemed to drain from Zonda's face.

"Err … my father showed me around. The palace used to be open to visitors."

"You never–"

"We can talk tomorrow. We need to get back to our rooms in case there's a bed check."

* * *

Sin closed his bedroom door and pressed his back against the woodwork. A long sigh escaped his lips. It had been one hell of a day. He patted his jacket, checking Lilith's envelope was still tucked inside. Turning the light dial, he let a dim glow fill the room. His stomach lurched and he inhaled sharply. A voodoo doll and battered top hat decorated with red ribbon rested on his bed. The desk chair slowly rotated. "Take a seat," rasped Noir.

The magician's presence seemed to suck all of Sin's strength. His knees gave way and he slid to the floor. He'd nearly died three times today, possibly more, but none of those experiences held a candle to the terror now racking his body. How did Noir trigger this senseless fear and why did he seem powerless to fight it?

Noir smiled; it contained no warmth. He held out his hand, the claw-like fingernails long and yellowed. "You have something of mine."

Sin didn't move. He couldn't; fear paralysed him. Anger flared in the man's eyes, mistaking inaction for insolence. Fire sprung from Noir's fingers. "Make no bones, boy. I could take it from you and extinguish you and your lady friend in an instant." He clicked his fingers and the flame died. "However, I'd rather we were friends. You hand over the envelope and vow to tell nobody on pain of a most horrible death and we can forget about your little indiscretion."

Sin's palms tingled with a cold sweat and his heart thumped loudly in his ears. It made no sense. He was used to pushing his fear down, locking it away, but somehow Noir held all the keys to releasing it.

He withdrew the envelope with trembling fingers. The man seized Sin's wrist, his skin rough as dead leaves. He plucked the letter from Sin's grasp and vanished it into his jacket. "Now for the vow." He scooped up his hat and removed the voodoo doll, placing it on Sin's palm. "Do you swear by the Lord of the Crossroad, Loa of the Dead, the vengeful Baron Samedi, that this shall be a secret well kept?"

The tiny straw doll rose upright, seemingly of its own accord.

Sin swallowed, his mouth dry, terror squeezing his heart. "I swear."

CHAPTER 15
DISAPPEARING ACT

A polished oak table, big enough to seat fifty, ran the length of the dining room. Students occupied one end, tutors the other, with the intervening space left empty, like an educational de-militarised zone. Giant gilt-framed portraits of COG members, past and present, adorned the walls. Sin gazed unseeing at a vivid oil painting of a dashing leather-clad aviatrix. A flight pistol in one hand, cutlass in the other, she battled Teutonian skytroopers aboard a burning airship.

"Mother trained her, you know," said Velvet from two chairs down the table.

"What?" said Sin, pulled from his thoughts.

Velvet gestured to the picture. "Captain Felicity Hawk. She's the youngest sky sailor ever to command her own aerostat. Mother wants her to join the Committee."

"Oh, I wasn't really looking," said Sin and returned to pushing a sausage around his plate. For the first time since his arrival at the palace, the food held little appeal. He'd woken with dread banding his chest, as if Noir's evil essence still haunted his room. The sense of malevolent unease had clung to him through his early morning classes, sapping his concentration. Now with Zonda not showing for breakfast, Sin worried that Noir had done something terrible to reinforce their deal. If all the magician wanted was his silence, then there were more terminal ways to ensure it. Sin was no stranger to the way blackmail worked; the Fixer had used it often enough against Coxford's Sheriffs and magistrates. You started with something simple, implying that would be the end of it, then asked for a bit more, slowly drawing the victim in. Noir would ask for more favours, and with each one, the magician's hooks would sink deeper.

Three mushrooms sat on Sin's plate, joined by a pool of melted butter. Velvet, Lilith and Noir; they were all linked, like a chain. Noir terrified him, Lilith intimidated him and Velvet – well, Velvet was the weak link. She may not be directly involved in their schemes, but she was Lilith's daughter. If he could find some dirt on Velvet, maybe he could blackmail Lilith into forcing Noir to leave him alone.

Skewering a mushroom with his fork, he smiled for the first time that morning.

* * *

The green room was painted the colour of summer grass and patterned with a gold bamboo motif. Glossy lacquered Chinasian cabinets hugged the walls, displaying all manner of unusual bladed weapons. From the ceiling hung paper lanterns in a multitude of shapes and sizes.

The special assembly hadn't been timetabled and an anxious feeling nagged at Sin. Was his nocturnal escapade the assembly's cause? Had Noir betrayed him? He'd be gutted if he was to be thrown out of COG now. Stopping the war still seemed beyond him but he enjoyed the lessons and he'd made friends, or one friend at least. His eyes sought out Zonda who was waiting in one of the angular teak chairs, and some of his unease lifted. She looked bleary eyed and had a pristine gauze bandage wrapped around her right forearm, but she welcomed him with a smile.

"Well, that was a spifferooney adventure."

Sin took her hand and examined the dressing. "Are you okay?"

"It was deeper than I thought. I had to go to sick bay and get it biobonded."

"Biobond?"

"It's the same stuff they used on your shoulder. It sort of glues wounds back together and speeds healing. When Nimrod was done with breaking bodies he turned his mind to fixing them. It's another part of his penance, I guess."

"Is there anything the man didn't invent?"

"He didn't invent the camera-nocturna."

Sin raised his eyebrows in question.

"It's like a normal camera," said Zonda, "except it uses chemicals that react to a different wavelength of light so it can take nocturnagraphs at night."

"Oh. Who invented that?"

"I did. Although it doesn't actually exist. I've drawn the plans and worked out the chemical formulas. I'm certain it would work. It's just, how would a girl build such a thing?"

"In detention," whispered Sin to himself. Gears in his mind whirred. Could he lure Velvet into the grounds at night – breaking a Cast-Iron Rule – and take a nocturnagraph that might give him the leverage he needed to get Noir off his back? Zonda would have to build the camera first, but he was sure Nimrod would help. Then all he had to do was draw Velvet into the trap.

Sin reached into his jacket and pulled out a waxed paper package wrapped in string. "Bacon and egg banjo. You missed breakfast."

Zonda seized the package. "Oh, I could kiss you."

Sin froze, but as Zonda eagerly opened the gift it was clear she had no intention of doing so and he dropped onto the chair next to her.

Major C marched to the front of the room, reflections of the coloured lanterns sparkling from his brassanium mekaniks. Behind him skulked Noir. The Major's gaze tracked over the candidates, settling on Zonda. "The Cast-Iron Rule banning you from the grounds at night exists to protect you. The estate is patrolled by the watchmek who cannot differentiate friend or foe and will attack on sight." In a series of small clicks, the Major's head turned so he looked directly at Sin. "If you were involved in last night's disturbance, now is the time to confess and accept the consequences."

Sin had no intention of fronting up, so the almost imperceivable shake of Noir's head as he glared pointedly at Sin was a wasted gesture. Zonda fidgeted in her chair. Sin gripped her bandaged arm and squeezed. She squeaked in pain but the distraction appeared to push any thought of confessing from her mind.

The Major straightened and his mekaniks clunked. "Very well. Combat lessons are cancelled due to an issue in the boiler room. However, we cannot afford any let up in your training so Staff Noir has agreed to bring forward your introduction to magic."

Major C left the room as an excited buzz ran through

the candidates. Noir removed his cloak. "What is magic?" he whispered.

Zonda half raised her arm. Noir ignored her and stuck out his tongue, which appeared to be covered with a blue flame. Exhaling, a stream of fire shot into the air, then with a click of his jaw, he sent a smoke ring drifting towards the ceiling. "Magic is science we don't understand yet." He coughed and hacked a glob of burning phlegm onto the floor. "Can I control the elements with secret dark forces or was that merely chemical trickery courtesy of Nimrod Barm?" He stamped on the flaming gob, his heavy leather boot extinguishing the fire. "I'll let you decide. Perhaps the more pertinent question is: does it matter either way?"

He pulled up a chair and with an exaggerated sweep of his arm gestured towards it. "COG Von Darque, please."

Velvet paraded to the front of the class. She wore a byzantium dress that cascaded in ruffles from her hips to her ankles. Neatly arranging her skirt, she perched on the chair, her feet flat on the floor, her back straight. She glanced sideways at Sin and the corners of her mouth turned upwards. Noir pulled a silk sheet the size of a tablecloth from his hat and covered Velvet. "Watch," he said and threw his hat in the air. It spun end over end then exploded in a shower of sparks. Noir whisked the sheet away and discarded it on the floor. Velvet was gone. Only her dress remained, draped over the chair. Noir clapped his hands together. "*Remember*, we *all dread that which* seems inevitable, but the war can be stopped. I will teach you the craft of magicians and mesmerists, sleight of hand and sleight of mind, the art of hypnosis, misdirection and illusion so that you can lie, cheat and steal as COG directs."

Lying, cheating and stealing. It was the only life Sin had known since running from the orphanage. He'd not thought about that day for years, but now the memory played bright in his mind, as if somehow triggered by Noir. It had been a Friday during penance. The children stood with their hands out waiting for Sister Alldread to deliver cleansing punishment. She was known to the orphans as the witch with the biter and had a wiry strength that belied her slight build. With a look of fervent ecstasy, she'd brought the biter down on Sin's palm and for the first time ever, time had slowed. The pain bit deep and prolonged and in that instant, Sin's fingers wrapped around the rattan cane and yanked it from the sister's grip. As the orphans cheered, he snapped her cherished biter and threw the pieces back at her. Then he ran from the orphanage and into a life of crime.

Sin jolted from the memory as Noir clapped his hands again and whispered, "Ta-da."

The doors opened to reveal Velvet. She now wore a short skirt, striped leggings and a suede bodice. Sin watched as she strutted back to her seat. The disappearance had been quite impossible, yet Sin had witnessed it with his own eyes. He felt a pain in his leg as Zonda pinched him. "You're staring."

"I was wondering how Noir did it."

"Well wonder with your mouth closed and your eyes elsewhere."

Noir reached into the air and a large coin materialised at his fingertips. "We are creatures of reason." He placed the coin in his palm and curled his fingers over it, making a fist. "Show us point A and point B and we will erroneously conclude point C." He opened his hand to reveal the coin had vanished. "We are also creatures of prejudice." He grabbed Sin's hand and squeezed it closed into a fist. "Show us point A and point C and our prejudices will fill in point B." He motioned for Sin to open his hand. Tentatively, Sin uncurled his fingers. A yellowed note covered in faded scrawl rested on his palm. Atop the note lay a length of broken rattan cane.

CHAPTER 16
HOUSE OF A THOUSAND DEATHS

Sin tramped to the shooting range, Zonda at his side. They were dressed in ribbed leather suits, reinforced with oval brassanium panels. On their heads they sported padded flying helmets and ironglass safety goggles. The timetable gave no details about the next lesson but whatever it was, they needed protection for it.

"So what was on that note Captain Creepy gave you?" asked Zonda.

"It was just some scrap of old paper; it didn't make any sense."

Zonda held out a gloved hand. "Can I see?"

"Nah, I chucked it. Load of old rubbish," lied Sin.

"And the bit of wood, what was with that?"

Sin shrugged, the rigid leather suit making the gesture

awkward. "Who knows? He's as barmy as the rest of them."

"You shouldn't say that. You know what it means?" said Zonda, wagging a finger.

"It means he's a nutter."

"Yes, but it comes from people implying you're as nutty as Nimrod *Barm*."

Sin flexed his hands. They'd been issued brand-new leather gloves and the stiff hide rubbed against his skin. "That don't make no sense. The man's a genius."

"It's a fine line between genius and insanity. Many are keen to suggest Nimrod's on the wrong side of it."

Sin remembered the previous evening, trapped in the boiler room, when he'd called the professor barmy. No wonder Nimrod had snapped at him. His swarthy complexion reddened and suddenly the leather suit felt as rough and prickly as the gloves.

They walked on in silence, Sin contemplating the note from Noir. It had been torn from a larger letter but Sin was certain it was about him.

The boy is lost to us, escaped and vanished. Perhaps we were too hard. He was wont to be unruly, and if you spare the rod you spoil the child. I will show you what he has done to my cane on your next visit. Let us hope he is soon found. I pray for his soul. Sister S Alldread.

Sin scuffed his boots through the dirt. Why did Noir have the note and what was his purpose in revealing it?

There was more going on here than Sin understood. He was a tiny cog in a complex machine, being turned and twisted by the biting teeth of bigger, more powerful gears.

* * *

Staff MacKigh waited for the candidates in front of a foreboding mansion situated in a wooded clearing at the edge of the steamrifle range. With his booted feet planted firmly apart and his barrel chest thrust forwards, his stern military bearing was only somewhat marred by the pink taffeta dinner dress he wore. "Welcome, candidates. Today you will enter the house of a thousand deaths where no one has ever come out alive."

The candidates exchanged fearful glances.

MacKigh smiled. "Och, let me rephrase that. No one has ever come out alive on their first attempt. You will enter in teams of two or three, retrieve a briefcase from the library and make your exit. Each team must contain at least one member from each wing. Choose your teams now, and choose wisely. Your life depends on it."

"Your brains, my good looks, what's the worst that could happen?" said Sin to Zonda.

"You do remember nearly being killed by a homicidal Battler Boy the last time you said that?"

"Nearly killed, not actually killed." Sin lightly punched

an armoured plate on her arm. "Besides, that's why we're wearing all this gear."

Velvet stepped between Sin and Zonda, putting her arms around their shoulders. "So team, what's the plan?"

"I don't recall inviting you to join us," said Zonda.

"You didn't, but no hard feelings, I'm letting you join my team anyway," said Velvet.

Sin surveyed the other candidates who were already sorting themselves into groups. "Don't seem like we've got much choice, Zon."

Velvet smiled but her eyes were tinged with hurt. "Great, we can be like the three steam-musketeers."

"Personally, I don't find a trio of sword-wielding Fromagians that appealing," said Zonda.

"*Unus pro omnibus, omnes pro uno,*" said Velvet.

"One for all and all for one," said Sin.

Both girls turned to him in surprise.

Sin shrugged. "Fixer used to say it, din' he."

"Maggot, front and centre with your team," barked MacKigh.

Claude Maggot, Skinner Grundy and Ethel Hope shuffled to join MacKigh who led them up three broad stone steps to the mansion's wide front door. "Goggles on. You have twenty minutes. Go."

Claude heaved on the iron doorhandle and the door swung open. A giant padded mallet arced down from the ceiling and thudded into his torso. He flew backwards down the steps, crunching onto the ground in a battered heap. "COG Maggot, you are dead. COGs Grundy and Hope, you may continue," said MacKigh, ignoring Maggot's groans.

As the afternoon wore on, the teams returned in various states of disarray and, according to MacKigh, all dead. Jimmy and Trixie had been dispatched to the sick bay with possible cracked ribs and Ada nursed a bloody nose.

"COG Chubb, you're up," said MacKigh.

"I hope you won't treat us unfairly because of the dress," said Zonda.

"Aye, lassie, it crossed my mind. Although to be honest, I quite like it."

They approached the front door. Sin held out an arm, barring the way. "Follow me. I have an idea."

As he led them around to the side of the house, Velvet put her hand on Zonda's shoulder. "It's just like the good old days. You and me playing at secret missions while the parents talk business."

"I don't remember them being that good," said Zonda. "You were the vivacious daring spy and I was the dowdy lackey who was destined to die in some horrible manner while you saved the day."

Velvet smiled. "That's right. Vice-Marshal Von Darque and Corporal Chubbs. Fun times."

Sin climbed some steps to a set of patio doors. "No one said we had to go in the front." He opened a tool pouch on his belt and using a flat-bladed file jemmied the lock. The doors swung open and, wary of traps, Sin stole inside. In the centre of the drawing room a charred sofa and armchairs nestled around a circular Persian rug. Opposite the sofa a fire flickered in a marble-mantled fireplace. Sin ran his hand over the sofa's wooden arm. The sooty residue clung to his gloves.

Velvet stepped onto the rug and an ominous click cut the air.

"Take cover," shouted Sin as a deep rumble built in the chimneybreast. He pushed Zonda behind the sofa and stretched for Velvet but she stood tantalisingly out of reach.

A fireball erupted from the fireplace and surged into the room. Sin dived on top of Zonda, flames licking across his back, the heat intense even through the protective leather suit. Sin pressed tighter to Zonda, squeezing into the pocket of safety created by the sofa. Velvet hurtled overhead, trailing smoke behind her as she hit the floor and rolled. With a whoosh the flames died, leaving a soot cloud in their place. Sin disentangled himself from Zonda and scrambled towards Velvet. Patting at the smouldering patches on her suit, Sin extinguished the last of the hot embers.

MacKigh appeared. "COG Von Darque, you are toast.

Return tay the others." He inspected Sin and Zonda. "COG Chubb and COG Sin, you may continue."

Velvet looked at Sin, a wounded expression on her face. "What happened to one for all?"

"I tried to reach you," said Sin.

"Not hard enough," answered Velvet and walked out of the patio doors.

Had he tried hard enough or had he just saved himself? If he'd helped Velvet, they'd probably both be dead and what was the point in that? But deep down he suspected if it had been Zonda on the rug, things may have played out differently.

With the caution of someone who'd nearly been barbecued, Sin opened the drawing room door and eased into the passage beyond. Testing the floorboards with each step, he progressed to a panelled door marked *Library* and nudged it open. The library walls were the height of the mansion. Dark teak bookshelves inset with chemlights climbed to the ceiling, where the room's only natural light filtered through a glazed dome skylight. Polished wood ladders ran on brass tracks around the shelves. At the room's centre a leather briefcase rested on a sturdy oak table.

"Does this seem a bit too easy?" said Sin.

"We were nearly burned to a crisp."

"Nearly, but not actually." Sin dropped to one knee and scanned the floor. "House of a thousand deaths and we've met one. Even I can do that maths."

They crept into the room, wary of potential threats. There were no hiding places for assailants and although the room had a fireplace, the furniture bore no signs of charring.

"So what do you think?" said Zonda.

"There are no windows and only one way out. If someone blocks that door, we're trapped."

"May as well get it over with then," said Zonda and reached for the briefcase.

"No. Wait," said Sin, and tilted the table. As the briefcase slid off the edge, he flipped the table onto its side and pulled Zonda down behind it. They waited, their bodies pushed against the heavy oak barrier, their faces inches apart. Sin stared into Zonda's eyes, his heart pounding.

Zonda eased her face closer to Sin so their lips nearly touched. "What now?"

The strawberry scent of Zonda's hair filled Sin's nose. He swallowed and turned his head away. "Nothing, I guess." He pushed himself up and contemplated the briefcase. "I was expecting something far more exciting to happen."

"Me too," said Zonda, her shoulders slumping. She took the briefcase and walked towards the door. "That was sooo disappointarooney."

A tapping sound overhead caught Sin's attention. A raven had landed on the ironglass skylight. The bird squawked and then Sin saw it. At the top of a ladder, almost hidden from view, hung a leather briefcase identical to the one in Zonda's hand.

"It's a trap. Chuck it away," shouted Sin.

Zonda hurled the briefcase into the corridor. It exploded in a flash of flame, showering her with red paint.

Time slowed. A hail of paint pellets spun towards Sin. He twisted and dropped behind the table. The wood shuddered, an onslaught of shot splattering the oak.

MacKigh marched into the room. "COG Chubb, you are dead. COG Sin, you are dea–" MacKigh paused and straightened his dress. Dribbles of paint ran down the table but Sin's leather suit remained untouched. "COG Sin, you may continue."

Mindful of further traps, Sin climbed the ladder to the other briefcase. Inside were stacks of neatly bound paperwork. He was about to descend when he noticed a small window in the skylight. If he could reach it, he could make his escape and avoid the corridor, which was an obvious choke point and no doubt contained more surprises.

He raised the case's leather handle to his mouth and gripped it in his teeth. The ledge at the base of the dome was just wide enough for his fingers. He curled them over the brickwork and kicked away from the ladder. Inch by inch, he worked his hands along the ledge, trying not to think about the hard library floor forty feet below. Forearms burning and injured shoulder aching, he hauled himself through the skylight. The fresh air smelled good and he was glad to be free of the confines of the house. At the roof's parapet he found a sturdy-looking iron drainpipe and gave it an experimental tug. He knew from experience that downspouts could peel away from the walls leaving you awkwardly suspended, but this one seemed firm enough. Once again, he gripped the briefcase's handle in his mouth and, monkey-like, shimmied down the drainpipe.

He dropped the last six feet to the ground and sprinted towards the woods, wary of any final deadly surprises. The broad trunk of an elm offered refuge while he took stock. No one had followed him and ahead he could see the bright pink of MacKigh's dress. He broke from cover and approached the instructor. "COG Sin, mission accomplished, Staff," he said and handed MacKigh the briefcase.

"And was it worth it?" said MacKigh.

Confused, Sin glanced over to Zonda.

MacKigh prodded him in the chest. "She canae help you, she's dead. Was her life a fair exchange for what's in the case?"

"I don't know, Staff. I've not checked," said Sin.

"Nae, you dinnae know. Nay one of you thought to ask why we needed the case." MacKigh pulled open the briefcase's leather flap and upended it. Out spilled the papers. The string on one of the bundles broke as it hit the ground scattering a jumble of old dinner menus across the dirt. "COG missions are dangerous. You need to make damn sure you know why you're doing them." MacKigh motioned in the direction of the palace. "The Committee are concerned with the big picture. To them missions have acceptable losses. But for you, returning without colleagues, whatever you've achieved, is ne'er worth it."

MacKigh's eyes glazed over and for a long while he stared into the distance. Nobody broke the silence.

CHAPTER 17
PHOTO SHOOT

The quiet murmur of Nimrod and Zonda poring over plans for the camera-nocturna was punctuated by the plink of bubbles escaping fermenting chemicals. The technical discussion was beyond Sin so he scanned the gardens through the telescope. Velvet loomed large in the eyepiece and he watched her walk to the fountain, the setting sun casting her long shadow across the water. Sin focused on her face and marvelled at how close she appeared. He now knew that a series of lenses in the brass tube magnified the image, but Noir was wrong – understanding the science didn't make it any less magical.

Velvet looked up. Her ice-blue eyes filled Sin's vision. He jolted back, as if, along with the light, the telescope had magnified the odd spiky feeling she gave him. He turned around guiltily but Nimrod and Zonda were still deep in conversation.

"This is good," said Nimrod, "very good. You designed it yourself?"

Zonda squirmed with pride. "Yes, sir."

Sin rubbed his hands together, his palms tingling. "So can we make it?"

The magnifying monocle hanging in front of Nimrod's face created a giant flickering eye. "We absolutely must. It's brilliant. I think a shopping trip is in order." He pulled a multifaceted brass watch from his pocket and turned several of the protruding buttons. "I've preparations to make. Meet me back here in an hour. We're going into town."

"Shouldn't we get permission from the Major?" asked Sin.

Nimrod raised his eyebrows. "Probably. Although as head of COG we'll just take it as read that I'm allowed. Carpe diem, young man, carpe diem."

Sin's brow furrowed.

"Seize the day," translated Zonda.

* * *

An hour later they headed to the stables, only half of which was a home for horses, the remainder given over to mekanikal beasts. There were polished hansom cabs with

155

shiny mekanika steeds between the yokes, sleek traction cars with graceful brassanium curves and all manner of chunky steam and clockwork gigs and carriages.

A burly stablehand met them as they entered. "We're just preparing the town coach as requested. Will you be needing a driver, sir?"

Nimrod paused, considering, then replied, "No. I'll manage fine tonight. Thank you, Clark."

Clark shuffled his feet awkwardly. "You sure, sir? You know the rules."

"I made the rules. I think I can break them once in a while."

"Very good, sir," answered Clark in a manner that suggested it was anything but.

"Professor, what are the rules?" Sin asked.

"The Committee's worried that I may be a target and so I'm not supposed to go out on my own. It's a load of old phooey and to be honest I'm fed up with being chaperoned."

They followed the stablehand to a streamlined scarlet and gold liveried machine. An ironglass dome covered the central driver's seat, behind which extended a more traditional passenger compartment.

Two more servants, dripping with sweat, turned a giant winding key thrust under the carriage's body, tightening the motor's spring. "She'll be good to get you to town and back, sir, but we've done no more than fifty turns," said Clark.

Nimrod jumped onto the lowest rung of a set of steps and heaved open the carriage door. "That's excellent, my good man." He stepped inside and held out a hand for Zonda who followed him up. Sin joined them, dropping into a cushioned seat. Nimrod strapped into the driver's position and pushed the steering yoke. The clockwork springs moaned and with a gentle twang the contraption began to move.

Sin had never travelled by carriage and the speed with which the estate zipped by was exhilarating and frightening in equal proportions. Nimrod threw the carriage into corners with reckless abandon, a huge grin on his face as the narrow wheels slid sideways across the gravel. Despite the driving style, the ride was incredibly smooth. A series of pistons and springs kept the passenger compartment level.

"This is incredible," said Zonda. "I was expecting a real bone shaker."

"Gyroscopic self-levelling. I designed it myself. It's an adaptation of the one I use in the watchmek to keep them upright." He glanced over his shoulder at the two candidates. "At least when no one's knocking them over."

"Where are we going?" asked Sin, changing the subject.

"William Henry Fox Talbot knows more about

photography than any man," Nimrod paused acknowledging Zonda, "or woman alive. He will undoubtedly have the lenses and chemicals we need to make the camera-nocturna."

"And he's expecting us?" asked Zonda.

"Oh yes, I sent a tweet. We're going to meet him at my gentleman's club, the Royal Society of Inventors."

* * *

They reached the cobbled streets of Coxford and their progress slowed. The city seemed different, grubbier and more run down. Or maybe he was different, thought Sin. It had only been a few days, could he really have forgotten the hardship and the squalor already? He looked down at his new boots and tailored clothes and a feeling of guilt stole over him. His old crew would be huddled together in a cellar, cold and hungry, or out on the streets, fighting for survival. Sure, any of them would have done the same in his position, but it didn't stop him feeling bad about it. And what would the Fixer think? He'd always been tough on Sin. It was his way of teaching Sin the ropes, training him for better things. Would he be pleased that Sin had escaped the life? Probably not – he'd be smarting that Sin still owed him money.

A motorbike roared past, belching steam from its

blunderbuss exhausts. The red-leathered driver bent low over the boiler, gunning the engine.

Nimrod waved a hand in the air. "That blighter's been trying to get past me since we left the palace. Still, we gave him a pretty good run for his money. I bet he hadn't reckoned on a race."

Smog lay heavy over the city and Nimrod hunched forwards, straining to see where they were going. Tall town houses and magnificent stone colleges loomed large through patchy gaps in the pea souper. A hackney cab pulled by horses wearing respirators clattered past and a traction-tram appeared from the murk like a ghost ship, gliding through the night on a cloud of steam.

"Here we are," announced Nimrod. He pulled back on the yoke and the carriage drew to a halt beneath the portico of an impressive stone manor house.

They disembarked and climbed the steps to the frosted ironglass doors. A porter rang a bell and raised a hand to his pillbox hat. With a muted hiss, the doors opened.

The entrance hall was spacious but cluttered with cased scientific exhibits. To the rear of a reception desk decorated with a multitude of cogs, gears and pistons, a wide central staircase swept up to a balconied second floor.

From behind the metallic desk a disembodied voice with a hint of a Ruskovian accent said, "As always, a pleasure to see you, Mr Barm."

"And a pleasure not to see you, Dimitrov," replied Nimrod.

"Ah-ha. Very good, sir."

A small man emerged from behind the desk. He was no more than four feet tall, including the height of his top hat. A goatee beard neatly trimmed to a point accentuated his angular face.

Nimrod dropped onto one knee and clasped Dimitrov's hand warmly. "Is Fox Talbot in?"

"Yes, sir, he's in the Arguementorium."

"Splendid." From his pocket Nimrod pulled a gift-wrapped parcel. He handed it to Dimitrov. "A present for the little one."

Dimitrov smiled – a smile of a genuine affection for the great inventor. "She's not so little these days. She'll soon be taller than me, sir."

"They grow so fast. How old is she now?"

"Nearly four, sir."

"Excellent, I'll send something for her birthday." Nimrod stood and with a wave of his hand marched further into the building. He lowered his voice as they moved out of earshot. "Don't be fooled by his size, that man is a giant. He saved my life once."

Sin looked back at the diminutive figure. It appeared no one in this new world he inhabited was quite who they seemed.

The hullabaloo of the Arguementorium reminded Sin of a rowdy Friday night hostelry, but without the aroma of stale beer and vomit. Groups of men, and the occasional woman, dressed in everything from fine evening wear to tradesmen's coveralls, exchanged forthright views on the latest scientific theories.

The cavernous circular room was furnished with clumps of leather armchairs interspersed with large potted ferns to provide segregated areas for discussion. Scientific tapestries hung on the walls and silk looped in swathes from the ceiling in an attempt to muffle the sound.

Nimrod brushed past the fronds of a fern labelled *Pteridophyte – Cyathea Medullaris*, although someone had neatly put a line through *Pteridophyte* writing above it *Monilophyte*?

Behind the fern an elderly scientist with wispy grey hair argued with a much younger man, whose bushy moustache was waxed into aggressive spikes.

"The formulas are nearly complete, but I must progress to real trials," said the scientist.

Moustache man prodded the scientist in the shoulder. "You'll get your money and the workhouse has plenty of test subjects but we need to see results. We don't care about the rats; we care about soldiers in trenches."

Across the room, a balding gentleman with overdeveloped jowls waved to them from behind a wooden box camera mounted on a tripod. He removed the lens cover and held up a glass jar. In one half sloshed a pink liquid, in the other half rested a green jelly. He shook the jar vigorously and the chemicals mixed, producing a blinding flash.

The room momentarily quietened then an uproar of complaints arose. Hazy images filled Sin's vision and he felt peculiarly off balance. He leaned on Zonda's shoulder for support and they stumbled over to the photographer.

"I got your tweet," said Fox Talbot, handing Nimrod a clockwork carrier pigeon. The bird's head and body were formed from bulbs of paper-thin ironglass covered with a filigree of iridescent purple metal detailing the pigeon's features. Constructed from the same metal, the wings and inner clockwork shimmered in the light.

Zonda gasped. "Is my vision still dubious or is that gravitanium?"

Sin blinked, his eyes watering. "What's gravitanium?"

"It's the lightest metal known to man. What makes it totally stupendous is when heated it throws off the pull of gravity."

"So, it gets hot and it floats?"

"Yes, but it was reported scientists only found a few ounces in a meteor crater. Hardly enough to experiment with, let alone make anything useful. That bird is worth a king's ransom."

Nimrod placed the tweet into a pocket of his jacket. "So, can you help us?"

Fox Talbot patted the camera. "That's the purpose of this beauty. It'll save starting from scratch." He handed a leather satchel to Zonda. "Lenses, filters and chemicals. I believe you're the genius behind this idea, so you'd better take charge."

Zonda slung the satchel's strap over her shoulder. "Thank you, sir."

"You're most welcome. Always a pleasure to help photographic entrepreneurs," said Fox Talbot. He folded up the camera's tripod and handed it to Sin. "You look like a strong fellow. If I let Nimrod near it, he'll probably turn it into some sort of fish-tography."

Fox Talbot's chuckle was silenced by the scream of a steampistol. Nails ripped through the air and the world around Sin exploded into chaos.

CHAPTER 18
NAILS AND NEEDLES

A Chinasian vase shattered in a shower of pottery. Nimrod crashed to the floor dragging Zonda with him. A metal nail protruded from his leg. Sin dived next to them, seeking cover behind a sturdy leather sofa. More pistol screams rent the air and nails zinged, thumping into the upholstery.

"The penalty for treason is death," shouted a voice full of malice.

"Steady on, old chap," said someone from across the room.

The pistol's shriek filled the Arguementorium closely followed by the thud of a body falling.

"Go," whispered Nimrod. "It's me he's after."

Sin peeked from behind the sofa. Throughout the Arguementorium startled scientists were either running for the exits, or cowering behind furniture; their raucous discussions replaced by panicked breathing and muted whimpers.

A man advanced towards them. He was suited head to foot in leather and brassanium armour, a black metal mask fixing his features into a hideous sneer. In one hand he brandished a pistol.

The buzz of adrenaline surged through Sin's veins, his quickened pulse strangely creating a sense of calm. Run or fight? Either way the odds weren't favourable. Sin tensed, preparing to leap. Zonda held his arm. "Wait." She rummaged in the leather satchel and pulled out a flash jar. "Close your eyes and get ready to run." She shook the jar and held it above the sofa.

A pistol screamed and a nail pinged off the jar, sending it tumbling from Zonda's hand. Sin screwed his eyes tightly shut, every ounce of his being telling him it was wrong to be under attack and not be able to see. The chemicals flared brightly. He leaped up, vision blurry. They were twenty feet from the exit. Zonda and Nimrod would never cover the distance before the man's sight returned. Sin could flee and save himself, but an image of MacKigh staring blankly into the woods lost in silent regret flashed before him. COG was his new crew. He didn't see how he could stop a war, but right here he could make a genuine difference. Legs pumping, he sprinted towards the armoured man. *Time slowed*. The puffs of steam pluming in slow motion from the assailant's long-barrelled pistol were quite beautiful except for the deadly nails bursting from their midst. Sin twisted and a nail ripped across his jacket sleeve. He thumped into the man and they tumbled towards the floor. Time back to normal, they crashed into the ground. The man slammed his metal masked head into Sin's face, knocking him backwards. Pain spotted Sin's vision. His head felt woozy and his limbs seemed heavy and not entirely his to control. A shadow loomed over him. The man, now on his feet, aimed his pistol at Sin's chest and squeezed the trigger.

"Urah!" shouted a voice in a thick Ruskovian accent.

The gunman spun and his pistol screamed but the nail flew over Dimitrov's head. The enraged Cossack lunged with his sabre and the would-be assassin collapsed to the floor.

"*Svoloch!*" cussed Dimitrov and spat on the dead man's chest.

Sin let his head fall back to the floor as nausea overtook him. He should be feeling relief or elation at having survived, at having saved Nimrod, instead all he felt was sick. Across the room, over the shocked murmurs of startled scientists, he heard Zonda chivvying Nimrod along and a smile crept onto his face. He'd saved Zonda too, and she was worth fighting for. Maybe when it came down to it that's what all soldiers felt. Yes, you believed in the cause, but in the end you were fighting for the ones you loved. *Loved*, where the hell had that come from? He must have smacked his swede harder than he thought.

Leaning on Zonda for support, Nimrod limped over. Behind them trailed Fox Talbot, his face white as an overexposed photograph.

"I told you. The man is a giant," said Nimrod.

Dimitrov helped Sin to his feet and pumped his hand vigorously. "You are now Dimitrov's friend and honorary Cossack, sir."

"That was a close one, what?" said Fox Talbot, his hands trembling.

Nimrod banged his fist against his chest, his breathing ragged as he struggled for breath. His eyes rolled back in his head and he collapsed onto the sofa.

Zonda pressed her fingers against his neck, checking for a pulse. "He's barely alive."

"Was he shot?" asked Dimitrov.

"A ricochet caught his leg but it's hardly bleeding," said Sin.

Dimitrov pulled the nail from Nimrod's thigh. Beneath the blood, yellow slime covered the point of the nail.

The sound of rushing feet thudded down the corridor outside. Sin tensed and Dimitrov's free hand went to his sabre.

His coat flapping around him, Eldritch charged into the room. "Damn it. What's happened?"

"Poison," said Dimitrov, waving the nail.

Eldritch hoisted Nimrod onto his shoulders in a fireman's lift. "We need to get him back to the palace," he said.

Sin snatched up the camera. Poison wasn't fair. It was a mean way of killing. Even the Fixer didn't use poison.

The entrance hall was a scene of devastation. Expended nails littered the floor and two more lifeless assailants sprawled amid cracked ironglass display cases.

"The first one, he is quick and slipped past me." Dimitrov kicked a body. "The others, not so quick."

Straining under Nimrod's weight, Eldritch pulled a mekanika pigeon from the pocket of his coat and thrust it at Dimitrov. "Tweet the palace and let them know what's happened."

Dimitrov clicked his heels together and bowed. Eldritch barged through the front doors and thudded down the steps. Behind the town coach, three motorbikes idled, steam trickling from their blunderbuss exhausts. Though each bike was individually customised, they all shared the military robustness of the Royal Enfield Company. Sin remembered the motorbike zooming past the coach earlier that evening. The lead motorcycle was without doubt the very same machine.

Eldritch heaved the carriage door open and lay Nimrod across the back seat. Zonda hurried after him. She pulled some spare cushions from the seat and placed them under Nimrod's legs. "It'll help with the blood flow," she said to Sin in response to his querying look.

"Hang on," Eldritch yelled.

The town coach lurched and Sin's head banged against the window. Outside, he saw someone ducking down an alley. Noir? Or at least he thought it was him. A heavy smog swirled around the coach and the chemlights' reflection from the window made it hard to be sure. Still, the white face and crooked hat were uniquely distinctive. Why was Noir there and why had he not helped? Sin leaned towards Eldritch in the driver's seat. "Did anyone else come with you?"

"No. Clark, the stablehand, was worried. Nimrod's not supposed to go out by himself. I rode straight down. It seems I was too late."

"But who'd want to harm him?" Sin asked.

"Workers' groups who blame his technology for the loss of jobs. Peace activists who still see him as the warmonger's puppet. Foreign governments who fear he'll return to his old ways and give the Empire crucial military technology. Take your pick; the list goes on."

The carriage swerved around some detritus in the road and the chemlights flickered.

"What about our own government, would they want him dead?" asked Sin.

"It's possible. Why?"

"'The penalty for treason is death.' That's what one of the attackers shouted."

"Some in the military take a dim view of Nimrod's withdrawal from the weapons program. However, I believe the consensus in government is that if the balloon goes up and the Empire is again at war, he'll do the right thing. That's why they leave COG alone; it's a ready-made army of spies to be cajoled into doing their bidding."

"And will we do the Empire's bidding?"

"Not if Nimrod has anything to do with it. Although after tonight that may not be a factor."

Zonda tugged Sin's arm. "I need your help. He's having some kind of seizure."

Eldritch twisted in his seat. "Do you want me to stop the carriage?"

"No. Keep your attention on the road and get us back as fast as possible," commanded Zonda in an uncharacteristically authoritative fashion. She pulled Sin closer so that he blocked Eldritch's view and hitched up her skirt. Strapped to her thigh was a small leather case. She flicked it open. Inside were five glass syringes, each containing a different coloured solution. Holding a finger to her lips, she gave Sin a conspiratorial look.

Sin's eyebrows raised. Sweet, innocent Zonda was apparently neither of those things. She wanted to inject Nimrod, the head of COG, with some bizarre chemical, and she wanted him to be a part of it. He glanced at Eldritch. He was a member of the Committee; someone with power and experience. The right thing to do would be to let him know. Except clearly that wasn't part of Zonda's plan. If she was trying to help Nimrod, why would she want to keep it a secret?

Withdrawing a syringe containing a milky liquid, Zonda eased the needle into Nimrod's arm.

Sin placed his hand on hers and she raised her head. He tried to read something in her expression, some definitive sign. She was either trying to save Nimrod or complete the assassination attempt. But which was it? Her eyes sparkled back at him and he nodded.

Zonda depressed the plunger and shot the fluid into the scientist's veins.

Sin shuddered. It was done. All he could do now was wait and see if Nimrod lived or died.

CHAPTER 19
KING'S KNIGHTS

The coach slowed to a halt outside the stables kicking up a shower of gravel. A waiting medical team yanked the doors open and the orderlies barged past Sin and Zonda. They attached a clockwork life support to Nimrod's chest before manoeuvring him onto a canvas stretcher. "Two, six, lift," shouted one of the orderlies and, with military precision, they carried the stretcher from the coach. Eldritch shadowed them as they marched towards the palace where Lilith waited, deep lines creasing her forehead.

Sin leaned against the coach in a state of shock. The evening had turned from a jolly jaunt into a nightmare. He played over the events in his mind. Could he have reacted differently? Why hadn't time slowed when the assassin first attacked? It had all happened so fast. Nimrod was shot before he even realised what was going on. And what was Zonda doing with a case of syringes strapped to her leg?

The whinny of a horse punctuated the quiet tick of the coach's clockwork cooling down. Major C marched from the stables, a harried expression on his face.

Zonda stood to attention and handed him a poison-coated nail. "He was shot with one similar to this, sir."

The Major's metallic fingers closed around the nail. "We will talk in the morning, but now I need to be with Nimrod."

"He's had an adrenalin injection with a wide spectrum antidote," Zonda said.

Gears whirred and the Major's head turned towards Sin. Zonda straightened her dress. "He knows. It couldn't be avoided. Eldritch doesn't."

"Loose ends need to be tied up or removed. Your choice." The Major marched after the stretcher, his metal boots crunching on the gravel, leaving a trail of dust.

Sin looked from the Major to Zonda, uncertain of what he'd just witnessed. "We need to talk," he said.

Zonda hastened towards the palace. "No. We need to go to the gym."

* * *

Sin padded along a balance beam. "What are we doing here?"

Zonda teetered across an adjacent beam. "I need the practice and this give us somewhere private to talk."

"So talk."

"I haven't been entirely honest with you."

"Yeah, I got that."

"My father works for COG. He's been training me over the years so I could become a candidate. I loved the technical aspects but it would be fair to say I shirked on the physical side of things."

"I figured you knew more than you were letting on. What's that got to do with a garter full of secret syringes?"

"Standard field kit." Zonda jumped from the beam. "You don't want to know what I had strapped to the other thigh."

"Maybe not. That still doesn't explain why Eldritch can't know about the injection."

Zonda reached up to the monkey bars. "There's a spy in COG sabotaging operations. No one would suspect a candidate of snooping so I'm undercover investigating. That's what I was doing at the arena and in the gardens the other night."

"Eldritch is a suspect?"

"Everybody's a suspect, except Major C, which is why I report directly to him."

Sin swung adjacent to Zonda as she steadfastly manoeuvred from bar to bar, a look of determination on her face. Noir had sworn him to secrecy, but this couldn't be a coincidence. They were hunting for a traitor and he knew Noir was up to no good. After their shared ordeal of that evening, Sin felt something for Zonda he'd never experienced before. Perhaps this was what real friendship was, knowing you can tell someone anything, knowing you can trust them with your secrets. Zonda had levelled with him and now he must do the same. "I've not been honest either," he said.

Sin unburdened himself of the events of the last few days: the overheard conversation in the Conserva-Observatory, spying Lilith through the telescope and the reclamation of the note by Noir. He didn't understand how it could be connected but now he'd started talking, the truth spilled out and he told Zonda about the photograph in his keeper, the note with the broken cane and how his recruitment to COG had been no accident. He nearly told her about how he could slow time, but the Fixer always said trust your gut, and something told him this wasn't the right moment.

It felt good to be free of the secrets. It felt good to be doing the right thing. Earlier that evening, when he'd charged the assassin, he'd known with the absolute clarity of someone about to die that he belonged in COG, and now he wanted to do whatever he could to help unmask the spy.

Zonda rested with her back against the wall. "Well golly-ghosharooney. Aren't you a dark horse?"

"No blacker than you, and I'm supposed to be a wrong 'un."

"Fair pointlington. And you've no idea why Nimrod wanted you recruited?"

"Not a clue. Somehow I'm going to find the truth of it, only …"

"Only what?"

"Can we keep it our secret until I figure out what's going on?"

"I should really tell the Major," said Zonda, twiddling a pigtail.

"Promise me you won't, or I might never discover what happened," said Sin. He took Zonda's hand. If she told Major C, who knew how he might react? It didn't matter that Sin was innocent of any wrongdoing. He'd seen enough kids sent down for a stretch to know that guilty or innocent, sometimes only the look of the thing counted. "I'm keeping your secret about the spy. Keep mine for me, please."

Zonda twined her fingers between his. "I promise."

"Thanks, Zon," said Sin, squeezing her hand.

"In the morning we need to tell the Major everything else, agreed?"

"We can tell him now."

"No. He's going to be focused on Nimrod tonight."

"Will Nimrod be all right? If there's a traitor at the palace, they could strike again."

"The Major will ensure he's protected, but the damage may already be done." Zonda pushed herself to her feet. "Come on, let's have another go at the slanted steam-pit."

"Don't you think we've done enough for one evening?"

"Posituitively not. Tonight's changed me, Sin. Until this evening it was all a game, and now it's suddenly real. It's life and death and nails and blades and next time I need to be ready. You ran straight at the assassins and saved Nimrod's life. I could barely get him to his feet."

Sin shrugged. "I didn't really save him, that was Dimitrov."

"And while it would be fantabulous, and sort of creepy, to have a homicidal Ruskovian always watching over us, I doubt that will be the case. So I need to get fitter and stronger."

"So no more sweet, happy, innocent Zonda? 'Cos I kind of liked her."

Zonda looked into his eyes. "I think I can still be sweet and happy; that's who I am. But I'm afraid my innocence is gone."

* * *

The early morning sun cast its warming rays over the cluttered bookcases, filing cabinets and trophies from far-off lands that adorned Major C's study. Sin and Zonda stood to attention and recounted the events of the previous few days. The Major listened intently from behind his desk. His eyes were bloodshot and even his mekaniks seemed weary, adopting a hangdog slump.

"Noir's as slippery as a bucket of eels, always secretive, always up to something, but he's the best agent COG has. I'll need more than this to convince me he's the spy," said the Major.

Zonda straightened. "What about his suspicious behaviour in the gardens?"

Steam shot from the Major's neck. "Goddamn it! Noir just breathing is suspicious behaviour. The man's a devil who plays his cards close to his chest but he's always come through for COG." He drummed his metallic fingers on the desk, the metal tips pockmarking the woodwork. "Sin, carry on working with Noir, and keep Zonda updated so she can report back to me."

"Yes, sir."

"Zonda, this camera-nocturna, can you still build it without Nimrod's help?"

"Absolutamon, sir."

"Get it made, and do it so a watchmek can operate it." He held up his mekanika hand and wiggled his fingers.

"They're more clunky than me so make it simple and robust."

"How is Nimrod, sir?" Zonda asked.

"He's not good. He's in some sort of coma. It's a miracle he made it through the night. You've given him a fighting chance but he's a scientist, not a soldier, so we can only hope he's got the strength to battle through."

Sin raised his hand. "Sir, do we know who did it?"

From a desk drawer the Major retrieved a small metal shield the size of a large coin. "The King's Knights are a group of fervent royalists hell-bent on starting a war. They're expansionists who believe war in Europe will weaken the nations that threaten Britannia's global dominance." He tossed the shield to Sin. "This is their insignia. We recovered it from one of the bodies. What we don't know is who sent them and why now."

The shiny brass shield was cool in Sin's palm. "What do you mean who sent them, sir?"

"We've long suspected that certain elements of the government and military are unofficially pulling the King's Knights' strings, although we've never been able to prove anything."

Sin ran his fingertips over the shield's embossed emblem, two crossed swords below a crown. A feeling of familiarity overcame him. He'd encountered this before, but where?

The Major picked up a report from his desk. "The

Teutonians have entered Montenegro claiming that they're harbouring Serbian terrorists. Political analysts believe the real reason is that the Teutonians are helping the Ottoman Empire in their war with Serbia but COG knows the *real* real reason is Serbia and Montenegro are allied with the Ruskovians."

At least Sin now knew on a map roughly where the Ruskovians and the Teutonians were from. And the events of the previous evening had made him realise that he had the power to make a difference. The assassination of one man could change everything.

Steam seeped from the Major's neck. "Europe is a powder keg surrounded by zealots waving matches. If COG can't put out the flames, we're all going to get caught in the explosion. And without Nimrod …" The Major sucked in a deep breath and exhaled, his mekaniks clanking as he pulled himself to attention. "Without Nimrod we're all going to have to try a hell of a lot harder."

CHAPTER 20

HUMOURS OF THE BLOOD

"Try harder or there will be consequences," threatened Lilith.

Sin pored over an account of the 1704 Battle of Lenheim, the very battle that the palace had been named after. A week had passed since Nimrod had been poisoned and he showed no signs of improvement. Lilith had made it her mission to take over Sin's "detentions", forcing him to have extra lessons during lunchtime and after the normal day's activities had finished. However, unlike the great inventor, who managed to make learning fun, Lilith was a hard taskmistress. Sin had even begun to feel sorry for Velvet. If her mother had been this tough on her all her life, no wonder she was a bully.

He traced his finger over a map showing the troop

dispositions. "So a saboteur introduced a virulent disease called glanders to Tallard's army, decimating the Cavalry and making them ineffective on the right flank."

"And what can we learn from this?"

"Marshal Tallard wasn't very good?"

Lilith slapped a ruler on the map. "Chemical and biological weapons can reshape the battlefield."

If something as small as bacteria could change the course of a war, then maybe the young candidates of COG could do so too. Sin raised his hand, and then felt slightly silly because it was only him and Lilith in the room. "And the actions of one agent can make a difference," he said.

For a moment Lilith's face softened and Sin saw the woman beneath the cold exterior.

"You think I am hard on you?" said Lilith.

Sin shrugged. It was one of those questions there was no good way to answer.

Lilith took a deep breath, the bone supports in her bodice creaking. "Today we hear that the Teutonians have sent a brigade of steam cavalry into the Carpathian Mountains." She raised a hand to her chest, her fingers splayed over her heart, the sharply pointed nails digging into her skin. "That is my home. Or it was. There could be nothing left of it now. My castle, my people, my history, they could be all gone, destroyed, and for what?" Her hand dropped to her side. "I am lucky. I have money so I have a choice. My people, they have no choice. They will fight and they will die. This is why you must study hard. COG needs you; my people need you."

Selecting a heavy textbook from a shelf, Lilith dropped it on the desk in front of Sin. "Your homework for today. Humours of the blood."

* * *

Sin curled in the crook of a willow tree overhanging the lake and thumbed through the book Lilith had given him. Below, Zonda did push-ups.

Sweat poured from Zonda's brow, trickling down her flushed cheeks. "I'm spent. You have driven me past my physical limits. It is an absolute impossibility for me to continue." She collapsed to the ground, the push-up incomplete.

"You've only done five, and one of those wasn't a proper one."

"I require sustenance. Maybe some cake."

Sin dropped from the tree, careful not to lose his place in the book. "We discussed this. The only way to get over that wall is for you to get lighter and stronger."

Zonda raised her head. "It doesn't have to be a very big cake."

"Think of it as an equation. Wall equals strength divided by weight."

"I do believe I preferred it when you were a moron."

Sin slammed the book closed. "You think I'm a moron?"

"Not any more." Zonda pushed herself to her knees. "You've definitely progressed to village idiot."

He knew Zonda didn't mean it but it still irked him. She took her intelligence and schooling for granted whereas everyday he struggled through his remedial studies and detentions, trying to catch up on fourteen wasted years. He supposed she must feel the same about exercise.

Sin removed a rectangular tin from a pocket and flicked the hinged lid open. Inside nestled a succulent slice of treacle tart. "Mmm, this looks really good. I can feel my mouth watering already. I'm not sure I'll be able to manage it all."

Zonda jumped to her feet, instantly energised. Sin snapped the tin shut. "Stick with me to the bridge and you get a bite." He jogged away, Zonda huffing and puffing behind him.

* * *

Elaborate carvings of mythical creatures decorated the bridge's parapet. Sin sat next to a three-headed chimera, running his hands over the smooth stone. "Why'd you want a lion, a goat and a snake all joined together?" he said.

Zonda rolled a large chunk of treacle tart around her mouth in a state of rapture. "The Greeks often made hybrids. I guess they were combining the animal's best qualities."

"I get the lion and the snake – fearsome and deadly – but why a goat?"

Zonda ran her tongue over her lips savouring the last few morsels of errant sugar. "The goat separates the snake and the lion. Perhaps it stops them fighting. If you only had the dangerous parts of animals, maybe it would be too much of a monster."

Sin returned the tin to his pocket. "Do you think we'll finish the camera-nocturna this evening?" Without Nimrod's expert guidance, converting the camera had proven trickier than expected. The Major had given them clearance to use Nimrod's lab and so every night after supper they'd worked on converting the camera Fox Talbot had given them. The mekanikal and optical alterations were now complete but each time they developed the photographs all that emerged were sheets covered in dark splodges.

Zonda licked her fingers. "Jasper's been helping me with the chemical formulas. He thinks if I tweak the composition of the silver nitrate it should work."

Sin bristled, imagining Jasper and Zonda having cosy

chemical discussions that he was nowhere near smart enough to understand. The science behind how light, or indeed dark, made pictures, might as well be magic as far as he was concerned.

A malignant ball knotted in his chest. He slid off the parapet and began jogging over the bridge. "Once around the lake and we're done."

Zonda stamped her foot. "I thought we were done now."

Sin carried on jogging. He'd got used to Zonda's tantrums and found ignoring them to be the best policy.

"I hate you," she shouted but Sin could hear her thudding footsteps and heavy breathing as she jogged after him.

"And I hate Jasper Jenkins," he whispered under his breath.

* * *

Their exercise finished, Sin showered and returned to his room. He slumped onto the bed and took out his homework book. A constant faint hiss, almost inaudible, vexed his ears. He sat up and turned his head seeking the source. On his desk a carved ivory hourglass trickled away time, the sand slipping not quite silently downward. Propped against the timepiece was a playing card, the two of spades. *The fountain before the sand runs out* was inscribed between the pips in spider-like handwriting. Sin flipped the card over. Adorning the back was a sinister skeleton in a top hat juggling more playing cards. There was no doubt who the message was from. Why couldn't Noir just write a note like any normal person? Because he wasn't a normal person, he was about as abnormal as they came. Sin tried to keep a lid on his fear as the last few grains slid from the upper bulb. Cursing, he snatched the hourglass and ran.

CHAPTER 21
THE LOST EXPERIMENT

Noir stood with his back to Sin, one hand extended, letting the fountain's water splash onto his palm. Other than the exaggerated thump of his own heart, Sin was certain he made no sound as he approached, but the magician seemed to sense his presence and turned. He held out his hand expectantly, the fingers bent claw-like.

His arm trembling, Sin gave Noir the hourglass, the top bulb conspicuously empty.

"You're late," said Noir.

Sin bowed his head, unwilling to meet the magician's gaze. "I came as soon as I got the message."

Noir clicked his fingers and sand flowed upwards into the top bulb. "No matter. We still have time." He clapped his hands together and the hourglass vanished, replaced with a key. "You will go to the Waterloo Room in the instructors' wing. Hidden beneath the desk is a file that you will steal and destroy. Under no circumstances will you look in the file."

Sin swallowed. Fear constricted his throat. "The instructors' wing is out of bounds. It's a Cast-Iron Rule," he said, pocketing the key.

"Better ensure you don't get caught then," rasped Noir. From beneath his jacket he produced a clockwork pistol.

"What's that for?" asked Sin, his mouth uncomfortably dry.

"There's a watch-dog. Shoot it between the eyes and you'll be fine."

The knot in his stomach tightened. Sin took the pistol and stuck it in his belt.

A silver coin appeared between Noir's fingers. He kissed it and threw it into the fountain. "For luck. Go now. The Committee has a meeting, which gives you the perfect opportunity and gives me the perfect alibi."

* * *

The instructor's wing occupied the central portion of the palace behind the gymnasium. Sin pushed the carved wood door, half hoping to find it locked, but it swung silently inwards. His pulse raced as he stole into the corridor expecting all manner of alarms to sound. He waited, breath held, body tense, but his crossing of the invisible boundary to where discovery meant expulsion proved uneventful. Ahead, a black and white chequered floor ran the length of the wing. On raised plinths, as if guarding the doors on either side, stood knights in armour holding sturdy double-bladed axes. The passageway looked like a giant medieval chessboard. *Sometimes you have to sacrifice a pawn*, that's what Zonda had said during her match against Jasper. Was Sin to be the sacrificial pawn in a game where he didn't understand the rules, or even know who the players were?

He crept past rooms named after famous battles: *Rorkes Drift*, *Balaklava*, *Lapsang Ridge*. The knights gave him an unnerving sensation of being watched. Reaching the door marked *Waterloo*, he drew the pistol and let himself in, locking the door behind him. The room was an instructor's living quarters. The scarlet leather coat hanging on the coat stand identified whose.

Expensive period furniture decorated the room, which combined private dining, lounge and study areas. A corridor led to further rooms but Sin had already spied the desk set between two full-length windows.

The patter of paws sounded from the corridor. Sin clasped the pistol in both hands, took aim and waited. The original watch-dogs were small mekanikal beasts made from scavenged watch parts, but as technology had improved they had become larger and more advanced. However, what emerged from the corridor was no watchdog, it was a clock-weiler. Its solidly built iron body stood three feet tall, with a row of brassanium hackles running along its spine. The beast's jagged jaws opened and it issued a low mekanikal growl. Gears whirred as it sank back on its spring-powered haunches, preparing to pounce.

Sin squinted down the pistol, aligning the front and rear sights just like MacKigh had taught them, and squeezed the trigger. With a twang, the neodymium magnet projectile shot from the wooden barrel. Striking the dog's head, it clung to the iron, the intense magnetic field locking the beast's clockwork brain solid.

Tentatively, Sin took a step towards the dog, unsure of whether the immobilisation was permanent. The beast remained inert so he edged closer and curled his fingers around the dog's tail. He twisted and pulled backwards opening a hatch to the mekanika's workings. Inside were a confusion of cogs, gears and ratchets. He depressed the spring release and the clockwork engine unwound. Sin lifted the beast back to its "bed" along the corridor and arranged it into a sleeping position before prising the magnet from its head.

Returning to the main room, he skirted a Persian rug and headed to the polished walnut desk. The inlaid leather top was littered with paperwork, but if Noir was correct, what he wanted was underneath. As he bent down, he heard voices outside in the passageway and a key rattled in the door's lock. He dived under the desk. It was not the best of hiding places but he was out of options.

Major C clanked into the room and with an elongated hiss lowered onto a sofa. "I wish all Committee meetings were that quick."

"Indeed. I expected far more resistance from Noir. Getting COG Brazil undercover should be routine but the rest of the mission is nigh on suicidal," said Eldritch.

"For anyone else maybe. Noir's special. If he catches the zeppelin for Bucharest tonight, he might just pull it off."

Sin frowned. So Noir had been sent on a secret mission and he'd taken Lottie with him. It didn't seem right. Sin knew they were training to be sent on undercover missions, but surely they weren't ready?

Eldritch joined the Major, taking a seat opposite. "So what did you want to discuss?"

"The boy. You were supposed to keep him away from Zonda."

"I tried. At the Aquarinomic Hotel. I thought I'd encouraged him to befriend Velvet, only–"

Steam vented from the Major's half-helmet. "I don't like the sound of this."

"Only Velvet swapped rooms with Zonda so I may

have inadvertently brought Sin and Zonda together."

"Good God, man. I should have you flogged and drummed from the ranks."

Eldritch held a hand to his chest. "It wasn't my fault. Apparently, Velvet objected to being housed near the 'urchins' as she called them."

Sin tried to process this new information. His whole standing at COG was based on misinformation. He'd only sided with Zonda and the East Wing because of Eldritch's encouragement, so where did that leave him now? And why had the Major not wanted him to associate with Zonda? Was it because he was from the streets or was it something else?

Sin pushed further back into the shadows as Eldritch approached his hiding place and threw something roughly onto the desktop overhead. Sin looked up, his eyes drawn by the noise. Pinned to the underside of the desk was a thin document file – the one Noir wanted him to steal. Written in capital letters at the top of the folder was *THE LOST EXPERIMENT*. Below it were a list of names, all except the last one struck through. Sin read the last name and shivered.

CHAPTER 22
LETTERS AND LIES

SIN. The last name on the list. He wanted to rip the folder free and riffle through the contents but he had to remain cautious. There was no need to rush, he wasn't going anywhere, so he peered from beneath the desk and waited for the right moment. Eldritch and Major C were hunched over a map resting on a low tea table. Sporadically, a bout of steam would issue from the Major's mekaniks. Sin eased back into the shadows. Noir had ordered him to destroy the folder without looking at the contents. There was no way that was going to happen. He reached up and using the noise of the Major's movements as cover he prised the pins free. Clipped inside the folder were several pages of notes and three photographs.

The top photograph was ripped and faded, the edges

tinged with age. The once crisp blacks were now muddy browns but the picture of a group of men posing in a laboratory was clear enough. They all wore pristine lab coats except for a central figure who sported a tweed jacket. He was much younger in the picture, yet there was no mistaking the scientist's identity. It was Nimrod Barm. To the right of Nimrod stood a young woman in a white coat, her belly gently rounded, her eyes tinged with sadness. Sin's hand went to his keeper, the torn fragment inside a perfect copy of the woman in the photograph. If the lady was indeed his mother, that meant Nimrod knew her. Was that why he'd been so insistent Eldritch recruit Sin? He could question Nimrod and finally, after fourteen years, get some answers about who he was. Elation gripped Sin and he struggled to contain himself. Then the reality of Nimrod's plight hit home. His stomach lurched. It didn't matter what the scientist knew. He was in a coma and may never recover. Sin flipped the photo over. Written on the back in a neat cursive script was *The Eugenesis Project 1876*. It was a lead of sorts. Perhaps he could ask around at the Society of Inventors, see if it meant anything to anyone.

He flicked to the next photograph, which lay facedown. Inscribed by the same hand was written *Escape – September 12th 1876*. Sin turned the photo over. It showed a small wooden crate of Sinclair's Medicinal Spirits, except the crate's contents were not twelve bottles of gin but a baby swaddled in newspaper, resting in a bed of straw. The baby smiled at a teddy bear held above its head. His teddy bear. The one that had been left with him at the orphanage. A sovereign ring made from three intermeshing cogs graced the index finger of the hand holding the teddy. He stared at the photo, at himself as a baby, helpless, innocent. Anger simmered. Why had he been abandoned? He turned to the final photo. It was a different size and shape to the others and was stamped on the back with the crest of the City of Coxford Police. The picture showed a nun holding the same crate although now it was empty, with several of the slats broken. A dark substance splattered the outside obscuring all except the first three letters of the writing, so it appeared to say only one word. Sin. So this was how he had been named. Not because his mother was a shameful harlot as the Sisters had always led him to believe but because of his makeshift cot.

The anger surged in Sin's chest. He'd been lied to all his life and even here at COG, where he'd decided to make his new home, they were keeping secrets from him. Eldritch must know something of Sin's past; he must have some of the answers. Sin fought the urge to leap from hiding and confront Eldritch. He couldn't afford to get thrown out of COG, not now. Taking a deep but quiet breath, he settled under the desk and picked up the notes. The first two pages made little sense to him. He guessed they detailed some of the science behind the Eugenesis Project but it was mostly too complex for him to understand. The final page, however, was written in a spider-like handwriting he immediately recognised. Noir's.

Dear Sister Alldread,

I am pleased to hear that my hypnosis has relieved Sin's night terrors. The events he witnessed as a baby have left deep scars that may never heal. I can suppress the memories for now, however at some point they will break free with unknown consequences. Each session is becoming more difficult and I worry that Sin may be projecting his fear onto me. I have used mesmeric-amnesia to make him forget my part in the sessions, but the underlying emotions may be harder to quell. Please advise me if his condition deteriorates.

Yours sincerely,

Magus Noir.

Sin re-read the letter. At least he now knew why the magician petrified him, and perhaps how Noir had come into possession of the letter and the broken cane. From under his shirt, he withdrew his keeper and unlocked it. The folder's contents were a clue to his past; he couldn't destroy them as Noir had instructed. He rolled the photographs and notes into a tube, and slid them into his keeper before sealing it closed and scrambling the combination. Under the cover of the boisterous conversation that now drifted from the table he pinned the empty folder back into place. He crossed his arms over his knees and hunkered down, waiting for an opportunity to escape.

* * *

Sin awoke in darkness.

He recalled Eldritch and Major C breaking out a bottle of scotch, which they had steadily worked through as they reminisced about past glories and toasted fallen colleagues. Sin peeked from beneath the desk. The room was now silent. His cramped muscles complaining, he crept from his hiding place. Anger still smouldered in his chest but the fear of being caught overwhelmed it. Fingers of moonlight reached through the long windows, painting the room grey. Sin navigated to the door and edged into the passage, thankful for the chemcandles casting a bluish light along its length.

In the midnight silence the metal hobnails in his shoes made a horrible tapping against the marble floor. He slipped the shoes from his feet and padded along the corridor. His thief's senses nagged him. He checked over his shoulder. There was nothing, just the armoured knights and a very faint ticking of clockwork. A knight's head twisted towards him, the eyes glowing red. Adrenalin surged in his veins, prickling his skin. Not armoured knights – watchmek. He sprinted for the exit, his stockinged feet slipping on the shiny marble. The mekanika clanked from their platforms, weapons raised. Ahead two more knights blocked the way, battleaxes swinging towards him. Sin dived between them, sliding on his belly. An axe cleaved through the air, and he felt the swish of the blade as it sliced past, a whisker's breadth from his face. He regained his feet and bolted through the door to the main palace. His pace slowed. The mekanika weren't following but he heard raised voices. He hurried past the green room and ducked into a servant's stairwell. Silently, he replaced his shoes then scurried up the back stairs and headed to his room.

He pushed the door open, his heart hammering, half expecting to find Noir waiting for him before remembering the magician had been sent on a mission. The grandfather clock next to his desk showed it was nearly one in the morning. Remedial lessons started in five hours. Not bothering to undress, he slumped onto his bed and drifted into a dream-rayaged world of magicians, mekanika and mad scientists.

* * *

Sister Alldread towered over Sin, cane in hand. She brought it down on his back with a loud knock. Sin jolted awake as another knock sounded on his door. He rubbed sleep from his eyes and tried to bring the clock into focus. Ten past eight. Damn. He'd missed remedial lessons and breakfast. He unlocked the door and Zonda barged in.

"Are you all right?" she asked. Then without stopping for breath continued, "Where were you last night? I couldn't find you anywhere. I was completely hystericalified. I thought something badiferous had happened. I thought they'd sent you on a mission with Lottie. Has something badiferous happened? Are you going on a mission?"

Sin struggled to find an answer, or even to work out which question he was supposed to be answering first.

Zonda hugged him. "We've not fallen out have we? I don't really hate you. It was a sugar rush making me say it."

"It was Noir," said Sin.

"I know. Noir and Lottie off on a secret mission. Everyone's chit-jabbering about it."

"No. I mean Noir had me doing his dirty work. I'll explain later. I need to get ready for lessons, but we're good."

From her pocket Zonda pulled out a rolled up tube of paper. She handed it to Sin, a huge smile on her face. Sin uncurled the paper. It was a photograph of the lab but instead of being black and white it was captured in hues of violet. No, it wasn't a photograph, it was a nocturnagraph. "You did it?" he asked, checking he'd understood.

"Correcterlington. We did it."

Now it was Sin's turn to hug her. "Nimrod would be so proud."

CHAPTER 23
ROOFTOP REVELATIONS

Eldritch stood at the front of the green room. His eyes were puffy and a thin sheen of hangover-induced perspiration covered his forehead. Sin struggled not to glare and so focused on the two identical carriage clocks that rested atop the table next to the instructor. The daily plan listed the lesson as *Beat the Clock: an inter-wing competition* and there was a certain tense expectation in the air as the candidates chatted noisily.

Stanley tapped Sin on the shoulder. "How come you weren't in remedials?"

"Overslept."

"Thought maybe you'd been sent on a mission like Lottie."

"No danger. They ain't going to send me overseas. I can

hardly manage English let alone Teutonian or Fromagian, or whatever they speak in Bucharest."

"What makes you think she's gone to Bucharest?" said Velvet, leaning closer.

Sin's heart leaped. He could hardly admit to eavesdropping on Eldritch and the Major. He stretched and gave an over-exaggerated yawn to buy some time. "Dunno. Didn't she say she used to live there or something?"

"Class," shouted Eldritch and a hush fell over the room. "We can teach you techniques and skills but a COG agent must be able to think for themselves and improvise. That is the aim of Beat the Clock." He picked up the two clocks, handing one to Isla Shank and the other to Jimmy Ace. "Each clock is to be placed in full view in your common room and must stay there. It is the objective of each wing to steal or disable the other wing's clock. You must do so without confrontation or discovery. The clocks are out of bounds during lessons or in the ten minutes before or after a lesson. Any questions?"

Mercy raised a hand. "How long do we have to complete the mission?"

"You have the morning to plan and if you'll excuse the pun, the test has no time limit." Eldritch waited to see if there were any more questions. None coming he said, "The test starts now. Take your clocks and go."

The East Wingers huddled around Jimmy, escorting him in a mob of bodies back to the common room. He put the clock on a solid oak dresser while the candidates pulled the room's chairs into an impromptu circle. Sin sat next to Zonda, but his mind was elsewhere.

Esra Trimble began scribbling on a pad of paper. "We need a roster to guard the clock. I'll draw one up, so let me know if you can't do your slots."

Jimmy punched a fist into his palm. "The best form of defence is attack. So how do we get to the West Wing clock first?"

Ethel Hope held up her hand, a serious expression gracing her face. "I don't want to be indelicate but Sin and Stanley were both thieves. Perhaps they could enlighten us as to how they would do it?"

"Best monkey-man in the business, I was," said Stanley proudly. "It would be a pleasure to let you la-de-das in on our villainous ways, wouldn't it, Sin?"

"What?" said Sin, dragged from his thoughts of Eldritch and his secret file.

"They want to know how to steal the clock," repeated Stanley.

"They'll be guarding it, same as us. We've got to take out the guard and then the clock's up for grabs. It's not steamrocket science."

Jasper Jenkins tutted. "As this test proves, violence is

rarely the answer. There's to be no confrontation so we can't take out the guard."

"We've just got to take the guard out of play," Stanley said. "It doesn't have to be physical."

"Plenty of ways to deal with a guard," said Sin, "distraction, chloroform, bribery, blackmail, take your pick."

Esra held up a gridded timetable. "Here's our guard duty for today. And if I may make another suggestion, we don't need to stick to just one plan. Stanley, Ethel, Jimmy and I can explore the guard option. Zonda, Mercy, Sin and Jasper can investigate alternative methods."

Sin stood and forced his shoulders back, flexing his muscles. "Just so we're clear. They'll be trying to bribe, threaten or blackmail our guards to get a run at our clock. When that happens you let me know so we can take measures." Sin lowered his voice to a whisper and gestured at Ethel. "Because not wanting to be indelicate, if anyone were to betray us, I will enlighten you as to how thieves like me and Stanley deal with disloyalty."

Ethel's face paled and she clutched at the lace frills on the front of her dress.

"I'm sure no one here would turn traitor," blustered Esra.

"Everyone has their price," said Sin flatly.

*　*　*

Mercy and Jasper followed Sin and Zonda from the common room. Mercy took Zonda's hand. "I had an idea but didn't want to say in front of everyone else. If we can get a line of sight into the West Wing, could you shoot the clock?"

"Absolutamon. From where do you think we'll get a shot?"

"The servant's quarters are directly opposite, or you might get a bead from the roof," said Mercy.

"We can check out the roof," said Sin. "Like Stanley said, we have a certain expertise in that area."

"I would have thought you'd feel equally at home in the servant's quarters," said Jasper.

Sin straightened. The comment, like so many others, could have been innocent enough, however the smarmy smile on Jasper's face that disappeared before Zonda saw it made the intent clear enough. "I may have been poor but I was nobody's servant."

"Sounds to me like you were a slave for this mythical Fixer you so often tell of," said Jasper.

"It weren't like that. We were family and family look out for each other."

Jasper raised his eyebrows. "My apologies. The man was clearly a saint."

Sin's fingers bunched into fists. Oh what he would give for Zonda to be gone and to have two minutes alone with Jasper. "He weren't that either. He was hard and cruel and quick to temper but if you were his crew, he had your back."

Zonda tugged Sin's arm, dragging him away. "Come on. I'll show you how we get to the roof."

Sin turned, pulling free from Zonda. It was easy for Jasper to mock. He'd never foraged in bins for mouldy bread or been beaten to the ground over a half-eaten apple. He'd never stood shoulder to shoulder with a crew, facing down the enemy, pretending not to be terrified. He pointed at Jasper. "You don't know nothing of survival. The Fixer was mean but I never once saw him back down. Thick and thin, he'd be there for you when you needed him."

Sin took a step towards Jasper, who scurried behind Mercy.

"Yeah, go with Mercy, 'cos you won't get none from me." He watched them leave, his body trembling with anger.

* * *

With a scowl set on her face, Zonda led Sin to where a ladder climbed upwards from the top floor landing to a small trapdoor in the ceiling. Sin scaled the ladder and

206

pushed the wooden flap open, revealing the clear sky above. He heaved himself through and into a world of chimneys, walkways and lethal drops. Zonda's head and shoulders popped through the trapdoor. Sin offered his hand to help. Zonda refused to take it.

"What is it with you and Jasper?" said Zonda, slamming the trapdoor shut.

"He's a coward. You can't trust someone like that."

"He's been kind to me and his chemical expertise has been invaluable getting the camera-nocturna working. Just because he hasn't had to be tough like you, it doesn't make it wrong."

"It's nothing to do with being tough." Sin clenched a fist over his chest. "It's here in your heart and Jenkins's heart pumps yellow as custard."

"Well, I like him and you should give him a chance."

Sin walked away from the trapdoor. Maybe that was the problem. Zonda liked him and Jenkins obviously liked her. He cast his mind back to the incident in the pipe-way when Jenkins had panicked. "Don't matter whether I like him or hate him, he's going to get someone killed. At best it'll be himself, more likely it'll be the poor sod he's teamed up with."

Sin stood at the roof edge and stared out over the grounds. The view from the palace roof was magnificent, formal gardens melting into wildflower meadows and lush woods. It was hard to imagine the countryside ravaged by war. The palace a burning wreck, destroyed by Teutonian zeppelins or Ruskovian cannon. He pulled a tin from his pocket and flipped it open revealing a finger of iced angel cake. "Peace offering."

Zonda shuffled over to join him.

"Let me tell you about Noir," said Sin.

They sat, Sin enjoying the sunshine, Zonda enjoying the cake.

"Noir had me break into Eldritch's room and steal a file of stuff," said Sin.

"Are you madakins? You could have been thrown out."

"It weren't like I had a choice. Anyways, Noir said I was supposed to destroy the file without looking inside but it was all about me so I kept it. Do you want to see?"

"Absolutamon."

Sin unlocked his keeper and handed Zonda the notes and photographs.

"So this is your mother?" said Zonda.

"I reckon, and she was involved in some kind of experiment with Nimrod but I didn't understand it. Can you have a read?"

For several minutes Zonda pored over the papers, a host of expressions traversing her face.

"This is mind-boggerlington," she said, lowering the papers to her lap and shaking her head as if she couldn't quite believe it. "It's not fully documented but they describe something called Super-Pangenes, which are responsible for creating abnormally gifted people. So someone may have a Super-Pangene for beauty or strength or intelligence or pretty much anything really. The scientists extracted these Super-Pangenes from a host of talented people, and then added them to the genetic material of a developing fetus hoping to create a superhuman."

Sin rubbed his hand over his head. If the pregnant lady in the picture was his mother could that mean he was the result of that experiment? Was that why time slowed for him? Was he a superhuman?

"It's scientastical," said Zonda. "Like something from a Mary Shelley novel, like from *Frankenstein*."

Or was he a monster, constructed from many parts? Sin knew he had a dark side when his anger flared. Why assume the scientists had given him the good bits? Nimrod himself had said he'd designed more and more lethal weapons for the military, better ways to kill. Sin had always been a fighter, and a good one at that. Perhaps he'd been created that way.

Zonda sighed. "It's a shame Nimrod's still unconscious or we could just ask him about the experiment."

"You think he'd tell us the truth?"

"I think it would be worth asking."

Sin had once overheard the Fixer talking to the Crabb

twins, a couple of hardened enforcers who were known for making problems go away. *Dead men tell no tales*, he'd said as he patted them conspiratorially on the back. Dead men tell no tales. Maybe there was another reason for the attempt on Nimrod's life. To stop him confiding in Sin.

Zonda returned the photographs and notes. "I wonder why Noir wanted you to find them?"

Sin eased the documents back into his keeper and locked it. "He didn't. He made it crystal clear I was to destroy the file without opening it."

"Sillies. He only said that to make sure you'd take a peek."

"Oh. So just because I'm a thief, I can't be trusted?"

Zonda twiddled her fingers. "You did look inside."

"That's not the point. It's the principle of the matter, ain't it?" Sin clambered to his feet. "Come on, we've got a job to do." He pulled Zonda up and they shuffled along a narrow walkway running the length of the palace's central wing. Across a courtyard to their right was the palace's East Wing and to the left lay their target, the West Wing.

"This seems like a grand spoteroo," said Zonda, clinging to a chimneybreast. "By my calculations the fifth window along is their common room."

Sin pulled out a shiny brass telescope from his jacket and extended it.

"Where did you get that?" asked Zonda.

"I nicked it from the science lab," said Sin, shrugging. "Guess Noir's right, I can't be trusted." He held the telescope to his eye and trained it on the window. Inside he could make out the blonde bob of Trixie Asp. She appeared to be talking to someone just out of view. She toyed with her hair, twirling it around her finger then held out her hands and the unseen figure stepped in front of the window.

"No way," said Sin and handed the telescope to Zonda. "You need to see this."

CHAPTER 24
A MAJOR DISCOVERY

"It's Esra Trimble," said Zonda in disbelief, lowering the telescope from her eye. "What's he doing there?"

"Sold us out for the price of a kiss, that's what," said Sin. "We need to get back and tell the others."

Zonda dropped to her knees. "Wait a mo-mo. I've still got to check whether I can get a shot at the clock." She lay on her belly and peered through the telescope like she would a rifle sight. "I've got a good view of the room but I can't see the clock. It must be further back."

"What's Trimble doing now?"

"Ew! I'm not sure it would be polite to say. I …"

Voices drifted over the rooftops. Sin dropped to his stomach and clasped a hand over Zonda's mouth. "Velvet and Beuford coming through the trapdoor," he whispered.

"They must have had the same idea." He released his grip and slithered to a slight rise in the roof that hid them from view. He eased closer to the ridge and peeped over. Velvet crouched next to the big Americanian who held a set of binoculars to his eyes.

"Shoot, she's just sitting pretty waiting for the taking. If I had my buffalo rifle, I could end this now," said Beuford.

"The windows are ironglass. You couldn't shoot through them even with your rifle," said Velvet.

"So what's the point of this little excursion?"

"I wanted to know if you can make the shot."

"Yes ma'am, but if it's going to bounce right off the glass it don't help us some."

"That's why we need to coerce one of the East Wingers. Get them to open the window. We work through the problems one at a time until we have a viable plan."

"Y'all think Trixie will turn someone? Esra maybe?"

"If she doesn't, there are other options. I'll do it myself if needs be."

Beuford walked back towards the trapdoor. "I just bet you would. I seen y'all staring with your big blue eyes."

Velvet stalked after him. "Esra? Seriously?"

"Not Esra. Sin."

Velvet blushed. "Well, why shouldn't I want to be friends with him? He's the only one in the East Wing who isn't a total buffoon."

Beuford disappeared through the trapdoor, followed by Velvet.

"The blinking cheek of it," said Zonda. "Who does she think she's calling a buffoon?"

Sin pushed himself to his feet. "I thought she was pretty clear. I'm not a buffoon, everyone else ..."

Zonda whacked him with the telescope. "It was a rhetorical question."

They headed to the trapdoor. Zonda pulled the iron ring screwed into the wood. The panel didn't budge. "We may have a problemoso."

Sin straddled the trapdoor and, muscles straining, heaved on the ring. The wood groaned but refused to move. "Velvet must have bolted the door." Sin let the ring drop and pumped his hands open and closed, encouraging the blood to flow back. "One of us has to climb down the palace and unlock it. You want to flip a coin?"

A look of incredulity seized Zonda's face. Sin chuckled and punched her lightly on the arm. "Just kidding. I'll be back in five. Don't go anywhere," he said and lowered himself over the roof parapet.

The bright sunshine made the climb down easier than his previous nocturnal foray. He traversed a second storey window to the slanted roof of a porch and something inside caught his eye. A film of dust covered the ironglass but he got as close as he dared without smudging it and peered into the gloom. A nearly empty scotch bottle stood on a desk next to which rested a shield-shaped plaque bearing the insignia of two crossed swords below a crown. The door to the room opened and with a hiss and a clank in stomped Major C. Sin ducked below the windowsill, his mind awash. Surely he must be mistaken. The Major couldn't be connected to the King's Knights. He peeked over the sill. The Major poured himself two fingers of whisky, sculled it down and slammed the glass onto the desk. His mekaniks hissed as he stood to attention and saluted the plaque. From a drawer he removed a swatch of velvet and carefully wrapped the plaque. Then he returned the bundle to the drawer and locked it.

Sin attempted to make sense of what he'd seen. Why would the Major salute the banner of the enemy? He tried to think of a reason that didn't involve Major C being a traitor, but there wasn't one. If the head of COG training was corrupt, who else in the organisation was a traitor? Sin could trust no one. He couldn't believe Zonda knew, although she'd lied to him before, so how could he be sure? Careful not to make a noise, he continued his descent feeling more alone and confused than ever.

Sin retrieved Zonda from the roof, his normal easy rapport replaced with an uncharacteristic awkwardness. Deception had been a part of his life for so long it should have been easy to lie to Zonda. Easy to keep his new-found knowledge from bubbling to the fore but the sense of betrayal he felt was overwhelming. She had fooled him once and he was okay with that, because he'd thought she'd done it to protect Nimrod and to protect COG. Now it seemed that none of that might be true. Could Zonda really be working with the Major to destroy COG from the inside?

"Cat got your tonguearooney?" said Zonda, as they headed along the East Wing corridor.

"You what? I ain't seen no cat," said Sin.

"I meant you're not your usual epigrammatic self."

"Still not getting your puff."

"You're abnormally quiet," said Zonda, knocking on the door to Jasper's room.

"Out of breath from the climb, ain't I," lied Sin. He followed her inside and took a position by the window. Zonda joined Jasper who sat with Mercy at a low table on which rested a half-played chess game. Despite his shaken trust in Zonda, it still irked him that she seemed completely at home in Jasper's room. Maybe Jasper was a traitor too. Maybe that was why Zonda was always so keen to defend him.

Mercy toyed with a gold locket she wore on a necklace. "We found a linen cupboard with a view straight to the clock."

"And you'll never guess what else we saw," said Jasper, smiling at Zonda.

"Esra and Trixie," said Sin, a flicker of delight on his face as he stole Jasper's thunder.

Mercy looked to Sin. "What do you think we should do?"

"We should front him up. See what he says."

"How very you. May I suggest going in fists swinging is not the best approach," said Jasper.

"Not for you maybe, but me and Stanley know how to get answers."

"Jasper's right," said Zonda.

Sin's jaw tightened, a sudden weight in his stomach. Zonda should have backed him, not that cowardly know-all. Just because he could play chess and knew chemistry and stuff didn't make him right, didn't mean he knew how to deal with a turncoat. Then again maybe they were both traitors together.

Zonda smoothed the lace frills on her dress. "We don't know that Esra betrayed us. He could be trying to win Trixie over to help."

"He should have told us first. Going behind our backs creates suspicion, don't it?" said Sin.

"We didn't tell the others about our plan," said Jasper.

"Yeah, but we know we ain't traitors, don't we?" said Sin. He fixed his gaze on Zonda, expecting her to flush.

"No, we're not traitors," she said, and held his stare,

her cheeks no more pink than usual.

The moment seemed to drag on forever, like when time slowed, except he could see her breathing as normal. He broke eye contact. Perhaps he was wrong. Was he really sure of what he'd glimpsed through the window? Maybe the hunt for the spy in COG had him jumping at shadows, seeing conspiracies where there were none. Could he be wrong about the Major and Zonda? Perhaps that was the real danger of a spy. It broke the machine apart so that it became nothing more than individual cogs, all operating on their own.

Sin straightened. "We should tell the others about our shooting plan, but don't say we've checked it out already. That'll give Esra a chance to be truthful. Agreed?"

The others nodded. They headed back to the common room. Sin pushed the door open and was greeted with a wave of merriment. Stanley paraded the room holding the clock over his head.

"What's going on?" asked Sin.

"Stanley's only gone and done it," said Jimmy.

"Done what?" said Sin, but even as he asked he knew the answer. Their clock was still on the dresser.

"It was beautiful," said Esra. "I'd gone over to talk to Trixie, to see if she might help us. Anyway, I'm chatting to her wondering how to broach the subject and I see Stanley bob his head around the door."

Stanley placed the clock alongside its duplicate. "I'd snuck over to get the lay of the land and thought I might just chance me arm. I mean it ain't like anything bad was going to happen if I got caught. There's no Sheriffs or nothing."

"There's no one else about, just me, Trixie and Stanley," said Esra. "Well, monkey-man here puckers up and makes this idiotic face."

"And Esra gets me drift and plants one right on Trixie's kisser. Her attention ain't on the clock no more so I'm in and out like a breath of wind. Course that's when the real problem starts 'cos I've got to leg it without being caught and suddenly there's West Wingers left, right and Chelsea. In the end, I bail out a window and climb down. Like I said, I'm the best monkey-man in the business."

Sin fist bumped Stanley. "Much respect to the Nobbs, much respect."

"Couldn't have done it without Esra," said Stanley. "He's the one who really put it on the line. I mean Trixie ain't going to be too happy is she?"

Esra shrugged. "The mission comes first. You can't put your personal interests ahead of the team."

An uncomfortable hotness itched Sin's neck and he fiddled with his collar. Zonda was staring at him in an almost predatory fashion.

The door burst open and the moment was lost. Ethel hurried into the room. "Eldritch wants us all downstairs right now and he seems mighty peeved."

* * *

The students reassembled in the green room, two distinct auras hanging over the candidates. The East Wing, in possession of both clocks, chatted and joked, while the West Wingers waited in sullen silence. Trixie glared at Esra, dark smudges below her eyes. Velvet glowered, her jaw tight and her forehead creased.

"You're gawping at her," said Zonda.

Sin kept his focus on Velvet. "Wait."

Velvet shifted in her seat and glanced in their direction. Sin held up his hand, the fingers forming a circle. "Zero," he mouthed. Velvet scowled and turned away with a flick of her head.

"That was posituitively karmarific."

"Thanks," said Sin. "I think."

Eldritch paced to the front of the room. "We seem to have a dilemma. Beat the Clock normally takes several weeks; sometimes it goes the entire length of basic training without a winner. Never before has it been done in the same week, let alone the same morning."

Stanley raised his chin and puffed out his meagre

chest. Eldritch acknowledged him with a wave of his hand. "COG Nobbs, excellent work. Now please return the West Wing's clock."

The instructor frowned as Stanley offered him the clock. "Not to me, give it back to the West Wing."

"Don't get too attached," said Stanley, handing it to Velvet.

Eldritch clapped his hands together. "The competition begins anew at midnight tonight. East Wing, as victors, you get the afternoon off. West Wing, it appears you need some additional motivation, so this afternoon you will be mucking out the stables as punishment."

The students began filing out, an air of gloom hanging over the West Wingers. Sin jostled alongside Zonda. Having the afternoon off would give him an ideal opportunity to search her room and discover if she was a willing conspirator with the Major, but he needed to ensure her absence. "You want to go for a run around the lake this afternoon?" he asked.

Zonda stopped, an incredulous look on her face. "Are you completely mentalafied? Of course I don't."

"Let me rephrase that: shall we go for a run around the lake this afternoon so that you will be in spifferooney shape to get over that wall on the assault course tomorrow?"

Zonda ground her toes into the floor. "Do we have to?"

A hand with a grip like a steampress took hold of

Sin's shoulder. "COG Sin, a word," said Eldritch. "COG Chubb, you may leave."

"I'll see you at the lake," Sin shouted after Zonda as she hastened from the room. He turned to face Eldritch, his heart thumping. Had his incursion into the instructor's quarters been discovered? Obviously the watchmek had triggered an alarm but he'd made good his escape unseen. Or at least he thought he had. He adopted a look of innocent surprise and said, "Yes, Staff?"

Eldritch held his hand like a pistol and pointed it at Sin. "I let you steal from me once." He dropped his thumb sharply, like the hammer falling on a duelling steampistol. "It would be a heinous error of judgement to believe you can do it again."

Sin's brow crinkled. Eldritch had to be bluffing. There was no way he could know who took the contents of the folder. No way he could know they were in touching distance, concealed in his keeper beneath Sin's shirt. He had to out-bluff Eldritch. Keep up the pretence of ignorance and ride it out. He intensified his expression of confusion. "I don't understand, Staff?"

"I promised Nimrod I'd watch over you but my goodwill only stretches so far." Eldritch massaged the scar-tissue bisecting his eye. "In the regiment the penalty for theft was trial by combat. Believe me when I say nobody stole from me twice."

"I do believe you," said Sin. Eldritch presented himself as a swaggering Britannia Army officer but Sin recognised the hardness in him. Tempered in combat, Sin had no doubt Eldritch could switch in an instant from an Earl Grey-sipping dandy to a ruthless killer.

"Do you mind me asking what's been stolen, Staff?" said Sin, holding his palms outwards in a gesture of openness.

With a tiny shake of his head, Eldritch said, "War's coming. Think about who you want as your friends and who you want as your enemies. And more importantly, make sure you can tell the difference. I want what's mine back by tomorrow, COG Sin."

CHAPTER 25
PHOTOGRAPHIC PROOF

Sin palmed his lock picks and prowled to Zonda's door. He'd already heard her leave for the lake so the coast was clear. The lock was simple, designed to ensure privacy rather than deter thieves and in a matter of seconds Sin was inside. He appraised the room: it was similar to his, only the bookshelves were better stocked. An unusual feeling twisted his stomach. He was used to rummaging through other people's possessions but never before had that person been a friend. He pushed the feeling away.

Her desk was littered with papers containing draughtsman-like drawings for various inventions. On a large roll of paper weighted down at the corners with empty teacups, Zonda's curvaceous handwriting detailed a spring-powered boot that would enable the wearer to leap over walls with ease. Behind the paper another design poked out; a pocket watch capable of concealing a mini Bakewell tart.

Fingers trembling, Sin rummaged through the desk drawers but he found nothing. His gaze drifted to the bookshelves above the desk. They were mostly weighty leather-bound tomes with scientific titles such as *Newtonian Physics in the Modern World*. He homed in on one book with a faded red cover: *The Diabolical Miss Hyde*. He pulled the book from the shelf and knew his thievery instincts had been right. It wasn't a book at all but a wooden lock box. "Let's see what Miss Hyde has hidden," he whispered to himself.

The keyhole was too small for his lock picks so Sin took a brass paperclip from the desk and unfurled it. He slid the metal into the lock and worked it around until the mekanism sprung free. Inside was a collection of keepsakes. There was a medal and ribbon, a bundle of letters tied together with string, a spiralled shell and a faded photograph. It showed Zonda, maybe six years previous, standing at the front of a group of smartly dressed soldiers. One of the soldiers rested his hands on her shoulders in a way that somehow radiated affection. Indeed, the whole picture could have been one that captured a moment of family pride were it not for the fact that all the soldiers wore black metal masks. The same masks as worn by Nimrod's

225

would-be assassins, the masks of the King's Knights.

* * *

Sin and Zonda jogged around the lake. In each hand, Zonda held a small dumbbell made from old traction gears welded to the ends of a steel bar. Sin watched her closely, trying to get some inkling of what was going on inside her head. He still found it hard to believe she was a traitor. There was no doubting what he'd seen in the photo but he'd been wrong about Esra – could he be wrong about Zonda too?

"I think I'd rather be mucking out the stables," puffed Zonda.

"I'm sure Velvet would be delighted to have the help. We can always run back that way if you want."

"Wouldn't be fair. I'd feel I was somehow depriving her of a valuable learning experience."

Sin pulled to a halt at a large tree stump, the light and dark concentric rings showing hundreds of years of growth. He placed his hands on the top and started pumping out push-ups. "Just do five. You don't want to tire yourself for the assault course."

Zonda dropped the dumbbells. "You say 'just five' like that doesn't require some sort of superhuman effort on my part."

Sin stopped. "Do you think I'm superhuman?"

"Superhuman! The boy's got an ego."

"I'm serious, Zon. Those photographs, the Eugenesis Project. It's got to make you wonder."

"You can't leap to conclusions. We don't know what the photographs or those papers mean. You're posituitively super, but superhuman would be something else."

Something else, like being able to slow time. He'd never told anybody about that and despite the urge he had to confess, he couldn't. Not after what he'd found in her room. Besides, the ability wasn't something he could control. It just happened when he needed it, most of the time anyway.

"What is it you want, Sin?" asked Zonda.

What did he want? When he was on the streets, living in a palace seemed like an impossible dream, but now he needed more. The photographs and notes had made him reassess his ideas of his past. As an orphan, he'd made up stories of how his parents hadn't really wanted to dump him at the church and would one day return. It was a common story all the kids clung to, imagining they were really loved and only unfortunate circumstances had led to their abandonment. Seeing the photographs had made him realise that in his case it might be more than just fantasy and Nimrod was somehow bound up in the story. He hadn't been recruited at random. Eldritch had targeted him and somehow Noir was involved too.

"I want the truth," he said.

"Do you really? Because the truth's never simple. It's all relative depending on where you're viewing it from." Zonda began doing press-ups on the tree stump. "And the truth you want to hear is not necessarily the truth you'll get."

"Truth's never been that complicated to me. Did you nick that thing or didn't you? Did you give him a smacking or not?"

Straining, Zonda pushed out her fifth press-up then straightened to face him.

Her emerald eyes pierced his soul. "Sometimes we lie for a reason. It can be kinder than the truth."

She turned away from Sin and began a slow jog back to the palace.

* * *

Sin knocked on the darkroom door, which had been hastily repurposed from a storage cupboard in Nimrod's lab and was now equipped with developing chemicals and photographic paraphernalia.

"Wait a mo-mo," shouted Zonda, her voice muffled.

Sin heard a curtain being drawn back, a clatter of pots and an unlady-like curse. Zonda appeared through a black velvet curtain, the large magnifying glasses on her head giving her a bug-eyed appearance.

"Quick," she said and ushered Sin inside.

She whisked the curtains shut and the room was plunged into a greenish gloom.

"I've removed the first set of plates from the watchmek's camera. They seem to have managed to take several nocturnagraphs last night."

"So what do you need me to do?"

"Put them in the developing fluid then pass them to me."

Sin peeled the photographic paper from the plate and using a set of wooden tongs lowered it into an ironglass tray full of an almond-smelling solution. Zonda hovered at his shoulder as the paper turned shades of violet. The arbour seat set back in the hedge materialised. Lilith sat in the centre.

Sin passed the paper to Zonda and she lowered it into the fixing solution as he removed the next sheet. The developer did its magic and MacKigh appeared, chatting with Sergeant Stoneheart at the fountain.

"It's working great," said Sin. "They're so clear."

"But it's not revealed anything suspect. We're still no closer to finding the spy."

Sin stripped the paper from the last plate and dropped it into the ironglass tray. He gently agitated the solution and the violet hues emerged. It showed a figure crouching down, reaching under the arbour seat but it was neither Lilith nor Noir. The figure's face was obscured yet there was no mistaking the distinctive outfit he wore.

"The King's Knights," said Sin. The man in the nocturnagraph wore the very same outfit as the assassins that attacked Nimrod.

"*This* is what we're after. A genuine lead. I'll let the Major know first thing in the morning," said Zonda.

Sin didn't want to wait and he didn't want to leave it to Zonda. He wanted to confront the Major with the nocturnagraph and see how he reacted. See if he'd try to brush it under the rug.

"Let's take it now." Sin reached for the photo but Zonda slapped his hand away. It collided with the ironglass tray sending it skidding from the bench. With a loud crash, the tray shattered on the floor. Sin jumped backwards avoiding the developer solution's splatter.

"Whoopserooney," said Zonda. "I had to stop you putting your hand in the chemicals. Sorry."

Sin stared at the ruined nocturnagraph lying amid the shards of broken glass, the unfixed paper now an inky black colour. Of course it could have been an accident. Zonda may genuinely have been trying to protect him, but the only proof they had of the King's Knights' involvement was now conveniently destroyed.

"Are you thinking what I'm thinking?" said Zonda.

"I doubt it," said Sin.

Zonda prodded a glass shard with her toe. "That tray

was ironglass. It should have left a dent in the floor, not shattered."

"So?"

"So the developer weakened the ironglass. Which means if we spray it on something like, let's say, the West Wing common room window, it becomes similar to normal glass and no longer nail-proof."

An idea began to formulate in Sin's mind. A way of killing two birds with one stone.

"Fancy a midnight hunt?" he said.

CHAPTER 26
A SHOT IN THE DARK

Sin waited with Stanley on the roof above the West Wing common room. Brass pressure sprays filled with developer solution were attached to their belts and large hammers were slung over their shoulders on pieces of rope. Somewhere in the servants' quarters, Zonda and Mercy were making their way to an impromptu sniper's nest in the linen cupboard. The boys were to wait until five to midnight and then climb down and spray the windows.

A cool breeze wafted across the rooftop. Stanley seemed completely at home, legs dangling over the parapet.

"Come on. Time for some window cleaning," said Sin, glancing up at the palace's clock tower.

Stanley grinned and disappeared over the edge. Sin followed more cautiously. It was an easy climb and there was plenty of moonlight but the hammer and pressure spray were cumbersome. Drawing adjacent to the window, he gripped the rough stone carving and eased a foot into a gap between two blocks. The window was in four parts, each divided by a carved stone column. He unhooked his sprayer and sent a fine mist of chemicals floating over the section of glass closest to him. Opposite, Stanley did the same, his white teeth shining in the moonlight, a huge grin on his face as he casually swung from one hand.

Sin risked a peek into the common room. Isla Shank sat in a chair by the door; a novel lay open in her lap. Her fringe hung over her eyes and it was impossible to tell if she was reading or had dozed off. Across the room, the clock rested on a bookcase. When planning the shoot, the boys had elected to stay by the window until the shots were taken. Mercy was to fire first. Her nail should destroy the ironglass and, if they were lucky, hit the clock. If the ironglass was only damaged, the nearest boy would finish the job with the hammer before Zonda took her shot. They'd all agreed that if there was any risk of hitting the West Winger on guard the mission would be aborted.

The clock's minute hand clicked to midnight. Sin swung his hammer back, ready. Although expecting it, he still started as the shot screamed out from across the courtyard. The pane closest to him fractured in a starburst, a nail caught halfway through the ironglass. Sin slammed the hammer against the window and the ironglass shattered. A second shot screamed and the West Wing clock exploded in a shower of springs and cogs.

From across the grounds, alarms sounded. Chemlights burst into life, bathing the palace and surrounds in a brilliant white glare. Sin hurried upwards, feeling exposed in the dazzle of the lights. The sounds of shouting and rushing footsteps echoed from inside the wing. As he'd expected, shooting a window in the middle of the night had thrown the palace into chaos, hopefully providing him with the distraction he needed. He pushed up with his legs and reached for the parapet. A hand grasped his arm. Stanley leaned over and heaved him upwards.

"We good?" asked Sin.

"Golden. You go do what you need to, brother," said Stanley, taking Sin's hammer and sprayer.

Sin pelted along the roof heading to where he and Zonda had been trapped earlier in the day. He hadn't banked on the whole palace being illuminated, but this was his one chance so he'd have to make do. Braving the glare, he scrambled over the edge and began his descent. He drew level with the window outside Major C's room and the floodlights dimmed then died. The darkness was a comfort but the killing of the lights signalled the end of the emergency. Time was running out.

There was the narrowest of gaps in the window's iron

frame. Sin forced a lock pick into the space, jemmying the catch free. The window swung easily open and he stole inside. From his pocket he fetched a chemlamp and twisted the brass shutters, allowing a glimmer of light to leak out. The desk drawer's lock was a matter of seconds work with the pick. He removed the velvet-clad package and unwrapped it. Up close, he could now read the inscription underneath the crown and crossed swords: *To a loyal servant of the King, Captain Chubb, Second Battalion, King's Steam Cavalry.*

Major C and Zonda's father had served in the army together and were both King's Knights. No wonder Zonda was the only person the Major trusted. The Fixer had a saying: "Keep your friends close, keep your enemies closer." Sin had stumbled upon the Major's plan and so they had drawn him in, pretending to hunt for the spy to ensure his silence.

The distinctive clank of Major C approaching roused Sin from his thoughts. He rewrapped the plaque and placed it back in the drawer. Killing the chemlamp he hurried through the window, pushing it closed behind him. He hadn't had time to lock the drawer and would have to hope to luck that it didn't raise any suspicions. Sin climbed back to the roof, hauling himself over the parapet as the office light flicked on below. He stared up at the half-moon, catching his breath, and imagined some of the Fixer's crew on Coxford's rooftops taking in the same view. Life was simple for them. Hard, but simple. You had your crew and no one else. You could make alliances and deals with the other gangs but not for one moment did you trust them. If you had a problem, you sorted it or you went to the Fixer. Here there was no Fixer so Sin's only option was to sort it himself. He walked to the trapdoor and heaved it open.

* * *

Once it had been established that the palace wasn't under attack and the shots were candidate-initiated, the commotion had died down. Summoned to the green room, the candidates from both wings stood to attention. With the exception of the hunting party, they were all dressed in their nightwear, having been dragged half asleep from their beds.

Sin had hoped that the shots would provide the diversion he needed, although he hadn't anticipated the level of panic they'd cause. Now his stomach churned and prickles crept up the back of his neck. He knew they were in a whole heap of trouble but he didn't care about that. So long as they didn't chuck him out of COG, he could hack whatever punishment they threw at him. Heck, if it wasn't for Nimrod he probably wouldn't care if they did chuck him out. The whole organisation now seemed toxic to him but Nimrod knew the truth about his parents and why he'd been abandoned, he was sure of it. He glanced at Velvet. And if he couldn't get the answers from Nimrod, there were others in COG who had information about his past.

A bleary-eyed Eldritch entered the room, lacking his normal flamboyant swagger. He glared at the candidates and upended a leather bag. The remains of the clock jangled onto the ground in a cascade of cogs. He motioned to Sin, Zonda, Stanley and Mercy who stood separated from the other candidates. "Congratulations. You have again humiliated the West Wing who will be mucking out the stables for the next two weeks."

Groans arose from the West Wingers.

"And I expect them to make a better job of it than yesterday because they are also going to be sleeping there until one of them does something worthy of redemption." Eldritch turned to the four East Wingers and began clapping. "You are to be applauded for your cunning, ingenuity and audacity." He motioned to the other candidates. "Please join me in congratulating them." A smattering of applause started from the East Wingers.

"Everyone," commanded Eldritch and the West Wingers reluctantly joined in.

Sin sensed his three accomplices relaxing, relieved by Eldritch's praise, but he knew this wasn't going to end well for them.

"Silence," barked Eldritch. The clapping stopped. "It was an audacious plan, and also a bloody stupid one." He approached the four candidates, his fists clenched. "We live under constant threat. There's been an assassination attempt on our founder, and you think it's a spiffing idea to start shooting out windows in the middle of the night?"

Sin kept quiet, his head bowed. He'd seen this kind of rage in the Sisters. Whether you were right or wrong there was no point in arguing your corner. The questions asked weren't meant for answering, and besides, Eldritch was right. They had been bloody stupid.

"You will join the West Wingers sleeping in the stables until I see fit to pardon you. Now back to bed all of you."

Sin turned to leave. "Not you, COG Sin," said Eldritch.

His heart pounded while he waited, stood at attention as the other candidates left. Eldritch glowered at him but it was clear no conversation would be engaged in until they were alone. Finally, as Beuford ducked out of the door, Eldritch spoke. His voice was quiet and measured, and all the more menacing for it. "Do you really think you have the skills to better me?"

"I'm not sure what you mean, Staff," said Sin.

"Nimrod had me find you, but I found more than he'd bargained for. You have no idea how important those notes could be. I know they're in your keeper so you will return them by the end of the day or I will take the keeper and its contents from you."

Sin had no doubt Eldritch could wrest the keeper from him physically but it would be no use to Eldritch unless he had the combination.

Sin squared his shoulders. "I don't think Nimrod would approve of you stealing from me."

"Nimrod's not in the equation. The Major's in command now, and he and I have fought together on all five continents." Eldritch pulled a pocket watch from his waistcoat and checked the time. "Twenty-three hours and change, COG Sin. The clock's ticking."

CHAPTER 27
HITTING THE WALL

Sergeant Stoneheart paraded along the line of candidates, her riding crop tucked neatly under her arm. "The last time you did the assault course, it was an embarrassment. COG Von Darque was the only one who acquitted herself with any distinction. I expect better things today."

Stoneheart removed the oblong metal key from her pocket and jammed it into the post, activating the obstacles before removing it. "COG Chubb and COG Shank front and centre."

Velvet snorted. "This should be fun."

"Zonda's not the girl you think she is," said Sin. "If she can get over the wall at the start, she'll get round. In fact, I'll wager you she completes the course."

"Mummy's the third-richest woman in England.

What could you possibly have that I'd want?"

Thanks to Beuford's rooftop conversation, Sin knew what she wanted – to be friends – but he had to be subtle, he needed to lure her in. Once she was hooked, he could play her for answers and maybe find out who the hell in COG he could trust. "I bet you my pride."

Velvet flicked her hair. "How can you bet your pride? That's ridiculous."

"If Zonda doesn't complete the course, I'm yours for a day to humiliate as you wish. I'll muck out the stables or perform other menial tasks. You never know, we might even be friends. If she does finish, the roles are reversed."

Velvet held out her hand. "She's got no chance. You're on." Sin gripped the slender fingers, Velvet's skin pleasantly soft and warm as they shook, sealing the deal.

That had been too easy. Now he just had to hope Zonda had done enough preparation. Sin relaxed his hand. Velvet tightened her grip and pulled him closer. "I know you're up to something, but this one's mine."

Stoneheart zeroed her watch as Zonda and Isla readied themselves on the start line.

Velvet stood to attention and raised her hand. "Staff? May we run the course in reverse today?"

"And why would we do that COG Von Darque?" said Stoneheart.

"So COG Chubb might complete one obstacle before failing, Staff."

The West Wingers sniggered.

Stoneheart appeared to contemplate this, eyeing Zonda. "Candidates, today you will be running the course in reverse. Three, two, one, MARK."

Sin's demeanour of cocky optimism deserted him. This was a disaster. Now Zonda would hit the wall when exhausted, if she even got that far. He watched, fingers crossed, as both girls dived under the boxing net.

Zonda dismounted from the monkey bars several minutes behind Isla. However, time was not part of the bet. All Zonda had to do was complete the course. She stumbled, her legs looking like rubber, but now she only had one obstacle to go. The wall.

Despite her betrayal, Sin found he genuinely wanted Zonda to finish the course, and not only because of his bet with Velvet. He could tell she was spent yet she staggered towards the wall, committed to finishing. This wasn't about COG or the King's Knights – it was about a girl he'd once counted as a friend, digging deep and battling the odds.

Zonda ran at the wall and jumped. There was no power in her legs and she slid to the bottom in a repeat performance of the first time she'd faced the obstacle. However, unlike the previous encounter, she pushed herself up and away from the wall, readying herself for another attempt. She stretched her arms and legs and loosened her neck. Her gaze sought out Sin. "You can do it," he shouted. She may have played him for a fool but he'd keep up the pretence of friendship to find the answers he needed.

Zonda thundered forwards and sprang. She kicked at the wall, pushing upwards, and heaved her shoulders and chest onto the top. For a moment, it looked like she might fall back, then she reached over and lugged her legs clear before toppling down the far side.

"To the finish, Zon, to the finish," yelled Sin.

Zonda gained her feet and staggered over the line. "COG Chubb completing the course, Staff."

Sin rushed to Zonda and threw his arms around her. "Proud of you, Zon," he said, as the East Wingers surrounded them in a joyous group hug.

"Candidates, you have been doing the practice course," said Sergeant Stoneheart. She inserted the metal key into a post by the wall. "This will be the obstacle's height on test day." Steam hissed from the wall's base, and it rose another two feet.

* * *

Sin huddled over his maths books, the chemlamp's rays bright on the square-lined paper. He raced through the sums, determined to finish them before heading down to the stables. It was funny, but now the numbers made more sense, the shapes had meaning and values. It was simple really; he didn't know why he'd struggled so much before. His tutors seemed amazed by Sin's improvement in both maths and English, and Sin wondered if it was possible to have Super-Pangenes for learning.

A knock at the door broke his concentration and his hand went to his keeper. He'd avoided Eldritch all day, and as the deadline neared, he found himself more and more on edge.

"Can I come in?" shouted Zonda.

Sin swivelled in his chair. A pale purple envelope poked out from beneath the door.

"Just a minute, it's locked," he lied. He padded silently to the door and retrieved the envelope. It was sealed with wax, into which a motif of three intermeshing cogs was stamped. A faint aroma of lavender wafted from the paper. Sin thrust the envelope under a pillow on his bed then walked noisily across the room. He rattled the key in the door then pulled the door open.

Zonda flounced into the room and collapsed into a chair. "It's not fair. I'm never going to get over the wall now."

"You did it before, you can do it again."

"I appreciate the vote of confidence, even if I have got all the chance of an ice-cream in a steam furnace."

Sin suspected she was right. He was short for his age, probably a side effect of years of malnutrition, but he was still taller than Zonda. Unless she grew considerably over the next few weeks, she was going to fail.

"Then we do it the hard way: double your training." Before, he'd forced Zonda to exercise out of concerned friendship. Now, the part of him that felt betrayed looked forward to making her suffer. "Don't worry. I'll push you harder, you can count on it."

Zonda extracted herself from the chair. "Anyway, I only came over to see if you're ready to go to the barn. Mercy and Stanley are waiting in the common room."

"I've got to sort a few things. I'll meet you there in a minute."

Zonda moped from the room and Sin locked the door behind her. He pulled the envelope from under his pillow and broke the seal, peeling the flap open and teasing a folded note from inside.

Rendezvous. The fountain at midnight. V.

CHAPTER 28
A MIDNIGHT RENDEZVOUS

The smell of horses pervaded the barn. Livestock had been cleared from several of the stalls to make room for the candidates. In the warm glow of the chemlanterns, the straw-covered flagstones and rough wooden walls held a certain rustic charm, although not necessarily for the candidates who had to sleep there.

The East Wingers claimed a stall near the door. Sin suggested the air would be fresher and the smell would be less as they were furthest from the animals. He didn't mention it would also make it easier to slip out for his midnight rendezvous. For similar reasons he made his "bed" nearest the stall's entrance. They had been allowed to bring a blanket and pillow, but despite these luxuries, Zonda fidgeted and harrumphed, unable to get comfortable.

Stanley's head poked out from under his blanket, a huge grin on his face. "Just like old times, ay Sin."

"You mean apart from the blanket, the pillow and the clean hay," answered Sin.

Stanley pulled his blanket closer around him. "Yeah, this is like a five-star stable. I bet even the rats are clean."

Mercy sat upright. "Rats! You think there are rats in here?"

"Bound to be." Stanley patted his blanket. "Don't worry, you can always cuddle up to the Nobbster if you're scared."

Mercy reddened. "I'd rather cuddle up to the rats."

"You say that now, but when the rat king scurries in and he's bigger than your head, you'll not be so brave."

The chemlanterns dimmed and the candidates' banter lessened as sleep took hold. Sin dug the prong of his belt buckle into his palm to keep him awake. Before meeting the others in the common room, he'd checked in his dictionary to make sure rendezvous meant what he thought. It originated from Fromagian meaning "present yourself", although now the more common usage just meant "to meet". He was certain the note was from Velvet, but why would she arrange a secret meeting? He had wondered if it was an elaborate rouse by Eldritch to lure him into an ambush. It didn't really seem like the soldier's style, but to be sure Sin had resolved to wait for Velvet to make the first move before he left the barn. After all, it was apparent there was no love lost between Lilith and Eldritch, so Velvet would never be part of his scheme.

Hay rustled further along the stalls. Through half-closed eyelids, Sin watched Velvet creep through the barn and out of the door. He checked the pocket watch COG had issued him – ten to twelve. He could go confront her now but the note had been clear: midnight at the fountain. He delayed another few minutes then slunk from under his blanket and padded into the night.

He drifted through the grounds, insinuating himself from shadow to shadow, ever vigilant for the watchmeks. From the edge of the formal garden, he saw Velvet waiting at the fountain, hands on hips. She glanced up at the clock tower and scuffed her boot through the gravel. Why at the fountain? It was a terrible place to meet, exposed with no cover and no easy escape routes. And what did she want? There was only one way he was going to find out. He stopped skulking and strode to the fountain.

Velvet scowled at him. "You won the bet so I'm here. But the fountain at midnight is just a little melodramatic, don't you think?"

"You're the one who wanted a secret meeting. I got *your* note."

They exchanged confused glances. "RUN!" shouted Sin, grabbing Velvet's hand.

Spotlights flooded the garden with their chemical glare.

Guards armed with steamrifles sprang out from behind the hedges.

"Do not move. You are under arrest," said a voice through a megaphone.

Sin scanned the gardens for a means of escape but all the exits were covered.

"On your knees," commanded a guard, jabbing the muzzle of his steamrifle into Sin's back.

Sin dropped to the ground, noting that Velvet was not subjected to such rough treatment. The guard pulled Sin's hands behind him and clasped them in irons.

Major C clunked across the formal garden, gravel crushing beneath his brassanium foot. "I don't know what disappoints me more. The fact that we haven't caught the spy we were waiting for or the fact that we have caught you. I have no choice but to retire you both from training for breaking a Cast-Iron Rule," he said.

"Sir, it weren't our fault. We was tricked," said Sin.

"No excuses, you both broke the rules. Ex-COG Von Darque, you will be released into your mother's custody until she can facilitate your departure from this establishment." The Major's head jerked towards Sin. "Ex-COG Sin, you will be held in the brig until we can arrange your removal." With a hiss, the Major about-turned and marched away.

There was something about the way the Major had

said "removal" that sat uneasily with Sin. He remembered the Major's words when he'd returned with Zonda and the poisoned Nimrod: *loose ends need to be tied up or removed.* He had no doubt he was a loose end. Zonda had tried to tie him up by pretending they were looking for a spy and when that hadn't worked they had decided to remove him. If he was lucky he'd be dumped back on the streets of Coxford to carry on his life of crime, but he wondered if the Major's tone suggested a more permanent solution than expulsion.

He strained against the irons. He'd once been caught by the Sheriffs after a botched robbery of a mail wagon. They'd put him in cuffs then, but he'd been younger and his skinny hands had slipped easily through the steel hoops, allowing him to escape. He heard the tick of clockwork from behind his back and the irons ratcheted tighter. Pain shot through his wrists, his body tensed and he stumbled forwards. A thickset hand secured his arm, stopping him from falling.

"Don't struggle, boy. Those are no ordinary bracelets," said the guard. "They're the Nimrod Barm Prisoner Retention System, or as we like to call them, the manglers."

If he wasn't in agony, Sin might have smiled. That about summed up his week. His captivity was being ensured by the man he was trying to save.

CHAPTER 29
THE EUGENESIS PROJECT

Sin stood to attention in the brig, his hands still cuffed behind him. It was small but comfortable. Compared to how Sin had lived much of his life, it bordered on luxury. There was a bed, a toilet and a sink, which even had hot running water. Nevertheless, the iron bars at the end of the cell left no doubt that he was a prisoner.

He was flanked by the two guards who had cuffed him and ahead stood Eldritch, a look of disappointment on his face. "I had such hopes for you," he said. Sin shrugged, a gesture that sent bouts of pain through his shackled wrists. He wanted to explain about the spy and Major C, but if Eldritch was in on it, that might prove fatal.

"You've thrown it all away, and over what? A girl?" said Eldritch.

"It weren't like that."

"So what was it? I'm fascinated to know."

"Don't matter now. You're going to chuck me out anyway."

"Yes, we are. Guards, take his shoelaces and belt, then uncuff him," said Eldritch. A triumphant smile curled his lips. "Oh, and you'd better take his keeper too."

Sin backed away. "No, that's mine; you ain't having it."

"There could be anything inside – weapons, a means of escape. We can't possibly let you hang on to it." Eldritch held out a hand. "Unless of course you want to show us the contents."

Sin's cuffed wrists pressed against the cell's stone wall. "I'll bloody kill you," he snarled and kicked out sideways. His foot connected with the nearest guard's knee who staggered backwards. A fist slammed into Sin's side and he crumpled to the floor. A hand secured a toxic-smelling cloth over his mouth and nose. He thrashed his head and legs wildly but, constrained as he was, his efforts were futile. Finally succumbing, he sucked in a breath of chemical-laden air and darkness overcame him.

* * *

Daylight streamed through the cell's high window. Gingerly, Sin eased himself upright, unsure of his surroundings. They'd removed his cuffs but deep grooves still marked his wrists. His hand went to his chest. They'd taken his keeper. He inhaled deeply, the events of the previous evening flooding back like a bad dream. Had Eldritch manufactured the whole thing so he could steal from Sin without reproach?

Footsteps echoed along the corridor. Zonda walked towards the wall of bars, on her face was the same cold, dead stare she'd had on the steamrifle range. Sin swung his legs from the bed and reached between the steel uprights. Zonda placed a rolled up tube of violet-tinted paper into his hand. "You told me you were my friend and nothing was going to change that. You were wrong," she said.

Sin unrolled the nocturnagraph. Captured in brilliant violet hues were Sin and Velvet beside the fountain, holding hands.

Lifting his gaze to Zonda, Sin said, "That picture don't show the truth of it, we was—"

"Save your lies," said Zonda flatly. "I'm not interested in fabricated words from a fabricated boy." Head held high, she turned and walked away.

Sin screwed the nocturnagraph into a ball and hurled it into the toilet. He flushed it away, down the drain into the sewers, like his life.

* * *

The clanking walk of Major C woke Sin from a fitful sleep. He was unsure whether to stand to attention. Part of him just wanted to lie on the bed and ignore the Major. He'd been thrown out of COG. He wasn't part of them any more so they could poke their rules. But the faintest glimmer of hope still burned inside him. Perhaps it was all another test and the Major was coming here to tell him he'd passed and could return to his room.

Sin stood before the bars, feet together, back straight, arms locked rigidly by his sides. The Major's mekaniks vented a puff of steam as his head turned, checking behind him, ensuring they were alone.

"I am aware that we put you in a difficult position with the secrets that we asked you to keep," said the Major. "Have you revealed Zonda's hunt for the spy to anyone?"

Sin hadn't told a soul, but if he let the Major know the truth, was he signing his own death warrant, ensuring the secret died with him? On the other hand, what if he was somehow wrong about Zonda and the Major and there was an innocent explanation? What if Zonda's father had been working undercover in the King's Knights as a spy for COG? What if the Major wasn't the spy? In the end Sin decided he'd had enough with lying and he'd tell the truth whatever the consequences. "No, sir, I've told no one," he said.

"Not Noir, or Eldritch?"

"No, sir."

"Good. I genuinely appreciate that. However, you broke a Cast-Iron Rule, so I'm afraid there's little I can do to help your predicament, unless there are any mitigating circumstances. Is there anything else you want to tell me, Sin? Anything at all?"

Sin hesitated. He'd bite his own arm off to stay in COG, but he couldn't trust the Major. "No, sir," he said. "I broke the rules and that's on me."

The Major stood to attention. "It may take a while to resolve how best to deal with you. You'll be comfortable enough here until then. Goodbye and good luck, Sin."

* * *

After the evening meal on the third day, Sin was handed a set of smart yet worn clothes and told to wash and change. Two guards escorted him from the brig and out of the palace by a tradesman's door. His heart beat faster. This was it. He was leaving COG, a loose end to be removed. A carriage waited on the gravel, venting steam across the stones. With a whirr of clockwork the door to the enclosed passenger compartment swung open. Sin paused. If he got inside what would happen to him?

"Hurry up, COG Sin," said Lilith from the dark confines of the cab.

Sin started. She had called him COG. Perhaps he still had a chance. He clambered inside.

Lilith sat deep in the gloom of the cabin. She held a finger to her lips and motioned with her other hand for Sin to take a seat. The door slammed, locked, and with a hiss of steam the carriage rocked forwards. Sin dropped onto the cushioned bench.

Lilith steepled her fingers. "You have been a vexatious thorn in our side with your spying and interference."

Sin glanced at the carriage door. There was no visible method to unlock it and the ironglass window offered little hope of escape. "So now you're going to murder me?"

"That would be a waste." Lilith leaned closer. "No, we are going to use you."

Sin caught a faint aroma of lavender, the same as had been on the note summoning him to the fateful meeting with Velvet. "You arranged the meeting. You set me up. It wasn't Eldritch."

"We needed you thrown out of COG so you could help us unobserved. You seem to think we are the nefarious ones, yet Noir and I are the only people you can trust. There is a spy that we've been scheming to catch but your blundering has thwarted our efforts."

"You're saying all that skulking about was you trying to catch the spy?"

"Precisely. We have been leaking information to give us credibility. They were non-sensitive papers, pieces of Nimrod's research with no military relevance, or so we thought. Last week we put out one of Nimrod's zoological investigations. It was an experiment on octopus blood, which seemed pretty harmless, except a contact in the King's Knights paid far too handsomely for it. When their courier collected the papers Noir tailed him to the St Aldates workhouse."

"What's this got to do with me?" said Sin.

"Noir couldn't get inside the buildings unnoticed and we can't sanction an official COG operation, so you are going to do it. No one's going to suspect a fourteen-year-old boy, and you have skills, training and a knowledge of COG. That's why I've been pushing you so hard in detention. I needed to get you mission-ready."

"What makes you think I'm going to help you?"

"You believe in COG. You saved Nimrod's life. Uncover the truth and I will petition to have you reinstated."

The noise of the coach changed as it passed through the palace gates, leaving the estate's gravel road behind. Sin sat back. If Lilith was being truthful, she wanted to catch the spy and was offering him an opportunity to redeem himself. He should grasp it with both hands. But they had orchestrated his expulsion and they needed him to cooperate so perhaps, finally, he had the leverage to get some answers.

Sin looked her in the eyes. They pierced him to the core but he held her gaze. "I want to know about the Eugenesis Project."

Lilith's face didn't so much as flicker. "I don't know what that is."

"In that case you may as well stop the coach, because I'm not interested." Sin folded his arms and adopted his best poker face.

"I swore an oath to Nimrod. My family does not break its word, though I'll tell you what I can." Lilith stared out of the window for what seemed like an age before continuing. "Fifteen years ago I answered an advertisement in *The Times*. A team of scientists were seeking extraordinary people, not just talented, they wanted 'extramundane humans' as they termed it. My family has always been considered bizarre because we never get sick, so I applied and was admitted to the project. That's where I first met Noir."

Sin inhaled sharply. "Why was Noir on the project?"

"He was a stage magician renown for his fire act but his passion was hypnotism and mesmeric states. He could enter a trance where time would slow, allowing him to carry out impossible feats of sleight of hand."

Noir could slow time. That couldn't be coincidence. What had Zonda said about the notes he'd stolen from

Eldritch? The scientists had taken Super-Pangenes from a number of talented people and given them to a baby. A queasiness gripped Sin. Did he have Noir's Super-Pangenes? He'd half suspected he was part of the experiment, but not that Noir might be involved too. He shuddered in revulsion. What other freaks' Super-Pangenes might he have? Could it really be that he was made from many donors? He had to know for sure. "Am I the result of the Eugenesis Project?"

"Only Nimrod can answer that."

"Well, he can't, can he?"

"And if we don't find the spy, the next attempt on his life may be successful and your answers die with him."

"Say I believe you. How do I know I can trust Noir?"

"He's a dark horse for sure but he adheres to a code of sorts. I trust him with my daughter's life. He wouldn't let anyone kill Nimrod."

"He was at the Royal Society of Inventors when Nimrod was poisoned."

"He went after Nimrod when the alarm was raised, only to find someone had unwound the other carriages, delaying him. I find it more revealing that Eldritch managed to spectacularly not arrive in the nick of time. In fact, the timing of his failure couldn't be more perfect."

"So Eldritch is the spy?"

"Eldritch, the Major, Stoneheart, MacKigh, someone

else entirely, it could be anyone at the palace. This is why we need you. You've got to discover what they're up to and bring them into the open." Lilith reached into a lace-trimmed reticule at her side and pulled out a set of lock picks. "Yours, I believe. I caught COG Nobbs trying to sneak them into the brig. He was planning some sort of daring escape for you but I managed to scare him off."

Sin took the picks. Good old Nobby. It was sad to think he may never see him again.

The coach had left the palace grounds and he had left the best few weeks of his life behind. If there was even the faintest chance that he might be able to rejoin COG he had to take it. He slid the picks into a pocket and said, "What do you need me to do?"

CHAPTER 30
MOTHER'S RUIN

The coach pulled to a halt between two street chemlamps, their light leaching through the evening's smog. Lilith pulled a carpetbag from beneath the seat and pushed it towards Sin with her foot. "We've got you a job as the doctor's assistant. We don't understand why they're interested in Nimrod's research so we need you to discover what they're up to. Once we know that we can set a trap for the spy."

Sin lifted the bag onto the seat beside him. From inside her jacket Lilith pulled a letter. "This is a reference from the Sisters of the Sacred Science Orphanage. You are Sinclair Grant, a recent discharge with a perfect record of behaviour."

Sin reached for the letter and noticed a sovereign ring on the index finger of Lilith's left hand made from three intermeshing cogs. Sinclair was the name stencilled on the crate he'd been abandoned in and the ring was the one he'd seen in the photo. He grabbed Lilith's hand and turned it to get a better view of the ring. "You were there when I was abandoned. You know what happened to me, to my mother."

Lilith swallowed, a watery sheen glazing her eyes. "Your mother, Eve Metis, was a great lady and a scientist ahead of her time. If it wasn't for her, my Velvet would never have been born."

Sin released Lilith's hand. "Tell me what happened. Please?"

After a long pause, Lilith spoke, her voice trembling. "When you were two months old Eve came to me convinced that someone was trying to take you from her. She asked for my help to smuggle you out of the country. Her house was being watched so we came up with the plan of hiding you in a crate of gin."

"So how come I ended up at the orphanage?"

"Noir was driving Eve and you to the aerodrome when they were ambushed. Noir conjured a rain of fire on their assailants buying enough time for Eve to escape but he was terribly burned in the process." Lilith dabbed a falling tear with a lace handkerchief. "What happened next we can't know for sure. Eve was later found murdered on the other side of the city. We can only presume that she left you on the orphanage steps before drawing her pursuers away."

Sin inhaled deeply. He had no memory of his mother and always knew it was unlikely that he'd ever meet her. Even so, the news was a shock. He felt like he'd been punched in the guts. What had Zonda said? *The truth you want to hear is not necessarily the truth you'll get.* Well, this certainly wasn't the truth he'd wanted. Before, he'd had hope, now there was just an empty space, like all these years he'd been chasing a ghost.

"Noir spent years in a sanatorium recovering from his burns. On his release he tracked you down to the orphanage. I didn't like to abandon you there but Noir persuaded me that it was safest. Anonymity was your best protection."

"Protection from who?"

"We still don't know for sure, so you need to keep this a secret. If you don't, Velvet and I will be in the gravest of danger, as will you."

If his mother was such a great woman, why would anyone want to attack her and what was she running away from? Sin had often wondered about his father and why no photograph was left of him. Could this be the reason?

"Was it my father who murdered her?"

"Most definitely not."

"But you knew my father?"

"Yes, and before you ask, I am honour-bound to secrecy on the matter, as is Noir. He may have tried to prod your memory with his notes and theatrics but he won't out-and-out tell you any more than I will."

"I'm done with all these secrets and lies. Why can't you just tell me the truth?"

"Because promises were made. I promised your mother and my family does not break–"

"Its word. I know, you said," concluded Sin.

"Complete the mission and return to COG. Then you may find the answers you seek," said Lilith, folding her arms.

Sin scowled. Because of course, it was going to be that simple.

* * *

Wisps of smog curled around Sin's legs like a friendly cat. The sounds and smells of Coxford filled him with a sense of comfort. After the evening's revelations it was a relief to pretend for a moment he was back to his simple life in the gang. This was his city and he walked the streets with a confident swagger. Sin Metis, that was his name. His real name. He couldn't tell anyone but just knowing it made him more complete, tempering the sadness he felt that he'd never known his mother and never would. Growing up among orphans, he'd been stoic about his fate, but now, discovering that his mother had loved him – had died to protect him – his stoicism was transmuting to anger.

A trio of young urchins stepped from an alley, mistaking Sin for an easy mark. "Spare some change, sir?" said the biggest of the three.

This wasn't Sin's old patch although he thought he recognised one of them as belonging to the JTS crew. "Jimmy Two Sticks don't need my money and he don't need the Sheriffs sniffing round neither."

The boys' demeanours changed, more wary now, and Sin knew he'd guessed their master correctly. Sin dropped his bag, his hands bunching into fists. "My evening ain't exactly been bang up the castle so if you want a battering, let's dance," he said, slipping easily into the patter of the streets.

The two smaller boys hesitated, waiting for direction from their larger leader. "Don't reckon you've got nothing anyhow," said the bigger boy. Seeming to sense the danger, he backed away, the three of them fading into the alley.

The workhouse was a large, foreboding brick building. It looked like a prison and for the poor, destitute and infirm unlucky enough to end up there, it was one. Sin's life under the Fixer had been tough but it was never so bad that he'd considered the workhouse. The poor were viewed as slackers and conditions in the workhouse were deliberately harsh to deter them. They toiled twelve-hour shifts, crushing bones for fertiliser or picking oakum, and in return they were crammed thirty to a room and received two meals of gruel a day.

Sin walked up the steps and into the entrance foyer. It smelled of urine and disinfectant.

"What do you want?" challenged a burly porter from the booking counter.

Sin pulled the letter of introduction from his pocket. "Sinclair Grant. I'm to be Doctor Hotchin's assistant."

The porter snatched the letter and shouted to someone in the office behind him. "Veronica? The new assistant's here. Sort him out."

A chair scraped back and then Veronica hurried into view. Sin did a double-take. Despite the dowdy dress and cloth mop hat, there was no mistaking Velvet's elegant features.

"Welcome, Mr Grant, we've been expecting you. I'll show you to your room then give you a tour of the workhouse."

Velvet took Sin past the porter's office and along a gloomy corridor, at the end of which stood a dirty wooden door. Someone had once tried to brighten it with a coat of green paint but this had succumbed to the malaise of the workhouse, the once glossy coat now cracked and peeling.

Velvet ushered Sin inside. The room was just big enough for the narrow, iron-framed bed pushed up against the wall. The brickwork glistened with damp and in one corner an impressive cluster of toadstools pushed their way up from the rotting floorboards. It couldn't have been more different from his room at the palace – even the brig had been more welcoming – but Sin had slept in far worse. He threw his carpetbag onto the bed and turned to face Velvet. "What are you doing here?"

Velvet pushed the door closed behind her. "You didn't think they'd trust this all to you?"

"So you were in on the whole thing. You set me up?"

"No, that was Mother."

"She had her own daughter thrown out of COG?"

"Mother does whatever it takes to get the job done and she expects the same of me." Velvet tugged the cloth cap from her head. "Even if it's wearing rags like this, or tempting candidates to break the rules at selection. Whatever Mother says goes."

Lilith had ordered Velvet to try to get him kicked out of selection, and if it wasn't for Zonda, she probably would have succeeded. Sin felt an unaccustomed pang of guilt. He missed Zonda. She had a way of making him feel like he belonged. He wished they'd parted on better terms. "What do we do now?" he asked.

"Settle in. Don't do anything stupid, and watch for clues. You're used to these sorts of people so you'll know if something's wrong."

"I never stayed at the spike."

Velvet's brow furrowed. "The spike?"

"It's what we call the workhouse."

"See, you know the vernacular; you'll fit in just fine. Me, well it's killing me to talk like these commoners, and the smell, don't even get me started on that." Velvet reached behind her and pulled the door open. "I'll show you around, and in the morning you can meet the doctor."

After Velvet had finished the tour, Sin dropped onto his bed and tried to make sense of the day. Was he the result of the Eugenesis Project? Surely, this now seemed to be the case. But who was his father, or did he not have one? Had his mother been nothing more than an experimental test tube for the mixing of Super-Pangenes? If he was to find the truth, he was going to have to get back to COG.

* * *

Sin guessed Doctor Hotchin was in his mid-thirties, although the permanent frown that wrinkled his brow made him seem older. He'd issued Sin with a leather and brass respirator, his watery eyes seeming oddly intense as he'd instructed Sin on its usage. Once Hotchin was satisfied that Sin was adequately protected they'd commenced the morning rounds. Sin manoeuvred a clockwork-driven dispensary cabinet through the infirmary. Pushing down on the brassanium steering handles controlled power to the legs, making the large battered box waddle wherever Sin directed. The peculiar device was a pig to steer but it took his mind off the squalor of the infirmary. There were no beds, only rag mattresses on the floor on which lay the sick, the dying and, in one case, the dead. In a corner, a wooden bucket served as a toilet.

Sin checked the fit of the respirator that clung limpet-like to the lower half of his face. It made breathing more difficult but the charcoal filters did an excellent job of removing the smells from the air, or at least replaced them with a more amenable sooty tang.

The doctor examined the patients, making copious notes in a large journal and administering spoonfuls of medicine and pills from the cabinet. When all the patients had been seen, the doctor led Sin to a copper-plated door at the end of the ward. He removed a heavy brassanium key from the cabinet and inserted it into the lock. He fixed Sin with his watery stare. "Never go in here without me. Always wear your mask and don't, under any circumstances, remove it."

Sin nodded. "What's behind the door?"

Hotchin's frown deepened. "Hell," he answered.

The door swung inwards. Eight brass beds lined the ward. Tied to each with ropes and rags were what Sin could only assume were patients. Their once-clean gowns were stained with blood and pus. On their hands, feet and faces bulbous boils pulsated.

"Rat Pox," said the doctor. "If there are worse ways to die, I've never seen them." From a bookcase that now doubled as storage shelves, he removed a set of thick black rubber gloves and pulled them on. "Touch nothing without these," he said and handed Sin a pair.

Sin's gaze met one of the patients. The pleading look of horror and hopelessness in the man's eyes twisted his insides. He felt bile rising in his throat and had to swallow hard. If he was sick in his mask, he'd have to remove it and there was no way he was going to do that in here. With a feeling of revulsion building inside him, he surveyed the other beds. No one should suffer like this. It would be kinder to let them die, even help them die, rather than prolong the suffering.

The doctor approached the final patient, an emaciated woman whose legs twitched uncontrollably. From his bag he pulled a foot-long flexible brass tube with an eyepiece at one end. "I need you to hold her head still while I insert the endoscope," he said.

Placing his hands either side of the woman's head, Sin applied gentle pressure. He could feel the heat of her fever through the rubber of his gloves. She struggled weakly as the doctor forced the metal tube between her lips and into her throat, but the pox had taken the fight from her and she soon went limp. Hotchin lowered his eye to the device's optics and twiddled a knob. "Sinclair. You should see this."

The brass eyepiece was cold against Sin's face. It was a bit like looking through the telescope, except that what he saw was not rolling hills or beautiful gardens but a garish pink tunnel lined with yellow pustules.

"The latter stages of Rat Pox, I'm afraid," said the doctor.

Sin lifted his head away and Hotchin pulled the endoscope free. He dropped it into a bucket of bleach before wiping it clean and putting it in his bag. He dipped his gloved hands in the bleach and directed Sin to do the same before they both returned the sterilised rubber gloves to the shelves.

Hotchin cast a final glance over the patients then ushered Sin from the room. He pulled the door closed and locked it. With the cuff of his jacket he rubbed a smudge from the shiny metal. "Interesting thing about copper and its alloys, bacteria can't survive on it. Can't even survive near it. I wish we could use it in here," he said, gesturing to the squalor of the infirmary. "But it's just too damn expensive."

They returned to the doctor's office and Sin walked the dispensary cabinet to a steam-powered clockwork winder on the wall.

"I don't think I'll ever get used to the misery, but I find most things seem better with a good strong cup of Earl Grey," said Hotchin, placing a conical kettle on a small gas burner.

"So I've been told," said Sin. "I didn't think people still got the Rat Pox."

"Mostly they don't. We've not had an epidemic for years. Any new cases are brought directly to us before they become contagious and so we're managing to control it."

"What will happen to them?"

The doctor took two fine china teacups painted with scenes from the Raj and placed them on his desk. "They'll die; everyone does. Patient Three, Miss Gordon, she's got a day, maybe two if she's unlucky. After tea I need you to run to the undertakers and tell them we'll need one standard and one sealed casket for cremation."

CHAPTER 31
BLACKMAN AND BELL

The undertaker was half a mile across the city. Sin dawdled through the streets, enjoying being free from the oppression and misery of the workhouse. No wonder so many like him turned to crime. Living rough with a gang was a far better alternative to the wretchedness of the spike.

A steamtram puffed past, belching soot and cinders into the air. He moved to the side of the road, avoiding the jetting steam from the carriages, and noticed a pair of young cutpurses watching him from across the street. There was something about their demeanour that made him wary. He was not the easiest or most lucrative target yet they focused on him rather than scanning the surrounds for other marks.

Sin ducked into an alley at the back of Briton College

and hurried into the sunken doorway that acted as the delivery entrance for the kitchens. He concealed himself behind a barrel of Mutton Joe's Finest Lambs' Offal and waited.

The cutpurses padded past him, their pace becoming more frantic.

"Told you he'd seen us," said the younger of the two.

"Shut up and run. We'll get a beat down if we lose him."

The sound of their footsteps receded. Sin darted from his hiding place and gave chase. They could have been sent by Jimmy Two Sticks, but it seemed unlikely. His encounter the previous evening was hardly worthy of interest or retribution. Was the spy onto him already? It wouldn't be out of place to hire the services of the gangs. He'd occasionally done work for the Fixer that didn't involve thievery and was simply following someone and reporting back.

At the end of the alley Sin slowed. He waited for a group of well-heeled students to saunter by and slipped onto the street using them as cover. The urchins tailing him would probably have split up, taking a direction each. On failing to find him they should return to the alley. He crossed the street and rummaging in his pocket retrieved a penny. Tossing it to a hawker, he plucked a *Coxford Herald* from the stand and sat on a bench with a good view of the alley. The front-page article showed a grainy lithograph of a multi-gunned battleship below the headline *BRITANNIA NO LONGER RULES THE WAVES*. Sin scanned the crowds for either of the urchins as he read the article, which detailed the launch of the first Teutonian ocean-going warship, the *Brandenburg*. A shadow fell over him. Overhead, a giant lozenge-shaped airship drifted across the rooftops. On its grey sides was painted a moustached man in an aviator's helmet and goggles. He pointed down at the ground, his face stern yet imploring. Next to him, in letters high as a house, was written *The Sky Navy Needs YOU!*

Across the street Sin clocked the urchins disappearing back down the alley. He tucked the newspaper beneath his arm and followed them. They looked pretty young and from the ease with which he'd lost them he suspected they were inexperienced, so it was odd that they would be tailing him. If a mark was worthy of surveillance, you put someone good on it, or at least partnered a greenhorn with someone who could teach them the ropes.

An uneasy feeling niggled at Sin as they turned into Blue Boar Street. He pulled his cloth cap lower over his face and dropped further back. His smart clothes and clean looks offered a certain disguise but this was his old turf and he was chancing it coming down here.

He slowed, lurking by a Georgian building that housed

a respectable apothecary and also, Sin knew, a discreet opium den in the cellar. The urchins headed to the back door of The Bear Pit, Coxford's oldest pub. It dated from Tudor times and had bowed white walls, gnarled oak beams and a warped tile roof. The inside of the pub was equally twisted, as was its most infamous resident, the Fixer. That explained the use of greenhorns; it had to be newbloods or Sin would have recognised them.

He retreated through Wheatsheaf Yard, back towards the undertaker's. The Fixer knew he'd returned. That couldn't be good. He'd never settled his debt and the Fixer wasn't the sort of man who let things ride. He'd be safe in the workhouse, probably, but the streets now held an additional danger. He scanned about him, even more vigilant of his surrounds.

The frontage to Blackman and Bell was sombre and understated. Either side of the dark wood door, satin-lined windows displayed caskets and headstones, tastefully arranged.

Sin pushed the door open and a single deep chime rang out. A gaunt, black-suited man with slicked-back hair looked up from a ledger. His gaze travelled from Sin's feet to his head. Sin shuddered, realising he'd been expertly sized for a coffin.

"Welcome. How may I be of assistance?" said the undertaker, his baritone voice filling the room.

"Doctor Hotchin sent me. We need a standard and a sealed casket for cremation."

The undertaker added a line to the ledger. The sound of the pen scratching at the paper seeming unduly loud in the deathly quiet.

"Is either to be a *special* casket?"

The pen paused on the word special, as if the raised eyebrow and insinuating tone weren't enough.

"Err. No, I don't think so. He just said a standard and sealed casket for cremation."

"Very good. Delivery will be late afternoon, removal by sundown tomorrow."

The undertaker plucked a business card embossed with gold leaf from a holder on the counter and fastidiously wrote the details on the reverse. He rolled a blotter across the writing, drying the ink, then proffered it, clasped between pale skeletal fingers. Sin took the card and the undertaker returned to the ledger, their business concluded.

Sin made his way back to the workhouse, double-checking for any unwanted followers. As far as he could see, there were none. Doctor Hotchin was in his office going through patient records. Sin had debated whether to confront the doctor about the special caskets. It could be entirely legitimate, but from the undertaker's demeanour he doubted this was the case. However, it was only his first day and so he decided to play it innocent, imagining how he'd behave if he were not on the hunt for a spy.

"It's all arranged. They're going to drop them off this afternoon," said Sin, "but they asked about special caskets?"

The doctor looked up. "What did you say?"

"I didn't know what he was talking about. So I just said a standard and sealed casket for cremation, like you told me."

The doctor's shoulders relaxed and he returned to his paperwork. "Good. Good," he muttered.

"What is a special casket?" asked Sin, an air of innocent curiosity in his voice.

Hotchin's head jerked upwards, his watery stare fixing on Sin.

Sin shrugged. "I thought I should know, in case we ever need one."

The doctor fiddled nervously with his pen. "Ah, well, we sometimes need a copper-lined casket, which the body is sealed into. It depends on how advanced the Rat Pox is when the patient dies."

The explanation sounded reasonable but from the doctor's discomfort it was obvious there was more to it than this.

"Well, let's hope we don't need one any time soon," said Sin. "Do you require me for anything else?"

"No. You can take your lunch now."

Sin reached for the door.

"You've done well, Sinclair," said Doctor Hotchin. "You've coped much better than your predecessor."

"What happened to my predecessor?" asked Sin.

"Patient number five," answered Hotchin.

CHAPTER 32
CARPE DIEM

The workhouse staff had a separate dining room from the giant hall where the inmates ate. Painted a drab green with a solitary portrait on the wall of Sir Max Dowell, the workhouse's founder, the room felt less welcoming than Blackman and Bell. Sir Max appeared to be a stern, austere gentleman with dark hair, dark eyes and dark clothes. Sin guessed he had no sense of joy or frivolity, a sentiment that seemed to be echoed in the food being served. He had a stale hunk of bread and a bowl of watery stew, on top of which floated fatty globules.

The dining room was empty, possibly an indictment of the quality of the food, and so he sat alone at the end of one of the two wooden tables. He was marvelling at the cook's ability to make something so devoid of any discernible flavour when the door opened and Velvet slipped into the room. She eased the door closed and dropped onto the bench next to him. "How's the food?" she asked.

"It looks better than it tastes."

Velvet took a knife and prodded a translucent glob floating in Sin's bowl. It sunk below the surface leaving an oily slick in its place. "I've not had the heart to try it. I normally pretend I've got to go to the post house and slip into Marmadukes for tea and cake."

The mention of cake made Sin think of Zonda and he wondered how she was doing. Would she be managing to abstain so she had a chance at getting over the wall? Or would she succumb to temptation without his encouragement? Despite all that had happened, he missed her more than he'd have thought possible.

"Don't suppose you could bring an eclair back for me?" said Sin.

Velvet eyed him contemplatively.

"I'll void our bet," said Sin.

"I'll think about it. Have you found anything?"

"A room of Rat Pox victims and something suspicious to do with special coffins, but nothing cast iron. You?"

"There's a discrepancy in the records. I'm sure of it, but I've not been able to go back and check. Harris won't leave me alone."

Sin fished something that he hoped was meat from his broth. "When does Harris take his lunch? I can keep cavey so you can have a proper search."

Velvet tilted her head. "Cavey?"

"You know, act as a lookout."

"Ah, you mean *cave* from the Latin beware."

Sin swallowed the tasteless lump. "Course I did. Well known for our fluency in Latin, us street kids."

Velvet checked a watch hung on a silver chain around her neck. "It's worth a try. Tomorrow's lunch?"

Sin dropped his spoon into the bowl and pushed it away from him. "Let's do it now." He winked at Velvet. "Carpe diem."

* * *

Sin hovered in the doorway to the office while Velvet sifted through papers.

"I thought you were keeping watch?" said Velvet.

"I am keeping watch."

"You're not supposed to be watching me."

"I don't tell you how to sip tea and eat cucumber sandwiches, so do me the courtesy of not telling me how to do my job."

"You really do have a dim view of the aristocracy don't you." Velvet tugged at the brassanium handle on a tall wooden filing cabinet that, unlike the rest of the battered furniture in the office, still retained its varnished sheen. "This one's locked."

"That'll be the one we're interested in then. Have a dekko for a key. It'll be hanging under the desk or beneath a chemlamp or something."

Velvet rummaged under the desk. "You were right," she said, retrieving a small brass barrel key. "How did you know?"

"People think thieves are stupid and assume they'll outsmart us but we're more cunning."

Velvet turned the key in the lock and pulled the lever on the side of the cabinet. Clockwork whirred inside and the drawers began to open with a mekanikal slowness.

Sin's head snapped around, towards the workhouse foyer. "Harris is coming."

Velvet froze. "You sure? I didn't hear anything."

Sin tapped his nose and darted from the doorway. He slowed his gait to an unconcerned saunter and wandered into the foyer, blocking the porter's way.

"Mr Harris, sir. Just the man I was hoping to see," said Sin.

"Out my way, boy."

The smell of cigarettes and beer wafted from the porter and Sin guessed lunch had been a mostly liquid affair. Continuing to obstruct Harris's path, Sin said, "Doctor

Hotchin has some coffins arriving later. I was wondering what the procedure is for receiving them?"

"There's no procedure, undertakers bring 'um and leave 'um where the doctor wants." Harris took a step forwards, forcing Sin back.

"Do I need to sign for them or make an inspection to make sure it's correct?"

"Do what you want, just don't bother me about it." Harris stuck out a thick arm and brushed Sin aside. The man had a natural strength in keeping with his size. Sin could have resisted but that wasn't the role he was playing. And besides, he'd bought enough time for Velvet to cover her tracks.

* * *

Late in the afternoon the undertakers delivered the caskets. One was a rough wood box with rope handles and misaligned boards, which served as the last resting place for the deceased from the infirmary. The other coffin was clearly the work of a craftsman, with no gaps in the wood and a lid that sealed tight with metal clasps. This they left outside the Rat Pox ward in readiness. Sin once again accompanied Doctor Hotchin through the copper-plated door on his evening rounds where he tended to the patients and where, against all odds, Patient Three was still clinging onto life.

Afterwards they sat in the doctor's office sipping Earl Grey.

"It makes you think, doesn't it, Sinclair?" said Hotchin.

"What does, sir?"

"Seeing the likes of Miss Gordon. She knows she's going to die, but she's not giving up. I saw the same in India with wounded soldiers. Some would pass without a fight, others, they simply refused to go, said they had unfinished business in this world."

"Do you think there'll be another war, Doctor?"

Hotchin blew on his tea. "There's always another war, Sinclair. It's just a question of how far away it is."

* * *

The workhouse quietened down after supper, save for the occasional wail of a mournful inmate. Sin drifted towards Velvet's room. No one had told him he wasn't allowed to visit but, unlike COG, the workhouse was strictly divided into male and female sides and Sin suspected his presence would be frowned upon. He knocked lightly on Velvet's door. There was the creak of bedsprings then the door opened. Velvet scanned the corridor then ushered him inside.

Her room was bigger than Sin's and in better repair, with no mould or damp. Beneath her window was a small mirrored dresser on which sat an array of glass bottles. Hanging from each bedpost was a pomander that gave the room a strong scent of lavender.

"You know you're not supposed to be here," said Velvet.

"Not supposed to do a lot of things but it don't stop me. Besides, I came to see if you found anything."

Velvet pulled open a drawer in the dresser and took out a cardboard box.

"I found this," she said, handing it to Sin.

He flipped the lid open. Inside was a chocolate eclair.

Velvet smiled. "Although I found that at Marmadukes. Unfortunately, Harris returned too quickly for me to have a proper search of the office. What about you?"

Sin bit into the eclair. There was something different about Velvet now that they were away from COG. Gone was the petty bickering and the arrogance. Instead, she was focused on making things work. Determined to complete the mission. He swallowed and said, "I didn't find much. Harris smelled of cigarettes."

"And?"

"He smokes Salmon & Gluckstein Dandy Fifth. That's proper gentry tobacco, not the floor scrapings you'd expect a workhouse porter to be burning."

"You think someone's bribing him?"

"Harris must see everyone who comes and goes in this place. Perhaps it's an incentive to turn a blind eye."

"Indeed, but to what?"

"Could we have a look at the file cabinet now the office is closed?" said Sin, flicking one of the pomanders and sending a shower of lavender over the bed.

Velvet shooed him away. "No. Harris sleeps right next door so there's even less chance."

"How about if I create some sort of misdirection to occupy Harris tomorrow? Could you use the time to check the files?"

"That might work. What kind of misdirection?" said Velvet, picking lavender from her covers.

Sin smiled. "Something they'll get all steamed up about."

CHAPTER 33
AN UNHAPPY REUNION

Steam spouted from the ruptured pressure pipes with an enraged hiss. Sin lead Harris through the sauna-like fug to a complicated control panel hanging half-off the basement's wall. Its fascia was covered in circular brass gauges, the needles of which oscillated wildly. Thick copper pipes sprouted from the panel in all directions. The largest pipe, the diameter of Sin's arm, ran from the bottom of the panel to a spherical boiler in the basement's corner. Halfway along the pipe a large valve-wheel dripped water. A metal plate hung on a chain from the valve, on it the words *DO NOT TOUCH*.

"Someone's tried to wrench it off the wall," said Sin, neglecting to mention that he was the someone in question.

Harris ran a hand over his bald head, which was

turning a vivid pink colour in the heat. "Better turn off the main pressure from the boiler," he said uncertainly. His chunky fingers wrapped around the valve wheel and he began to turn.

"NO!" shouted Doctor Hotchin, appearing through the steam. "There's important medical equipment connected. It can't lose pressure." The doctor ran to the panel and tapped some of the dials. "Only the pipes to the workshop are broken. We can reroute them." He moved away from the panel, tracing a pipe until it reached an inline gauge. The needle on the gauge was slowly dropping. He pointed to a brassanium valve. "Sinclair, you've got the return bypass. Harris, the auxillary frunge wheel. I need you to both turn them off when I say."

The doctor returned to the control panel. "Three, two, one, now."

Sin's muscles strained as he worked the valve wheel. It was rusty and grated with each turn, seeming to fight harder against him with every revolution. He glanced up at the doctor who scrutinised the panel, feathering a lever as the gauge's needles played back and forth.

"My valve's closed," shouted Harris.

Sin turned the wheel twice more until it refused to budge any further. "Mine's closed too."

The doctor moved a handle on the control panel and the escaping steam stopped. He dashed to the gauge on the pipe and watched the needle climb.

Sin looked from the doctor to where the pipe ran through the wall. The brickwork appeared new, not having yet succumbed to the workhouse's melancholy and the pipe was shiny and untarnished. It seemed strange that the doctor was familiar with the boiler and control panel. On their rounds Sin hadn't seen any medical equipment more complex than the endoscope, certainly nothing that would require steam power.

Hotchin scribbled a note in his diary. He ripped out the page and handed it to Harris. "Take this to Pratt and Witney Boilers and tell them we've got an emergency."

The doctor hurried to his office with Sin in tow. "I need to check on the Rat Pox patients," he said. Donning his respirator, he took the large brassanium key from the dispensary trolley. Sin reached for his own mask and Hotchin blocked him. "Wait, Sinclair. I need you to stay here in case …" Hotchin's gaze darted about the office, coming to rest on the business card from Blackman and Bell, "… in case they need to collect the casket. Harris normally deals with it but you'll have to manage."

"Shall I come and get you if they turn up?"

Above the leather mask strapped to his face the doctor's eyes widened. "No. It's vital that I work undisturbed. Just stay here."

Sin relaxed back in his chair. He put his arms behind his

neck and lifted his feet onto a stool as if settling in for the afternoon. Hotchin checked his mask was secure then rushed from the office. Sin waited a moment then pulled open the doctor's bag. It was curious Hotchin hadn't taken it with him to check on the patients. From inside he retrieved the endoscope and shoved it into his pocket. With a footpad's stealth he eased the door open. The corridor was deserted and he slunk to reception undetected. Harris's normal space at the counter was empty, but Sin heard the rustling of paperwork from somewhere inside. The reception door was locked so, quiet as a cat on the prowl, he vaulted the counter and stalked into the back office.

Velvet hunched over the filing cabinet, riffling through paperwork. Sin's shadow fell across her and she jumped, spilling a sheaf of papers onto the floor. Her head snapped up. "Piston heck! What do you think you're doing?"

"I thought you might need a hand."

"I was doing dandy until you showed up and nearly gave me a heart attack."

"Found anything?"

"For sure. I need to do some crosschecking."

"Seriously, though. Can I help?"

"I don't mean to be rude but these records are pretty complicated and not for the semi-literate."

For once Sin got the feeling that Velvet wasn't putting him down, she was simply stating a fact. "I'll leave you to it. I think Hotchin's up to something. I'm going to check it out."

Velvet reclaimed the scattered papers. "Let's meet up this evening and share what we've discovered."

* * *

The infirmary's foul stench assaulted Sin's nose and he wished he'd thought to wear his mask. The patients moaned and groaned but paid him little heed as he approached the copper-plated door to the Rat Pox ward. He kneeled down and removed the endoscope from his pocket. Pushing the disc covering the keyhole aside, he threaded the endoscope into the hole. Fortunately, Hotchin had removed the key from the lock and, with some gentle coercion, Sin guided the endoscope clean through. He lowered his eye to the optics and saw a circular section of the Rat Pox ward. For some reason the endoscope had turned the image upside down but the detail was clear enough, the bodies strapped to the beds, the shelves of equipment. No Hotchin. Sin manoeuvred the endoscope sideways, panning his view back and forth in case he'd missed the doctor. Other than the patients, the ward was empty.

Sin pulled the endoscope clear and thrust it into his pocket. He needed to get back to Hotchin's office in case the doctor returned. As he reached the infirmary door, a voice behind him said, "'Ere, I knows you."

Sin turned to see a young scraggy-bearded man eyeing him from a rag mattress on the floor. "I couldn't place you earlier, been spinning me cogs trying to remember. You're one of the Fixer's lads."

There was something familiar about the man. Sin tried to picture him without the beard. He had a horrible suspicion the man was right; their paths had crossed. Still, he had to try to bluff his way out, convince the man he was wrong or the mission would be blown and he'd be out of COG for sure. "I do believe you're very much mistaken, sir," said Sin in his poshest accent.

"No, it's you all right. You running some sort of scam for the Fixer? What is it? Nicking drugs?"

Sin raised a hand to his mouth, pretending to be shocked. "I say, how dare you?"

"Bet the doctor don't know. Bet he'd make it worth me while if I told him. Unless of course you wanna make it worth me while not to?"

Sin raised his eyebrows. "Really, sir. I don't know you, I don't know this Fixer and I don't know how you can suggest such a thing."

The man grinned and tapped a finger against his temple. "I can suggest such a thing 'cos I used to run with the Barrel Lane crew and 'cos I stabbed you in the arm."

CHAPTER 34
AN UNWELCOME GUEST

Sin walked closer to the man. He was perhaps five years older than Sin and, despite being in the infirmary, he had a wiry strength to his frame. Sin suspected he wasn't even ill merely on the wag, dodging work and getting extra rations of food. Sin remembered when they'd fought before. The man had been a right handful and Sin didn't fancy his chances now. He was only going to get one shot at this.

He eased the endoscope from his pocket and, behind his back, wrapped it around his hand, forming an impromptu knuckleduster. Punching from his waist and twisting his hips like Eldritch had shown him, his fist connected with the man's chin and he collapsed onto the mattress.

"That's for stabbing me," whispered Sin to the unconscious man, then louder so the room could hear, he said, "This man has been abusing Doctor Hotchin's kindness. Don't let me catch any of you causing trouble or you'll get the same." He thrust the endoscope into his pocket, then clutching one end of the rag mattress dragged it and its occupant from the infirmary.

Sin's legs screamed in complaint by the time he reached his room but with a final effort he pulled his cargo inside. The man moaned groggily and Sin knew he didn't have long before he regained full consciousness. He tore strips of material from the mattress and bound the man's limbs. With a scrap of rag rolled into a ball he made a makeshift gag, which he forced into the man's mouth. It wasn't pretty but it would keep his prisoner silent and secure while he figured out what to do.

The situation had turned to horse dung. When things went south the Fixer always said the sweetest flowers grew from the biggest piles of crap. Even so, Sin struggled to see how was he going to come out of this smelling of roses.

He hurried back to Hotchin's office and eased the door open. The doctor hadn't returned yet and all was quiet save for the gentle tick of the infirmary cabinet's clockwork rewinding. Sin slid the endoscope from his pocket. Superficially, it appeared undamaged, but the tinkle of broken glass that came from within told another story. He returned the endoscope to the doctor's bag and latched it closed, hoping Hotchin wouldn't have cause to use the instrument in the near future. Sitting back in his chair, he tried to relax, as if nothing had happened. But his mind wandered to the man in his room, while his eyes seemed unnaturally drawn to the doctor's bag.

The office door swung open. Sin's heart leaped but he forced himself to remain still, outwardly presenting a facade of the bored assistant. Velvet stepped into the room. "Some men from Blackman and Bell are at reception for Doctor Hotchin."

Sin sucked in a deep breath and stood. "We've got a problem," he whispered.

Velvet glanced down the corridor. "What have you done?"

"It weren't my fault. A patient knew me from the gangs."

The sound of the door to the Rat Pox ward clanging shut echoed through the infirmary.

"That'll be Hotchin," said Sin. "We'll have to sort it later."

"Sort what?" hissed Velvet, but before Sin could reply the doctor stepped into the corridor.

Velvet straightened and squared her shoulders. "Thank goodness you're here, Doctor. I have two tradesmen at reception to pick up a casket."

"I'm afraid they're going to have to take the sealed casket back too." Hotchin turned to Sin. "And I need you to go with them, Sinclair. Tell Mr Blackman we're going to need that special casket after all."

* * *

Sin returned with the undertaker's assistants and the special casket just before tea. It looked like a normal coffin but was about a hand's width deeper and had an additional set of locks to secure it closed. Mounted on a clockwork-powered trolley it was easy to manoeuvre despite its additional size and weight. Under Hotchin's direction they wheeled it into the infirmary and positioned it by the door to the Rat Pox ward. Hotchin withdrew a purse from his pocket and handed each assistant a shilling for the extra trouble he'd put them to. Doffing their caps, they departed, their normal sombre demeanour replaced with large smiles.

"I'm going to need your help with this, Sinclair, and I'm afraid it won't be pleasant," said Hotchin, handing Sin his respirator.

"I'm getting the impression that not much of your job is pleasant, Doctor."

Hotchin smiled. "You're a quick learner, Sinclair." He secured his own respirator across his face and withdrew the brassanium key from his pocket. He opened the door and Sin wheeled the casket inside and next to Patient Three. It had only been a day since he'd helped Hotchin examine

Miss Gordon with the endoscope, but what lay in her place was an unrecognisable mess of pustules and bloody burst boils. Sin understood now why Hotchin gave them numbers. It was hard to think of the corpse as human, let alone a particular person.

"This can get icky so we'll need the gloves," said Hotchin.

Sin wriggled his fingers into the black rubber, grateful that the long gloves extended almost to his elbows. He wasn't a stranger to death but what he saw on the bed wasn't death; it was an abomination.

Hotchin unfastened the casket's lid and lifted it upwards. Hinged on one side and aided by chunky internal springs it swung easily open despite the copper-plated lining. The springs vibrated, making a boinging noise that would have been quite comical in any other situation. "We're going to wrap the body in the sheet and lift it into the casket," directed Hotchin. "You get the feet."

Sin untucked the bedsheet from under the mattress and folded it over the body's legs. Hotchin did the same at the head end, cocooning the remains in a makeshift shroud.

"Two, six, lift," he said and between them they heaved the morbid parcel into the casket.

"Why 'two, six'?" asked Sin. He'd heard the term used before and it hadn't made sense to him then.

Hotchin pulled the casket's lid closed. "It's a military

term. Six men to a steam-cannon gun crew. Numbers two and six lift the shell into the breach."

"Where did you serve?"

"I had a short stint in a field hospital attached to the King's Steam Cavalry. Then the Tea Wars ended and I returned to civilian life. Why do you ask?"

"I've often thought about joining up," lied Sin.

"Well, don't." Hotchin gestured to the patients in the room. "I said earlier there aren't worse ways to die, and that's the truth, but from what I saw in the war there are worse ways to live." He leaned on the casket, a haunted look in his eyes. "I can finish up here, Sinclair. Go get some supper before the kitchen closes."

Sin placed his gloves in the bucket of bleach and Hotchin ushered him from the room, locking the door behind him. Sin walked noisily away in case Hotchin was listening, then crept back to the door. He peeked through the keyhole but without the endoscope he could see nothing. Resting his head against the copper plates, he pressed his ear to the keyhole and listened. Inside, he heard a scuffing noise and then the boing of the casket's springs as the lid was reopened.

CHAPTER 35
COFFIN FIT

Sin let Velvet into his room. The man lay on the floor. An additional rag strip now covered his eyes so Sin didn't have to face his accusing stare. The man tilted his head, listening to the peal of bells that rang out across Coxford as myriad church and college clocks struck eight.

"What did you bring him here for?" said Velvet.

"I had no choice. He was going to tell Hotchin."

"You should have smothered him and left him in the infirmary. Half the patients never make it out anyway."

Sin looked at her in disbelief. "I ain't no murderer. He may be a wrong 'un but he don't deserve that."

The man blindly nodded his head in agreement. Velvet poked him with the toe of her boot and he squirmed backwards. "There are no rules or chivalry. That will only get you dead," she recited Eldritch's words.

"It's not chivalry. It's basic human decency. He's not the enemy, is he?"

"If he's going to get in our way, he is."

Sin folded his arms. It was all well and good Velvet standing there in judgement but she'd not been the one who'd had to make a spur of the moment decision. "Fine. You kill him then," he said.

The colour drained from Velvet's face and she stepped away from the man. "Why should I? You're the one who created the problem, you should sort it."

"I am sorting it. He'll have to stay here until we're finished."

"Great plan. What could possibly go wrong?"

Ignoring the gibe, Sin said, "So did you find anything in the files?"

"I was right; there are discrepancies. Certain residents vanish from the records for no reason and their disappearances coincide with Doctor Hotchin's orders of special caskets."

"What does that mean?"

"It means we need to take a look at that special casket."

* * *

Sin knocked on the door to Hotchin's office. He knew the doctor should have gone for the evening but it paid to be cautious. He tried the doorhandle. True to form Hotchin had locked up when he left. Sin selected a serrated metal rod from his lock picks.

"What are you doing?" asked Velvet.

"I've got to pick the lock."

Velvet rolled her eyes. "How quaint, and so last century." She pulled a brass hemisphere from the folds of her dress, just like the one Eldritch had used, and held it over the keyhole. The clockwork inside the device clattered and then the door swung open. Sin hurried inside and grabbed his respirator and the brassanium key.

"You'd better take Hotchin's mask if you're coming along," he said and handed the doctor's respirator to Velvet.

She examined the sweat-stained leather with an air of disgust and placed it back on the doctor's desk.

"It's really not my colour. It'll clash terribly with my hair."

"You've got to have a mask. It's Rat Pox."

"Von Darques don't get sick. We die of old age or violence."

"But it's Rat Pox."

"So you said."

Sin shrugged. "Suit yourself, it's your funeral."

"It actually isn't," said Velvet and strode from the room.

Sin and Velvet entered the Rat Pox ward, locking the door behind them. The casket still rested on the trolley beside Patient Three's empty bed. Hotchin had secured the locks, sealing it closed.

Velvet placed the metal hemisphere over the first lock and waited for it to do its magic. It rattled and clanked and rattled some more but as the clockwork ran down the lock remained closed. Beneath his mask, Sin grinned. "Time to go old-school," he said. Inserting a pick into the lock, he gave it a jiggle and the lock sprang open. The second lock was more troublesome.

An amused expression on her face, Velvet said, "I guess I must have loosened the other one."

"No, it's the tension on the catch," said Sin. "Lean on the lid, will you?"

The springs creaked as Velvet pressed down on the casket.

"Splendiferous," said Sin and the lock clicked open. The casket's lid lifted a fraction and a bluish vapour seeped from the seal with a hiss.

Sin heaved open the lid. Inside, resting on the wrapped remains of Patient Three, was the body of a man. The corpse was emaciated, the wrinkled skin tinged the pale blue of a blackbird's egg. From his eyes and nose leaked a sapphire-coloured liquid.

"You just put the one body in the coffin, right?" said Velvet.

"Yeah. Patient Three." Sin scanned the ward in case it was another patient but all the beds were occupied. He dropped to his knees and checked under the beds. Other than an accumulation of dust and cobwebs there was nothing.

"What are you doing? The mystery's in that casket," said Velvet.

"Maybe. Earlier today, when I messed with the boiler, Hotchin did his swede. Said there was important medical equipment connected that needed steam pressure but there ain't nothing here."

Velvet prodded the corpse with the tip of her knife. Where it punctured the skin more of the sapphire liquid seeped out. "I guess we know why the caskets are special. You get two cremations for the price of one." A smile crept onto her face. "And it's a foolproof scheme, because only a complete idiot is going to open the coffin of a Rat Pox victim." She looked pointedly at Sin.

"Hey, you opened it too."

"No. I just watched."

Sin pulled the casket closed and secured the locks. He wished Zonda was here. She'd probably say something oddball like "*weirdelicious, bluerooney blood*" but she might have had some idea of what the heck was going on.

He tried to remember what he'd read in the book Lilith had given him on humours of the blood. Nothing like this was mentioned, he was certain. "So the doctor's disposing of strange blue corpses, which is pretty suspect, but how does that help us find the spy?" said Sin.

"I have no idea. It's got to be connected. We need to search his office."

* * *

Perching on the corner of Hotchin's desk, Velvet examined her nails. "Going through all this paperwork has played havoc with my cuticles and we've not found a thing."

The lock of the final drawer in the desk was proving to be as tricky as the ones on the special coffin. Sin was certain Hotchin was up to no good but Velvet was right, they'd found nothing even remotely incriminating. He finessed the pick along the lock's tumblers and was rewarded with a satisfying click.

"What is it this time?" said Velvet as Sin slid the drawer open. "More riveting journals of Hotchin's exploits in India? You'd think he'd won the Tea War by himself from the amount he wrote about it."

Sin withdrew an ornate ivory box the size of a large book. Carved on the lid was a king cobra. Its fangs dripped venom and two red jewels sparkled for eyes. "What do you reckon this is?"

"Probably just some curio from the Raj," said Velvet dismissively.

The box's lid had no hinges and no visible way of opening it. Sin ran his fingers over the ivory, feeling its cool sheen. He traced the shape of the snake until his fingertips came to rest on the Cobra's jewels. He pressed down. Clockwork whirred.

"How'd you know to do that?" said Velvet, suddenly interested.

Sin had no idea. It had either been some innate thief's instinct or blind luck. Still, there was no reason to let Velvet know that. "I could see the signs of wear around the gems and it was obvious to the trained eye that they'd been repeatedly moved," he lied.

The box's lid rotated open. The inside was lined with soft velour and housed five small glass vials. Each vial contained a viscous yellow liquid.

Sin removed one of the vials. Sounding out the syllables, he read the fine italic handwriting penned on the lid: "Naja Oxiana."

Velvet levered another vial free. "Naja Kaouthia," she said.

"It must be some sort of code," said Sin.

"I don't think so." Velvet carefully replaced the vial

and wiped her hands on her skirt. "You should put yours back too."

"Why? What is it?"

Rummaging through Hotchin's journals, Velvet selected one. She folded the book open and began to read. "… breakfast today was the subject of much excitement. Some rather fine Cumberland sausages had just been served when the Chai Wallah burst into the mess tent waving a formidable stick and shouting 'Naja, Naja'. The poor man's eyes were like saucers and he danced from foot to foot like he was on burning coals. Eventually, Captain Marx abandoned his sausages and followed the Wallah outside to where a magnificent cobra swayed most hypnotically next to the latrines …" Velvet closed the book. "If I'm right, these are vials of snake venom."

CHAPTER 36
DOCTOR FRANKENLINE

Sin awoke to the sound of a fist hammering on his door. "Sinclair, get up. I need you in my office immediately," yelled Hotchin.

Sin pulled the blanket back and swung his legs from the bed. Had the broken endoscope been discovered? Or had he and Velvet left some telltale sign of their search of the office? Whatever the reason, Hotchin didn't sound happy. "Coming, sir. Just got to get dressed," answered Sin, trying to keep the panic from his voice.

"Quick as you can. No time to waste."

Sin heaved on his breeches as Hotchin's footsteps receded down the corridor. He eased past the gagged and bound man on his floor. At least the doctor hadn't burst into his room. Even with Sin's prowess at lying he may

308

have struggled to talk himself out of that one.

He slipped on his shirt and laced his boots while trying to make sense of the previous night's discoveries. Had Hotchin poisoned the second man in the casket? It seemed likely, but why? And what did any of that have to do with their hunt for the spy?

Sin fetched his jacket from the back of the door and steeled himself to face Hotchin. Whatever the doctor accused him of he would play the innocent and deny any involvement. He would keep calm and lie through his teeth if necessary.

Hotchin was hurriedly scribbling something on a piece of paper as Sin stepped into the office.

"That bloody idiot Harris has let the boiler men from Pratt and Witney turn off the steam. It's an absolute disaster." He thrust the piece of paper at Sin. "I need you to fetch Doctor Frankenline from this address. Tell him I need his help with the patients. Tell him we've lost all steam."

Sin read the address. Sixty-three Merton Street, right in the middle of his old thieving grounds. He should have felt comforted by the fact, instead it filled him with unease. He'd not spotted any urchins following him since the two he'd lost in the alley but that didn't mean they weren't there. The Fixer could have put more experienced members of the crew on it.

"Yes, sir, I know the street."

The doctor dabbed his forehead with a spotted handkerchief. "Be as quick as you can, Sinclair. It could be a matter of life and death."

* * *

Sin rushed along Crooked Row, his feet pounding the cobbles. The last time he'd been here he'd been running too, away from Eldritch. How much his life had changed in a few short weeks. He needed to find the spy or it would all change back again. When he'd not had two halfpennies to his name it hadn't particularly bothered him. Simply lifting a pie from one of the street vendors was a gratifying victory and enough to brighten his day. However, now he knew better, the thought of going back to the gangs was far from appealing.

Merton Street was a mixture of old stone buildings that formed part of Merton College and much newer brick townhouses. Number sixty-three fell into the latter category. Sin climbed the steps leading to the glossy black door and pressed the porcelain knocker-button. Steam spurted from a piston that raised the fist-shaped door knocker before it pumped back and forth rapping three times in quick succession. He heard hurried but measured footsteps inside and the door swung open.

"Yes?" said a dour-faced butler. His posture as stiff as his starched shirt.

Sin inhaled deeply, trying to calm his breathing. "Urgent message for Doctor Frankenline from Doctor Hotchin," he said.

The butler appraised him, staring down his nose. Sin knew he was deciding whether this was some type of con to get into the house and thieve. It was exactly the sort of thing the Fixer had him do in the past, and despite his better clothes he probably still had an air of urchin about him.

"I'm his assistant at the workhouse. I think it's to do with the Rat Pox," Sin added.

The butler ushered Sin inside and directed him to an ornate Georgian chair. "Wait here. I will see if the doctor is available."

Sin dropped into the seat, grateful for an opportunity to rest his legs and regain his breath. The butler sauntered away, obviously having a different understanding of the word urgent than Sin.

After what seemed like an age, but was probably only a matter of minutes, an elderly man in a herringbone suit hobbled towards him. Sin recognised Doctor Frankenline's ruddy face. He'd been in a heated discussion with a younger man when they'd visited the Arguementorium with Nimrod.

"You have a message for me?" said the doctor.

"Doctor Hotchin needs help with the patients. There was a problem with the steam system and he's worried about the medical equipment and the Rat Pox patients."

It was an overelaboration of Hotchin's instructions, but Sin wanted to gauge the doctor's reaction. Frankenline didn't query the message, but he took a sharp intake of breath and his pupils widened, confirming Sin's suspicions. There was something more going on with the Rat Pox patients than he'd so far seen.

"I need my bag. I'll get Pennyweather to summon a cab. If what you say is true, speed is of the utmost importance."

* * *

With a whoosh of steam, the cab complained to a halt outside the workhouse. Frankenline handed the driver a crisp pound note and then hobbled to Hotchin's office with as much speed as his old bones could muster.

"Bring your mask," he said to Hotchin. "You too, Mr Sinclair. This could be a three-man job."

Hotchin's brow furrowed deeper and he shot Frankenline a look Sin couldn't decipher.

"Where's the key?" snapped Frankenline.

Sin pulled his mask over his face as Hotchin removed

the key from the trolley. Frankenline hoisted his bag and hobbled from the room.

Hotchin inserted the key into the copper-plated door in the infirmary and checked his mask.

"You first, Hotchin, then Mr Sinclair. I'll secure the door," said Frankenline, his voice muffled by the respirator.

Hotchin turned the key and stepped into the room. Sin followed close behind, his eyes fixing on the special casket. He heard the door clank closed, then a sharp pain stung the back of his neck. He whipped around. Doctor Frankenline stood with his medical bag open and an empty syringe in his hand. "You're spying on us. You were in the Arguementorium when Nimrod was attacked," he said. "I'm afraid you're going to join Patient Five."

Sin's legs gave way and he slumped to the floor.

CHAPTER 37
WHATEVER IT TAKES

Sin tried to open his eyes but his eyelids refused to respond. They were as dead as his arms and legs. Not that he could have moved them anyway – they were bound at the wrists and ankles. He remembered Doctor Frankenline's words, and a vision of the Rat Pox patients, secured to their beds, played through his mind. He inhaled, the air flowing easily into his lungs. His mask was gone.

"You may feel a little pain as I inject a stimulant," said Doctor Frankenline from somewhere behind him. "You've been out for nearly two days."

He felt a needle slide into his arm and then fire ran up his veins, spreading throughout his body. In his head he screamed, while from his mouth came only the faintest of complaints. His eyes popped open. He wasn't tied to a bed in the Rat Pox ward but in a low-vaulted room surrounded by machinery. He managed to lift his head an inch and gaze down at his near-naked body. Thick leather straps secured him to a padded table. Needles skewered his arms and legs from which clear rubber tubes snaked to an ominously humming machine.

"Try to remain calm. You probably don't have Rat Pox yet," said Frankenline, twisting a dial on the machine. "Doctor Hotchin assures me he told you nothing of our experiments, so it appears we have a problem. How did you know about us?"

"I don't know anything. I've only just started here," croaked Sin.

"I'm a scientist. I seek truth from chaos, and you, Mr Grant, are not being honest. You are going to die here. That is the truth. I can make it quick and painless or you can die in the prolonged agony of Rat Pox. The choice is yours."

"Honestly, I don't know what you're doing. I was just helping Doctor Hotchin."

"I'm afraid I don't believe you. It matters not. The syndicate's sending you a special visitor and they can decide your fate."

Frankenline strapped a gag across Sin's mouth. "You've got some time to consider your options but perhaps this will help motivate you."

The doctor tilted the table forwards so Sin was nearly upright. Opposite him, strapped to tables identical to his, were the emaciated forms of two men. Both had the same odd pallor to their skin as the corpse in the casket. A piston on the machines attached to them pumped up and down forcing a translucent blue liquid around their bodies. Secured to a third table was the man from Sin's room, his face contorted with fear. Above his head on a chalkboard was written *Patient Twelve*.

"We're transfusing them with an artificial blood I've developed," said Frankenline. "It's a super-efficient oxygen carrier and provides an immunity to Rat Pox and other poisons. It really is jolly clever stuff."

Frankenline adjusted the dials on the machine connected to Patient Twelve and it began to vibrate. "Doctor Hotchin came up with the immunity concept after seeing a mongoose attack a cobra in India. A most remarkable creature and totally immune to the cobra's venom." He pulled a lever and the piston on top of the machine began to pump up and down, drawing blood up the tubes from Patient Twelve's body. "I was already working on the oxygen-carrying properties of octopus blood and a sponsor brought us together. Imagine our soldiers charging unhindered through clouds of poisonous gas as our enemies choke in their trenches."

Frankenline walked to a wrought-iron spiral staircase.

"I'm not sure we've got the formula quite right yet. They're dandy for a week then suffer complete organ failure and die in agony." His expression glazed over, momentarily lost in thought, then his eyes fixed on Sin. "Thanks to Nimrod's notes we've modified the formula and are nearly ready to test it. You can talk or be Patient Thirteen. The choice is yours."

* * *

Sin wasn't sure how much time had passed when he awoke. He didn't even remember falling asleep. He'd made a number of futile attempts to escape from his bonds and had tried to stay alert but had obviously succumbed to fatigue at some point. His mouth was dry and his stomach ached from hunger. Above him he heard a door scrape open and then footsteps. A flash of purple silk appeared at the stop of the staircase and Velvet descended. His body filled with relief then mild embarrassment as he realised he was practically unclothed.

Velvet fixed her eyes on his as she crossed the room. Fiddling with the buckled strap at the side of his jaw, she removed his gag.

Sin sucked in the cellar's tainted air. "You've got to get me out of here. They're going to poison me, or give me Rat Pox, or both."

Her hands tracing the route of the pipes, Velvet examined the machine connected to Sin.

"Whenever you're ready. No rush, I'm not going anywhere," said Sin.

"Stop complaining. I need to make sure I can remove these without you bleeding to death."

"I can get them out; just undo me," urged Sin.

"Relax, will you? These are tight," said Velvet, struggling with the buckled strap securing Sin's arm.

"It's hard to relax when you're expecting some special visitor who's going to pump you full of blue goo if you don't answer his questions."

Velvet's hand paused on the buckle. "What special visitor?"

"I don't know. Someone more important who can decide what to do with me."

"Someone like the spy?"

"Maybe, they didn't say."

Velvet stared at the emaciated bodies strapped to the other machines. "Whatever it takes. Whatever it takes," she murmured to herself and tightened the buckle back up.

Sin pulled at the restraint. "What are you doing?"

"This might be the break we've been waiting for."

"No. You're not leaving me here. Don't even think about it."

"They're not going to send this important visitor if

you've escaped, so I'm afraid you'll have to stay a little longer."

Sin's eyes widened. "Velvet. Unstrap me now."

Velvet reached for the gag, her hand trembling. "We all have to make sacrifices for COG. I'm sorry, Sin, but what I'm sacrificing is you."

Sin turned his head away. "Don't you dare. No. Don't ... *mmph.*"

Sin strained at his bonds.

"Conserve your strength," said Velvet. She looked across at Patient Twelve, his body racked in agony as the machine pumped blue blood through his veins. "We should have killed him. At least it would have been quick," she said and walked back towards the stairs.

CHAPTER 38
STRUGGLE IN VEIN

It was hard to judge the passage of time in the gloom of the cellar. Sin tried counting the strokes of the pistons rhythmically pumping blue blood around the other patients, but the monotony made his mind wander. A sudden nearby clicking brought him back to full alertness. A dial on the machine attached to him began to rotate. Each click brought an arrow on the dial a fraction closer to a green chemlight. *Click, click, click*. Sin had an ominous premonition that when the arrow reached the light something terrible was going to happen. *Click*. The arrow pointed upwards and the chemlight changed to red. The piston protruding from the machine's domed top shuddered then began pumping up and down. The needles puncturing Sin's veins twisted, sending a spasm of pain through his body. The piston pumped faster and he watched in horror as his blood was sucked into the transparent tubes. A light-headed euphoria overcame him as with each stroke, more blood was drawn from his body.

The dial continued to click around. Blackness encroached on Sin's vision, the world distorting. *Click.* The dial completed another revolution and the chemlight turned blue. The piston stopped and the machine vented steam. Gears clunked, then the pumping resumed, but now it was pumping blood back into Sin's body. Up and down went the piston and blue blood flowed into the tube. Up and down, blue blood pushing red blood along. Up and down, blue blood getting closer to the needles, closer to Sin's veins.

A set of heavy boots appeared on the top of the iron staircase. They clanked down the steps and a scarlet leather coat spiralled into view.

Blue blood surged into Sin's veins, burning like acid. Eldritch dashed across the room, eyes wild above his mask. Sin screamed through the gag, his pleas unintelligible. Eldritch yanked the leather strip from Sin's mouth.

"Turn it off! Turn it off!" yelled Sin.

Eldritch lunged for a lever on the metal tower's side and dragged it down. Steam dumped from the machine's base, billowing across the floor. The piston wheezed and slowly sank downwards.

"Got the blighter," said Eldritch.

Fire burned in Sin's veins, the caustic pain spreading throughout his body. "The blue blood, it's in me."

Eldritch teased the needles from Sin's arms, sapphire droplets forming over the puncture wounds. Sin shuddered. Maybe it was his imagination but despite the burning the blue blood felt cold inside of him.

"How long have you been on the machine?" said Eldritch.

"It's only just started but I'm infected for sure."

Eldritch unbuckled the straps that bound Sin to the table. "No, I don't think so. I think you're fine. Here, put these on." He handed Sin a respirator and a pile of clothes that had been stacked behind the machine.

His fingers shaking, Sin secured the mask over his face. His muscles ached from confinement but with Eldritch's help he managed to dress.

"Come on, we need to get you out of here," said Eldritch, draping Sin's arm over his shoulders.

Half carried by Eldritch, Sin shuffled to the spiral staircase. "Can you manage the stairs on your own?" said Eldritch.

"Too right I can," said Sin. He gritted his teeth and clasping the metal railings hauled himself upwards. Each step was agony, the pain making it hard to think straight. How had Eldritch known he was here? Another step, his veins stinging. It didn't matter, he was rescuing Sin. His muscles felt cold and leaden and his lungs struggled to pull air through the respirator. He'd saved Sin from certain torture, when the special visitor arrived. Not that he would have talked. Step by heavy step, Sin wound his way upwards. Eldritch eased past him and put a shoulder to the door at the top. "Let me get this," he said.

The door swung open, beyond it the horrors of the Rat Pox ward. Sin stumbled into the room, confusion gripping him. The ward only had one door, the one with the brassanium key, and it was right in front of him. He turned to see Eldritch pushing the bookcase back into place, concealing the hidden entrance.

Pulling Sin's arm back over his shoulders, Eldritch helped Sin across the ward. He heaved the copper-plated door open and guided Sin through before securing it closed behind them. Eldritch unbuckled his mask, letting it hang from his face. "What are you doing here?"

Sin reached up to his own respirator and unclipped it. "We were hunting for a traitor. We thought it was you."

"Me? Don't be ridiculous. Who thought that?"

"Lilith and Noir."

"And they put you in that lab?" asked Eldritch as they shuffled across the infirmary.

"No. That was Doctor Frankenline. We didn't even know about the lab until I woke up there."

"Who's *we*? Are Lilith and Noir here?"

"No, it's just–"

"Me," said Velvet, stepping into the infirmary, a steampistol aimed squarely at Eldritch.

"What are you doing?" asked Sin.

"I'm catching the spy."

Sin held his hand out to Velvet, his arm shaking. "It's not him. He's helping me escape."

"No. He's pretending to, so you'll tell him everything you know."

"COG Von Darque, lower your weapon. We need to get Sin medical assistance," commanded Eldritch.

Velvet cocked the pistol. "I don't take orders from traitors."

Eldritch turned to Sin. "There may be a traitor in this room, but it's not me."

Sin rubbed a puncture wound on his arm, thinking hard. "The machine in the lab. How did you know where to turn it off?"

"What does it matter? I saved you."

"It matters because you didn't hesitate. It was like you were familiar with the machine's workings."

"I didn't hesitate because I was concerned about you. I got you into this. I recruited you."

That night in the market seemed so long ago. Memories surfaced like bubbles from the deep. His hand in Eldritch's pocket, brushing over an odd shield-shaped coin, the embossed emblem only now having meaning. Two crossed swords below a crown.

"It is you," said Sin. "You and the Major."

Eldritch grabbed Sin, hauling him in front of his body. "Alas, just me. I tried to turn the Major but he was having none of it." A blade shot from the sleeve of the leather cloak into Eldritch's hand. He pressed the point to Sin's throat. "Out of the way, Von Darque, or I'll slit him ear to ear."

Velvet's hand wavered. "Go ahead. It'll give me a clear shot."

Eldritch pressed the tip of the knife into Sin's flesh and Sin felt a trickle of warm blood on his neck. "You may think you have a chance because your mother trained you. She could never beat me and even with that pistol you won't."

Sin needed time to slow, only his body felt too exhausted. He sensed the new blood circulating through his veins, reviving his muscles, but not quickly enough. He had to stall Eldritch. "If the Major's not one of the King's Knights, why did he have their shield in his room?"

Eldritch dragged Sin towards the doorway. "The King's Knights were formed by disgruntled members of the King's Steam Cavalry. The crests are similar but the swords cross differently. Major C has a regimental plaque awarded for bravery."

Sin flexed his fingers as pins and needles spread through his hands. "Why does he keep it hidden?"

"War's complicated. He's proud of the battles he won but ashamed of leading friends to their deaths. We toast them on the battle's anniversaries."

"If you fought with him, why turn traitor now?"

"I'm not the traitor. I'm still loyal to my regiment and our cause." Eldritch pressed the blade harder against Sin's throat. "Enough with the questions. Time to see how this plays out."

Energy surged through Sin's veins, as if his body was accepting the new blood, and another memory surfaced. Eldritch flying across the canal. He kicked back hard against the heel of Eldritch's boot and flames shot from the sole. Unbalanced, Eldritch's grip loosened. With new-found strength Sin pulled the knife from his throat and ducked away as the pistol in Velvet's hands screamed.

The nail punched through Eldritch's coat, impaling his leg, yet he still lunged at Velvet, slicing down with the blade. The pistol took the full force of the blow and in an explosion of steam it flew from her hand. Eldritch barrelled into Velvet, knocking her to the ground. She rolled and pulled a knife from her boot but Eldritch had already limped through the infirmary door.

Sin hauled Velvet to her feet. "Come on. We need to stop Eldritch," he said.

CHAPTER 39
TRAITOR'S GATE

Outside, the street was deserted. Fortunately, there was only a light smog this evening and Sin caught sight of a figure limping away.

They sprinted after Eldritch, hurtling down back alleys and side streets.

"He's heading for Doctor Frankenline's," panted Sin.

"How far?" asked Velvet.

"Couple more streets." Sin pushed harder, his new blood flooding his muscles with energy.

"He's messed up," shouted Sin eagerly as they turned into Crosses Court. To their left an archway led to Patriot's Gate but Eldritch had taken the right-hand arch, Traitor's Gate.

"City council welded the gate shut. We've got him."

They ran through the arch and their pace slowed, pulling to a halt halfway down the street. It was deserted.

"Where's he gone?" said Velvet.

A cruel laugh behind them answered the question. Eldritch stood, blocking their exit. He had a curved blade in one hand and a rapier in the other. "Did you really think I was running scared from you two?"

"More limping scared," said Sin. His gaze darted around the street, looking for anything he could use as a weapon, but there was nothing.

Eldritch advanced. "Please. I had to slow down so you could keep up."

Velvet stepped to one side and drew a second long dagger from the folds of her dress. "So why lead us here?" she said, tossing the dagger to Sin.

"I could hardly kill you in front of all those patients in the infirmary. Far better to have you meet your demise away from the lab. That way the experiments can continue."

Sin circled right. "What are the experiments? What am I infected with?"

"It's not an infection. It's an enhancement. This new blood will make our soldiers quicker, stronger and immune to disease and poison gases. We will decimate the enemy in their trenches while our forces advance unscathed."

"What do you mean, 'our soldiers'? I thought you

worked for the King's Knights, not the government," said Sin.

"The King's Knights are the government, or as good as. We do their dirty work and they turn a blind eye. We will ensure that Britannia stays great and the sun will always shine on the Empire."

Sin scuffed his soles over the cobbles making sure his feet were firmly placed. He could sense Eldritch was about to attack. "You seem pretty confident considering you're outnumbered and have a nail in your leg."

Eldritch lunged at Velvet, twirling the rapier. She jumped back but not before Eldritch had put a long gash in the sleeve of her dress.

Sin glanced at Velvet and saw the fear in her eyes. For all the training and practise Lilith had given her, Velvet had never been in a real fight.

Eldritch turned the blade towards Sin. "You couldn't escape me when I recruited you. Nothing's changed."

But something had changed. He had. COG had taught him that one person could make a difference. One person could be responsible for taking or saving hundreds of thousands of lives. He now had something bigger than himself to fight for and, if necessary, something bigger to die for.

"Velvet, listen to me," said Sin. "Don't argue, and don't hesitate. I'm going to delay this piece of crap traitor. You need to get clean away. Tell COG about the lab and tell Zonda I'm sorry."

Velvet nodded. Sin grasped the dagger tightly, his knuckles turning white. "On three. One, two …"

Sin charged towards Eldritch. *Time slowed*. Eldritch's rapier arced towards him. He parried with the dagger and the blade slid past his chest. He barrelled into Eldritch's midriff and, in a huff of exhaled air, they clattered to the cobbles. Time snapped back. Sin rolled away but Eldritch speared forwards with the rapier, skewering his shoulder. Sin screamed as the metal cut deeper. Eldritch clambered to his feet, pinning Sin to the ground. Fighting the pain, Sin glanced down the street to see Velvet fleeing around the corner.

Eldritch raised the second blade. "She'll not get far. I'm going to enjoy killing her once I've finished with you."

"You'll be leaving that boy alone," said a gruff voice from along the street.

Sin turned his head. The Fixer prowled through the arch into Traitor's Gate, his long rag coat flapping in the breeze. Behind him slunk a rabble of urchins, their eyes burning with malicious intent.

A warm sensation spread through Sin, taking away some of the pain in his shoulder. The Fixer had been like a father to him. Not a good father, but a father all the same. Sin knew the Fixer didn't forget, and he certainly didn't forgive, and Sin owed him. But if he was going to die here at Traitor's Gate, it should be at the hands of the Fixer, not Eldritch.

With a click of the Fixer's fingers, the urchins flowed from behind him, spreading across the street. "That boy's mine, and don't let it be said that the Fixer don't take care of his own."

"You think a bunch of kids are going to stop me?" sneered Eldritch.

The Fixer flashed a gold-toothed smile. "You ever seen a fighting dog taken down by a pack of rats? Razor teeth ripping flesh from bone. Sure it don't end well for some of the rats but it ends a lot more nasty for the dog."

"You come at me and more than one will die. I just want the boy. Do the maths."

"A pack's not about science. It's about heart, knowing you belong, knowing someone's got your back. Knowing whether you fight or fall, you do it together." The Fixer made the tiniest of gestures with his fingers and knives, clubs and all manner of weapons appeared in the urchins' hands. "Something tells me you're not part of a pack. I reckon you don't have the heart to die over this boy."

Sin screamed, the blade in his shoulder twisting as Eldritch lowered his head and whispered, "You're dead already, boy. Let Doctor Frankenline continue your legacy. He has your blood and with the formulas in your keeper he can create a legion of pangenetic warriors. Don't let the secret die with you. What's the keeper's combination?"

Sin raised his head. "One ... two ... damn you," he said.

Eldritch pulled the rapier free. "No lifesaving injections for you, boy."

Sin saw the yellow poison coating the blade and his head sunk back onto the cobbles.

Eldritch kicked his heels together, flame billowed from his boots and he shot into the air as his coat transformed into wings.

The Fixer pulled a blunderbuss pistol from his jacket. The angular Teutonian pressure pipes gleamed gold, matching his teeth. "Nobody said you could go."

The pistol screamed twice and two massive holes appeared in Eldritch's wings. The spy careened out of control, crashing into the facade of Oriel College, before tumbling to the cobbles with a loud crack.

Sin felt cold and his vision blurred. Above him the smog swirled, blocking out the stars. The Fixer's pockmarked face loomed over him. "I ain't letting you die, boy. You owe me."

Sin closed his eyes and shuddered. His lungs rattled as all breath left his body. There were some things even the Fixer couldn't fix.

CHAPTER 40
THE LIGHT

Bright white light filled Sin's vision and his ears rang with the voice of an angel.

CHAPTER 41
GEARS OF EXCELLENCE

"… and Lottie returned this morning, she's in excellent spirits despite a broken arm. So if you did decide that today was the day you were going to come round that would be posituitively fantabulous because it's test day tomorrow and I still can't get over the wall. Stanley's been helping me since you left but it's not the same and if you were there it would mean so much to me. And I know you broke into my room and saw those photographs that I keep hidden, however I've forgiven you for that and they're not what they seem. Well, they are exactly what they seem although not what you think. My father was in the King's Knights but not the traitorous ones, the real ones, the secret elite guard that protect the King and I'm so very proudilicious of him. He'd never betray COG and neither would I and I wanted you to know that so when you do come back to us there isn't any ill feeling or doubt."

Rising from a fug of dark dreams and half memories, Sin became aware of the fingers on his right hand. They felt warm, coddled by the hand holding his. He gently squeezed and the voice resumed.

"I'm choosing to believe that you did indeed intend to do that and it wasn't just some random response like all the other times because you have to come back to me, Sin. So I'm going to squeeze your hand and if you're hearing me squeeze back."

Sin tightened his grasp and Zonda squealed.

"I'm sorry I said horrible things to you before, I didn't mean them. Well, I probably did at the time. I was upset and was suffering from cake deprivation so my brain wasn't thinking straight. If you returnarooney now I will posituitively always be nice to you foreverington."

Sin tried to speak but his lips and throat were too dry and he could only murmur.

"I should probably get the nurse now, only they'll make me leave and so first I need you to know something. I love you, Sin, and I don't know if you'll remember any of this when you awaken but I had to tell you."

He felt a pleasant warmness on his lips and the sweet strawberry scent of Zonda filled the air around him.

A bell rang and Zonda shouted, "Nurse! He's trying to speak."

Feet scurried and Zonda's aroma was replaced by the harsh tang of smelling salts. Sin coughed and his eyelids flickered open. The ward was bright, sparse and sterile, a far cry from the infirmary at the workhouse. A uniformed nurse leaned over him, her auburn hair tied back under a white nurse's cap.

"Nod your head if you can understand me," she said in a no-nonsense tone.

The muscles in his neck were stiff but Sin managed to move his head.

"Good." She took his wrist, looked at the fob watch hanging from her apron and checked his pulse. "You've been unconscious for several weeks so you can expect to feel a little sore."

Behind her Zonda jiggled on the spot. She pirouetted, her frilled dress puffing out around her.

"COG Chubb, you need to leave now," instructed the nurse.

Sin licked his cracked lips. "No. She stays," he croaked.

"Mr Sin, you are in no position to give orders." The nurse's tone was stern but the corners of her mouth turned up and she made no further effort to enforce Zonda's departure.

The nurse reached under Sin's arms and hauled him into a sitting position. She plumped his pillows and made sure he was comfortable. "That's better. We don't want you falling back to sleep. The Major's going to want to see you."

* * *

Zonda had left for lessons and Sin waited for the arrival of the Major. He knew he was back at the palace but on its own that meant nothing. The nurse had referred to him as Mr Sin so he must still be expelled. They were good people and had nursed him back to health but that didn't mean he'd been forgiven. In the distance he heard the clank of the Major approaching and sat up straighter.

The hospital doors swung open and in marched Major C flanked by Lilith and Noir. The magician limped badly using an ebony walking stick to take his weight. To his surprise, Sin found that he was pleased to see him, pleased the COG agent had survived his mission, although apparently not without injury.

The Major hissed to a halt at the end of the bed and saluted. Sin raised his arm to salute back and a dull pain twinged his shoulder where Eldritch had skewered him.

"As you were," barked Major C.

Sin relaxed his arm and massaged his shoulder.

"How are you, soldier?" asked the Major, his bushy moustache quivering.

"Dazed and confused to be honest, sir. How did I get here? Why am I not dead?"

Lilith stepped forwards. "Velvet alerted us and your friend the Fixer was happy to hand you into our care … for a finder's fee of course."

Sin smiled. The Fixer, always on the make but a heart of gold. Admittedly, gold that he'd murdered, cheated and robbed to acquire, but a heart of gold regardless.

"We don't know why you're not dead," said Noir. "We think the blue blood has given you immunity. It was designed to protect soldiers from biological and chemical weapons."

"And the lab?" asked Sin.

A small flame appeared in Noir's hand. "It caught fire. As did Doctor Frankenline's house, and indeed Doctor Frankenline."

"Eldritch is refusing to cooperate," said Lilith. "He has denied any involvement in the attempt on Nimrod's life. He claims Nimrod's genius will be crucial in the next war."

"A war which, if not prevented, you have certainly delayed," said Noir. "Britannia's plan to march over Europe, poisoning all in their path, is now thwarted."

The Major straightened. "You and COG Von Darque have done a great service, exposing the spy and for that we owe you our thanks. However, you deliberately broke a Cast-Iron Rule and I'm afraid that is something I cannot reverse."

A whistle tooted and the hospital doors burst open. Puffing steam behind him, Nimrod piloted a walking chair towards Sin's bed. "I think maybe you can, Major."

Sin smiled, relieved to see that Nimrod had recovered, at least partially.

"Nothing would delight me more than to allow this young hero back into COG but the Committee's manual is unflinching on the subject of Cast-Iron Rules," said the Major.

"Indeed it is, though there is a precedent," said Nimrod. "Only once has a candidate broken a Cast-Iron Rule and been allowed to stay in COG. Felicity Hawk broke the rules while preventing a surprise zeppelin raid. The Committee agreed she should be given a chance to redeem herself and if she won the Gears of Excellence trophy she would be reinstated."

The Major smiled. "How fitting. I put forward the motion that if Sin is triumphant on the assault course tomorrow he shall be reinstated. Does the whole Committee agree?"

"Aye," said Nimrod.

"Aye," said Lilith.

Noir fidgeted on his walking stick. "How's your shoulder, boy?"

"Good enough. Just give me the chance to prove it," said Sin.

"Aye, you'll get your chance," Noir said.

With a delicate touch, the Major lowered his mekanikal hand onto Sin's good shoulder. "Get some rest. Tomorrow's a big day."

CHAPTER 42
RELATIVE TRUTH

The East Wingers crowded around Sin as he entered the gym.

Stanley clapped him on the back. "Good to have you back, brother."

"Yeah, well, I may not be back for long if I don't win today," said Sin, staring across the gym at Velvet.

"She only beat you before because she cheated. You've got her number for sure," said Esra.

Sin rolled his shoulders and grimaced at the dull pain deep in the muscle. He may have her number, but as the knot of nervousness built in his stomach he wondered if that number was a big fat zero.

Steam belched and spurted from the course's mekaniks, an ever-present reminder of the difficulties ahead. Adjacent to the course, pistons had raised a platform from the floor on which were seated the Committee and staff. Major C occupied the central chair, a pensive look on his face. Beside him Nimrod was in a heated discussion with Noir, who adamantly shook his head. The scientist placed a hand on the magician's shoulder and whispered something in his ear. For the first time ever, Sin saw a genuine smile on the magician's face. Noir held out his hand, which Nimrod clasped.

"I don't believe it," said Stanley.

Sin cocked his head. "You didn't know Nimrod was better?"

"No. Nimrod's been clattering about for days. There, walking onto the stage, that's only Captain Felicity Hawk."

Sin followed Stanley's gaze to a young lady in a leather aviator's outfit. Behind her, two staff manoeuvred a veiled portrait and easel onto the stage. Hawk carried the Gears of Excellence trophy in one hand while directing the placement of the portrait with the other.

So that was what the Major meant when he'd said it was fitting. If he won, Hawk would be the one to award him the trophy. Sin looked across the course to where Zonda fidgeted next to Trixie on the start line. His was not the only fate that would be decided today. He strode towards his friend, his attention so focused he walked straight into Sergeant Stoneheart. It was like hitting a wall. He bounced back, his shoulder in agony.

"Watch where you're going, candidate," barked Stoneheart.

"Sorry, Staff," he managed to gasp and limped over to Zonda. He wrapped his arms around her in a big hug. "I think this will help you get over the wall," he said and slipped her the perforated metal key he'd lifted from Stoneheart's pocket.

"I can't. That's cheating," said Zonda, her voice trembling.

"No, it's improvising. Besides, if by some miracle I win, it would be for nothing if you weren't here too. So do it for me."

Her eyes darting about guiltily, Zonda held her hands to her stomach hiding the key. Stoneheart raised her watch. "Candidates, on my mark. Three, two, one, MARK."

Zonda sprinted to the post by the wall, inserted the key and tapped in a code. Steam erupted from the wall's base and it sank into the ground.

"Stop! That's cheating," shouted Stoneheart.

Major C rose to his feet and his voice boomed across the hall. "No rules were broken. Continue." Then after a short pause, he added, "You go, girl."

Zonda waved a triumphant fist in the air and dived for the monkey bars.

Her run wasn't elegant but over the weeks Zonda

had improved dramatically and she crossed the line in a respectable time. She collapsed to the floor and lay on her back panting.

"I think I'm going to die."

Sin stood over her. "I knew you could do it." He held out his hand and hauled her to her feet.

"I was deliberately slowerooney, just so you'd have a chance," said Zonda, still puffing.

"Thanks. But I doubt Velvet will show me the same courtesy."

* * *

The wall remained down so that all the candidates would face the same course. Running East Wing versus West Wing, the candidates ran in pairs until only Velvet and Sin remained. They stood on the start line awaiting Stoneheart's count. Velvet was uncharacteristically quiet. Sin wished she'd goad him or make some outrageous slur but she stared at the course in thoughtful silence.

"So how come you weren't thrown out of COG?" asked Sin.

Velvet shrugged. "I didn't actually break any rules. When I met you at the fountain I was acting under the direct orders of a member of staff."

"Your mother!"

"I guess that's just the advantage of having a parent on the Committee."

"Candidates ready," shouted Stoneheart. "On my mark. Three, two, one, MARK."

Sin sprinted off the line and leaped onto the monkey bars. He fought through the pain in his shoulder, matching Velvet swing for swing. His blue blood gave him an abundance of energy and the cheers of the East Wingers spurred him onwards, but by the time he reached the balance beams the physicality of the obstacles was taking its toll. He vaulted onto the beam as Velvet dismounted, an obstacle ahead.

Battling the pain, he was determined to make up the ground, however Velvet gave no quarter and as he reached the boxing net she was already halfway through. The steam-powered gloves slammed down, and unlike their previous encounter Velvet ignored them, driving towards the finish.

A leather glove pounded into Sin's shoulder and he choked back a scream. Frozen in agony, he watched Velvet heave herself from beneath the net and sprint for the line. It was over. He'd fought hard but his injured body just wasn't up to the task. His fate was sealed.

Inches short from crossing the finish Velvet drew to a halt. Smiling, she sat down and waited.

Sin scrambled out of the net, his heart pounding. Could this really be a last-second reprieve? Clutching his shoulder, his arm hanging limp, he stumbled past Velvet and collapsed across the line. Velvet stood and stepped over the finish in second place.

Sin raised his head. "Thanks."

Velvet shrugged. "If anyone deserves to be in COG, it's you. Besides, it's more fun with you here."

Sin looked about for Zonda. She stood to attention with the other candidates in front of the stage. Zonda smiled at Velvet and, lifting her hand, smartly saluted. Velvet returned the salute, then hauled Sin to his feet. "Come on, you've got to get awarded my trophy."

"This doesn't make up for leaving me in the lab," said Sin.

"Are you sure, because I kind of thought this made us even?"

"Not even close."

Captain Hawk took centre stage. "And the winner of the Gears of Excellence trophy is COG Sin," she announced.

Sin felt a burst of joy in his chest. She'd called him COG Sin. Amid the cheers of the other candidates he mounted the stage and received the bronze and brassanium cup.

"I am honoured to be here today," said Hawk, "not only to see the next generation of COG operatives but also because I have been invited to join the Committee. An invitation that I duly accept." She walked over to the covered easel. "As is tradition I would like to present COG with a portrait of one of its members. An individual who is the most honourable, brave and determined man I know. I present to you Major Churchill Chubb." She pulled the sheet away revealing a brightly coloured painting of Major C in all his mekanikal glory.

Sin's gaze shifted from the picture to Zonda, who clapped enthusiastically. Sin took her arm and pulled her closer. "He's your …"

"Father, yes. We were trying to keep it a secret but I guess the cogs are out of the clock now."

Major C smiled, his bushy moustache quivering. "I believe we are going to take some photographs so please mingle and enjoy some rather fine tea and refreshments."

* * *

Across the assault course the camera flashed, capturing candidates in dramatic poses. Zonda sat with Sin on the now half-raised wall. On Zonda's lap rested a piece of cake nearly as large as her head. "I've soooo missed this."

Sin puffed out his cheeks. "I can't believe you didn't tell me."

"You've always known I like cake."

"About your father, cake for brain."

"Wouldn't have been a secret then," said Zonda through a mouthful of cream.

Major C detached himself from a conversation with Lilith and joined them. He grasped Zonda in a hug, his brassanium arm hissing softly. "I'm so proud of you."

Stepping back, he held out his hand for Sin to shake. "And I believe I have you to thank for helping her."

Sin patted the wall with his free hand. "I just got her past one obstacle. The rest was all your daughter's doing, sir."

The Major lifted Zonda from the wall. "If you'll excuse us I want Zonda to meet Captain Hawk." He put an arm around Zonda's shoulder and guided her away.

Immediately, Nimrod, who had been lurking nearby, filled their place. His fingers twitched nervously at the mekanikal chair's controls. "I have some things to discuss. Will you walk with me?" he said in hushed tones.

Sin dropped from the wall. "Of course. What is it?"

Nimrod guided his chair away from the celebrations. "Have you heard of Cinderella?"

"Don't think so."

"It's a fairytale where a princess is identified based on the fitting of a glass slipper she left behind at a ball."

A furrow formed on Sin's brow. He hadn't been sure what Nimrod wanted but he'd not expected princesses and fairytales.

Nimrod nodded. "I know, the logic of selecting monarchy based on podiatry is flawed in so many ways, but the point is the prince knew he had the correct person because of what she left behind." Reaching inside his pocket, Nimrod withdrew Sin's keeper. "We recovered this from Eldritch. He claimed it was yours but I didn't believe him so I constructed a machine to find the combination. Last night it succeeded and inside I found my equivalent of Cinderella's slipper."

From his pocket Nimrod withdrew the photograph of the Eugenesis Project, except it wasn't the one Eldritch had possessed. This one had a piece missing from the bottom centre. A piece that Sin had carried for fourteen years.

Nimrod turned to face Sin, putting his hands on his shoulders. "I want to tell you about the Eugenesis Project. How we made you better than human. But all that can wait. What you really need to know, right now, is your mother would be proud of you, *son*."

Sin's heart leaped and the world came into precise focus, colours sharp and vivid, sounds crisp and clear.

"You're my father?" he asked, not daring to believe it.

"The truth of the matter is that you were enhanced with the Super-Pangenes from various extramundane donors," said Nimrod. "But in as much as the normal sense of the word can be applied to you, yes, I am your father."

It was almost too much to take in. Sin pressed his fingertips against his temples, trying to make sense of it all. He had a father. A billionaire, genius father who was head of COG. The palace was his home, the candidates and staff his family. He belonged.

There was so much he still didn't know, so much he didn't understand. Was he normal? What Super-Pangenes did he have? But one question burned brightly in his mind ahead of all the others.

"What was my mother like?" he asked.

ACKNOWLEDGEMENTS

This has been an epic journey. Without the navigational prowess of a number of people I may have fallen into many traps on the way.

Thanks to Storylines, Tessa Duder and Walker Books for giving me this opportunity.

Thanks to my mentor, Alex Smith, for her guidance, and to Adele Broadbent and Phoebe Wilton-Stuart for scribbling all over my first draft, and to Jackie Rutherford and Anna Mackenzie for scribbling on subsequent drafts.

Thanks to my editor Mary Verney for her time, patience and expert advice.

Special thanks to Alex and Max for listening to all my stories over the years.

And most importantly, thanks to my wife Louise who when not walking beside me on this journey was carrying me through the difficult bits.

ABOUT THE AUTHOR

GARETH WARD (aka The Great Wardini) is a magician, hypnotist, storyteller and bookseller. He has worked as a Royal Marines Commando, police officer, evil magician and zombie, and as a writer and compere of Napier City's inaugural steampunk murder mystery evening. Born near Oxford in the UK, he currently lives in Hawke's Bay, New Zealand, where he runs two independent bookshops with his wife Louise. His first novel *The Traitor and the Thief*, a rip-roaring steampunk adventure, won the 2016 Storylines Tessa Duder Award. You can learn more about the fantabulous world of Gareth Ward at **garethwardauthor.com**